A SUMMER

OF

GOOD-BYES

Blue Triangle Press

#2

2017

Also by Fred Misurella

Fiction:
Arrangement in Black and White, a novel
Only Sons, a novel
Lies to Live By, stories
Short Time, a novella

Non-fiction:
Understanding Milan Kundera:
Public Events, Private Affairs

A Summer of Good-Byes

By

Fred Misurella

Fred Misurella

Library of Congress control number: 2017904885

CreateSpace Independent Publishing Platform

Charleston, SC

Acknowledgements:

Thanks to Beth Seetch for editing the manuscript so carefully and providing positive and encouraging feedback. In all cases, mistakes are the author's. Author photo from East Stroudsburg University. Chapter One, "Unto Us a Son", was published in different form in the Spring, 2014, *Summerset Review*.

ISBN: 1537721119
ISBN 13: 9781537721118

For Kim, Alex, and our new family love,

Filipka.

(And in memoriam: Jimmy Garrison.)

"Fish, flesh, or fowl, commend all summer long

Whatever is begotten, born, and dies."

–Yeats, "Sailing to Byzantium"

PART ONE:

UNTO US A SON

I.

"Absolutely," I said, though with many, many secret doubts.

My wife, Lee, was talking about a baby — a photo of a baby. The child was big, round-faced, and laughing — or crying — at any rate, making what looked like a horrifyingly loud sound.

"He," she said, "is the one. Let's do it now."

I've often wondered what provokes love, or constitutes its image, in real life or photos. I'm not thinking about beauty queens or musclemen, or pleasing glimpses of naked flesh. But certain lines and shades coalesce, certain movements, rhythms, or gestures attract and make, somehow unconsciously, an impact on the viewer that can change a life.

Art, we used to say in college, moves the world.

I still remember my first genuine aesthetic experience, the one that committed me to a life in art, both as practitioner and critic. It made me fall in love, just as my wife fell in love at the moment this story begins. During my junior year in high school, our French teacher arranged a one week summer visit to Paris, and of course that included a tour of the Louvre. Our first afternoon there I felt tired and listless, partly because of jet lag, partly because I had been up late the night before. A girl and I had walked along the river, holding hands and kissing at several moonlit bridges,

6

with the result that, next morning, we both missed the tour bus from our hotel. She had decided to sleep in, but I wanted to go to the museum, and so, armed with directions from the hotel concierge–two or three Metro stops away as I recall–I arrived at the sprawling museum beside the river more than an hour late, alone, and not quite sure where to find our group.

I paid the modest student entry fee and wandered around the halls, trying to get my bearings. The rooms were hot and crowded, and I was surprised to hear American voices all around me as I strode the length of the main gallery–stopping at Giotto's portrait of St. Francis receiving the stigmata and Mantegna's *Martyrdom of St. Andrew*—arrows sticking from the saint's body. But I could not find our group, and I decided to make the best use I could of this time alone. With a floor plan of the museum, I continued down the main gallery to the small, crowded room where the *Mona Lisa* hung, encircled by a small crowd of tourists listening to a guide. Then I walked to the end of the gallery and down the stairs to the classical area. I saw the *Venus de Milo* first, standing before another crowd. Feeling groggy from the heat, I went to sit in a small day-lit courtyard to rest.

The Louvre is huge, as everyone knows, impossible to tour completely in one day, and I felt the length of all that I still had before me to see. I closed my eyes and dreamed, dozing for a good half hour to the sounds of home—more American voices, in other words—but none of them from my French class. "I'll do

7

it alone anyhow," I said to myself when I awoke, and so
with a stretch and a quiet yawn I resumed my tour of
classical works. But I soon grew weary of all that lost
human time and, taking a deep breath, decided to
mount the stairs in search of more modern things. I left
the classical gallery, passing another naked Venus as I
approached the hall, then lowered my head, leaned on
the handrail, and pulled myself up the stairs. As I
turned on the first landing — and this is the true order of
the moment as I remember it — I dropped my hands,
looked up from my shoe tops, and gasped: A winged
figure loomed above my head, soaring toward the
ceiling.

It was a statue, not a dream-monster: headless,
armless, but leaning toward me with broad, outspread
wings. Its position at the top of the stairwell gave it a
rising, ascending quality that was half eagle, half
mythological spirit on the way to the heavens–and yet
all very distinctly human, female. I stood on the landing
in awe, absolutely outside myself and, as I think of it
now, outside the contemporary moment, too. What
startled me was my gasp–the loudness of it–before I
noticed the looming figure. It was a sound, I am sure,
caused by the statue and something primitive in me that
responded blindly with surprise. I had never seen this
piece before, in pictures or reality, and so I had to ask
someone about it.

"*One of ze sree great treasures of ze Louvre,*"
someone said next to me in passing. I saw a tour guide
leading a group of Americans past me up the stairs.
"*Voici La Victoire du Samothrace,*" she said, fairly

8

shouting. As the group filed past, I noticed my high school French teacher among them with five or six of my fellow students behind her. They all greeted me loudly, joking about my late night out and my flushed, excited face that seemed to imply some extended sensual pleasure. With a laugh and a shrug, I told them nothing but joined them for the walk to the top of the stairs.

I have seen the *Victory of Samothrace* hundreds of times since, occasionally spending an hour or more staring at it. I try to recreate and understand that moment of first perception, especially the nature of my visceral gasp. Something moved me to feel love at that moment–for more than the statue — grand and impressive though it was. Small birds and other animals respond suddenly to the shadow of a hawk flying above them, and because of its flourishing wings, I have thought that the *Victory of Samothrace* affected me that way — a sudden manifestation of threatening power, which turned out to be friendly.

I felt no fear in the moment–especially not physically. I felt energy instead, then inspiration and happiness, as if the wonder of life had revealed itself to me. I was amazed, in other words, but in a very solemn way.

Doubter that I am, I dislike describing the experience in quasi-religious terms. Still I cannot deny the impression of being stricken, as I remember it, chosen to perceive something special. Beautiful women have affected me similarly sometimes, as have passages

9

from music–Puccini, especially with a great soprano's ardor producing it–scenes of the countryside in France or Italy, and one or two paintings by Cézanne and Van Gogh.

A mystery, yet it cleared many years later when the photographs arrived from our adoption agency a few days after a phone call about Russia. I saw my wife reveal in her eyes something intense, like my own moment of wonder, although I must confess I did not share her feeling. The pictures came in a thick brown-paper-wrapped package, as if it were hiding something. Nervous, we sat next to each other on a couch, tore apart the wrapping, and, tensely, as if it enclosed a dangerous or contraband item, carefully opened the envelope of photographs. I felt my wife's body sag against me as we leafed through them–black and white portraits of lonely-looking, modestly dressed Russian kids smiling to look inviting for the camera.

"They're trying so hard. Even the very little ones," Lee said. "It's as if they know they're trying to sell themselves."

"They probably do–or at least sense something from the photographer."

"Look. Her socks are mismatched."

Lee pointed to a girl. Eight years old, the information said, named Sonia. She stared at the camera with her arms outstretched.

"If she were here, how could you not pick her up?"

I turned the picture over, continuing to look through the others. To be honest, I felt frightened now,

10

fearful of what we had started. The children looked pathetic, defeated, and terribly underfed. I wondered what kind of character could survive such gloom as they had experienced from the very beginning of their lives. Selfish, I know, but could they be happy, could they achieve?–Russian painters, writers, and musicians had succeeded greatly, but I could think of none who had started with so little support behind them. Could Lee and I make up for it? Could we love enough, care enough, act unselfishly enough to fill in the great void of their first few days, months, even years?

I looked at one boy–age five, thin, smiling, rumpled sweater and trousers barely covering his lanky wrists and ankles—and something in his huge, dark eyes made me think we could never make him happy. Another five-year-old, a girl, stood with her little brother–he was one–and looked away from the camera. I saw no tears or other evidence of crying, but such a stoic coolness covered her face that I wondered if she could ever give a loving hug and smile.

"They're sweet," Lee said. Then, evidently thinking thoughts similar to mine, she added, "They reveal a lot about us as well."

She turned the photo over and, with a little gasp, held the next one very still.

Swaddling clothes are wraps to bind and control an infant as well as warm it, and I am sure Lee's reaction to the photo stemmed from the child's obvious attempt to break through the body wrap that bound him. It was a boy, on his back, facing the camera with

11

his left arm reaching toward us from a blanket as his mouth, contorting into either a laugh or a howl, expressed an explicit invitation to be aided. Handled.

We both stared at the photo in silence, I, I admit, from intense fear, Lee, I am certain, out of absolute and intense love. "Mikhail Alexandrovich," appeared beneath the photo, "May 30."

"Four months," Lee said.

I stared at the yellow cast of the photo (this one in color, for some reason) and attempted to think rationally. The boy's round, baby-cheeked face looked distinctly argumentative, as if I could see already future disagreements about cars, schoolwork, and friends. His cheeks, flushed pink, brought to mind hefty Russian weight lifters and wrestlers, and I knew that while I held the advantage now in strength and endurance, each year would alter that–imperceptibly at first but with increasingly obvious results. Would he love a doddering father (and mother) as much as a strong one? Would he remain loyal without blood ties? Would I be a good parent under these circumstances?

"This is the one," Lee said, smiling. "I'm ready to call the agency."

"There are others to look at."

"No use. This is the one. I can feel it. I don't want to lose the opportunity."

"We've always said we would prefer a girl," I reminded her.

Lee paused at that, looking cursorily at other photographs. She returned and stared for a long time at the girl with her arms extended toward us. "Sonia

12

would be lovely," she said, "but she's already formed. I want a chance to bond."

"So do I."

"Then it's all done," Lee said. "I'll go call the agency about ... Mikhail. Let's call him Misha."

Within a day or two the official process had started, and the agency told us to plan on flying to Moscow around Thanksgiving. The idea of bringing a child home at that time struck us both as wonderfully poetic and a sign of some larger human plan. Certainly the wall had fallen in Berlin, and the Russian empire that had smothered Europe's central and eastern cultures as long as we had lived now seemed more American and free than anyone had ever dreamed. But cold war memories of pale imprisoned people, artists starving or executed because of independent thought, and philosophers and writers told what to think or write made the idea of escape to liberty and plenty an indivisible part of Misha's entrance in our home.

We renewed our passports, applied for visas, submitted medical and financial statements to Russian authorities in charge of the adoption process. By early October we felt ready to go at any time, but at the same instant bad news and information started to reach us.

As most people would, I suppose, we had begun to pay more attention to adoption stories in magazines, newspapers, and books. Much of what we read discouraged us. In addition to the stories of overturned American adoptions, we began to read and hear about disappointments overseas: unhealthy, drugged or alcoholic children, babies who were physically or mentally damaged at birth, large sums of money taken with no child being delivered–all this in a process that had very little international regulation and over which our legal system held no power. In addition, Russia's increasing crime rate worried us. Bloody stories of gunned down tycoons mixed with ones about duped or assaulted tourists led to real apprehension, especially since, the agency told us, all transactions in Russia would be conducted on a cash basis, with American dollars–not rubles–required. Russia's Chechnyan campaign also filled the news, so essentially, as one psychological expert analyzed it, we would be starting family life in a lawless, war-torn country whose currency had very little value and whose people regarded all Americans, no matter their profession, as wealthy capitalists with yachts, private planes, and dollars to burn.

"Don't wear good shoes or clothes over there," someone told us. "It marks you as a target. And leave your baggage at home–it won't reach you at the airport."

Prejudice?–Who could know?–But we decided not to take a chance. We bought money belts, chose jeans and sneakers to wear, and looked for the most worn sweaters and jackets we could find in our closet. Then we started to read press releases from the American State Department and its embassy in Russia. The most frequent notice we found said that foreign adoptions had been halted by the Russian Duma (the country's legislature), and so the State Department

14

advised against Americans proceeding with Russian adoptions.

"Disinformation over adoption," the adoption agency called it. "The American State Department is trying to discourage people. It's the old Cold War attitude, distrust of Russians and probably a resistance to bringing more immigrants into the country."

"Immigrants!–He's a baby."

"No, he isn't. Not to them."

The notices, along with the war, crime, and political confusion continued, and while several respected experts and family members cautioned us against proceeding, Lee stubbornly kept the photograph of Mikhail–enlarged now–taped to our bathroom mirror. When I shaved in the morning, looking out the window onto Riverside Drive, I saw a glimpse of our future in the yellow shawl, the hand reaching toward me, the eyes and open mouth shrieking silently for ... what? Food? Attention? Love? Obviously, we couldn't turn him down. We had to proceed.

In early November the adoption agency called to inform us of a slight problem. Because of personnel matters, there would be a small delay–perhaps till December. I remember the letdown Lee and I felt, as if once again a pregnancy had ended suddenly and once again we needed to take a deep breath and start over.

"No, Mikhail Alexandrovich will be your son," the agency contact said. "This delay is merely procedural–because our Russian program is so new, we have to get the proper people in place to help you when

15

you are there."

At the same time we read more discouraging articles about difficulties with Russian adoptions: One writer told of a severely handicapped child passed off as normal, another of an adopted infant who had disappeared–kidnapped by a distant relative not wanting the child to leave the country. Either scenario, especially the latter, struck us as awful, and when we read about doctors in Minnesota and Baltimore who offered advice on foreign adoptions, we called their offices. One knew of our agency and its primary contact in Russia and saw no reason not to continue, the other advised us to ask for a measurement of the child's head to gauge its health. Upon receiving the measurement a few weeks later, along with Misha's age and weight, she told us he was within normal ranges and advised us to continue.

"But when you get there," she cautioned, "pay attention. Hold him, look in his eyes, talk. If there's something that doesn't seem right, follow your instinct. Tell them he's not what you expected. If need be, you can choose another baby."

"Another?–"

"You haven't adopted him yet. They can't force you. And in Russia there are plenty more."

"It will be hard. My wife is already committed."

"But you can do it. I've advised many people who have."

With 1984-like images of Russian officers and cold-hearted, imperious women acting as civil servants in adoption institutions, I had real doubts we could say

16

no. But Lee saw it as a real alternative and felt more certain of moving on. In mid-November the agency called to say that things were falling in place in Moscow and that we should prepare to leave for Russia any day. We sent them a certified check to pay for legal services and the caring and feeding of—yes, this is the way we phrased it—our son. A friend passed along a crib that her child no longer used, family members bought or lent clothes, basinets, and toys. "It's like a real birth," Lee said, smiling as she arranged things in his room. We bought mobiles, colorful pictures, and bright, cheerful music tapes (need I say Mozart, Bach, and Tchaikovsky?) along with a player to put in Misha's room. We repainted the walls, decorated them with hand-painted Disney cartoons, found an abandoned wooden rocker in the street that we had repaired, and hung a huge picture of Winnie the Pooh and Tigger over the crib to give him company.

Two days before Thanksgiving, the agency called and told us to finalize our travel plans. In Moscow and Perm (a small city at the base of the Urals where Mikhail lived) people were in place and expecting us shortly. Russian people who were fluent in English would meet us at the airport, chauffeur us to necessary appointments, and put us up in their homes.

"Great!—And when should we arrive?"

"Around Christmas," the agency liaison said. "You should have a child before the new year begins."

We found an agent who specialized in Russian travel, received our visas in a surprisingly short time

17

because of his contacts, and bought toys and mobiles for children at the orphanage in Perm, as well as token gifts for the administrators there. The adoption agency also told us that from the moment we accepted the child he was ours–our responsibility–and we should therefore bring clothing, diapers, travel equipment, and formula to feed him.

We packed all that, bringing only underwear and toilet articles for ourselves. On Christmas day, wearing old down ski jackets and the only jeans, shirts, sneakers, and sweaters we would use on the trip, we drove to Kennedy Airport, checked our bags and traveling bassinet, then went to the lounge to wait for the plane that would take us to Misha. "A nice Christmas present," one of the checkout people at Kennedy said. We nodded and smiled, but we looked on it differently–as the true beginning of a brand new life. The august sounds of Handel's *Messiah* had accompanied us for most of the drive to Kennedy, and now the dull glow of multi-colored lights flecked the landscape beneath us as we flew toward Frankfort, Germany, where we changed planes and, in a heavy, beautiful snow that seemed to beg for sleigh bells, reindeer, and little children waiting for them in warm fire lit rooms, headed toward Moscow, landing finally in the early morning on a dark, seemingly smoke-filled day.

***

The Moscow terminal was crowded, underlit,

more like a rush hour subway station than an airport, with mustached, soldierly men bumping into us and brusquely pushing us aside as we followed our young English-speaking guide, Oleg, through the halls. He led us to various counters and offices to have papers checked, exchange money, retrieve baggage, and, eventually, be admitted officially into Russia for a short time.

Oleg brought us to a car waiting outside the main building and introduced us to the driver, Gennady, a retired Soviet Colonel. He drove us to his apartment on the outskirts of Moscow, fed us a meal of hard boiled eggs, beets, and other crudités he had grown and pickled at his country *dacha*, and then, after a quick tour of a dark downtown (the Kremlin, the U.S. Embassy, and Red Square among other sights), brought us back to his apartment for the night, letting us sleep in his bed while he slept on a living room couch and sent his wife and daughter to a friend's apartment.

It was a whirlwind, with Lee and me rising at three or four next morning, drinking coffee and tea, then gathering our things to ride to the airport again for a pre-dawn flight from Moscow to Perm and the Urals where our new life awaited.

Gennady and Oleg left us in the airport waiting room because they had to drive another set of new parents to the airport for a flight to the United States, and so we waited among tall, heavily-jacketed men and women for a sign or announcement to tell us when we should board the plane. Nothing came, at least nothing

19

that Lee or I recognized. All I remember is that at some point all the men and women impatiently standing–and smoking–near the outside doors, opened them, marched down slippery ice-covered metal steps onto the tarmac and stood together, showing more impatience than they had inside, at the bottom of the steps to a plane.

Great, but the problem was that three or four other planes stood there too, each looking ready to take off, and we had no idea which would leave for Perm. A man in a leather jacket and fur cap shoved me aside to stand in front of me at the base of the steps. He carried an attaché case in the left hand, puffed a fat tan-papered cigarette that he held in his right hand, and glowered menacingly at the open door of the plane where two disheveled stewardesses straightened their hair and worked to keep their blouses inside the waistbands of their gray skirts.

"*Peeermm?*" I said, attempting the Russian pronunciation I had heard from Oleg and Gennady. I pointed to the stewardesses and the door at the same time I prepared to duck should attaché, cigarette, leather-clad elbow or shoulder swing in my direction out of annoyance.

The man turned to me, his dark eyes sizing me up while his down-turned mustache brought to mind classical images of Ivan the Terrible or worse. But instead of a threatening rebuke he let his face soften as his mouth turned up into a smile and his eyes brightened with a glance at Lee.

"*Amerikanski?*" he said. "Americans?"

"*Da,*" I answered, imitating countless Soviet

20

soldiers I had encountered in Cold War films. "Americans."

His smile broadened, he tugged at the tickets I clutched near my chest in my right hand, studied what showed between my fingers and his, and abruptly shook his head.

"*There*," he said, or some Russian-accented equivalent. He pointed to a different plane where a second group of about two dozen people huddled at the bottom of a stairway, passengers mounting it one at a time to enter the airplane. "*Peerm*," he repeated, smiling, and led us to the crowd, pushing his way past people roughly while beckoning Lee and me to follow. At the bottom of the steps he elbowed two men aside, called up to the stewardesses at the top of the steps, stuck his cigarette in his mouth, dropped his attaché to the icy tarmac, and placed one hand on my back and the other on Lee's. "Go," he said. "*Peerm*," and shoved us up the stairs.

We smiled, thanking him, and found seats (unreserved since this was a commuter flight) immediately fastening our seatbelts, noting with amazement that even on take-off no one else, including the flight crew, did. The plane was old, rickety, with very little insulation against noise. One man lay across two seats on the other side of the aisle from us, another opened a bag and ate hard-boiled eggs; the stewardesses, like the ones in the other plane, let out curlers and rearranged their hair. We had several cups of tepid tea, a pale lemon-colored view of dawn

21

spreading over the snowy landscape, and a surprisingly smooth flight that landed us on a sunny white field at Perm.

No one waited at the base of the airplane steps; no one stood with our names on a sign (as we had been promised) inside the terminal. We carried our bags and backpack out the front door to a cab stand and stood near the curb, trying to look like we knew where our ride would be. Men in fur caps leaned against cars and smoked as they eyed us carefully. Toward our right I noticed several cars leave what appeared to be a parking lot, and for no reason except another place to stand, I motioned Lee toward it. We slogged through several inches of snow on an uncleared sidewalk, and, reaching the corner of the terminal building, stood at the curb again, staring at the lot in one direction and the cab stand in the other. No one, including the men leaning on the cars, looked expectant.

"Well?" I said, looking at Lee.

She shrugged and said it would be alright. "They're only a few minutes late."

We had a name, Olga, for our contact, but no address or phone number though we had addresses and numbers for Oleg and Gennady in Moscow. I had just resolved to enter the terminal and try to phone one of them when a young woman in black wool coat, leather boots, and a tall, fur Siberian hat strode up to us and, nervously, pronounced our names.

"Lee? Ben?–I am Olga Kolarova." A young man, clean-shaven, stood just behind her left shoulder holding a black worker's cap. She introduced him as

Andrei, and he stepped forward immediately, extending his hand warmly, first to Lee, then me. They led us through the parking lot to their car, Andrei taking Lee's bag and letting me manage on my own. Bags and backpack in the trunk, Lee and I took the back seats while Andrei drove us out of the airport grounds and Olga laid out the day's activities.

"First," she said, turning to face us from the front seat, "we'll meet Katharina, of the Child Welfare Office, who arranges adoptions for our children who need it. Then we'll go to the hospital and meet the child."

I looked at Lee, suddenly feeling my throat clench while my hand reached for hers. She smiled warmly, her face flushing a deep, pleasure-filled red. "Mikhail," she said aloud, as if tasting it. "Alexandrovich."

"Yes, Mikhail. He awaits us at the hospital. Katharina may go there with us, too."

I nodded, looking out at the snow piled high above the car's roof line beside the highway. As we rode, we began to see buildings, more brick here than the ubiquitous gray cement in Moscow, and, as if I would find a clue to future behavior in my son, I observed people closely along the streets, noting orderly queues at bus stops, well-dressed boys and girls on the way to school, and here and there along the streets intricate ice sculptures with individual men and women working on them as people walked past.

"It's a very nice city," I said to Olga, remarking to myself that no one looked miserable, oppressed, or shabby in the way many, especially men, had looked in Moscow. I had read something about Perm–that it had an artistic tradition, having housed the Bolshoi Ballet during World War II, that it was the birthplace of the ballet impresario Sergei Diaghilev, and that it had a respected university as well as several prosperous theaters and industries. Seeing it firsthand still presented surprises, among them its quaint, European appearance that reminded me more of Switzerland than some backwater economic power with a city trying to survive.

"Yes," Olga said, smiling. "We are very proud of our *Peerm.*"

She spoke a few words in Russian to Andrei, and as we drove through town she pointed to landmarks: the state theater and museum, the university campus, several schools and shopping areas, and then the principal river, the Kama, iced over in the center of town.

At some point we turned off the main road into a driveway and parked amid a group of stolid red brick buildings. Lee and I stayed in the car while Olga entered one. Andrei turned and smiled at us but said nothing since he apparently knew very little, if any, English. In about fifteen minutes Olga returned to the car with a tall, blonde woman in a plaid wool coat whose smile lit up the day as well as her face. She opened the car door, slid into the seat beside Lee, and introduced herself as Katharina. When she took my hand and shook it, immediately calling me "Ben," I felt my throat relax at last and my voice regain a little of its normal timbre.

"Well," she said. "Let's go meet your child."

Lee nodded and smiled. I felt a bit of a clench return to my throat, and I must say it grew tighter as we drove, passing several more ice sculptures that Katharina said formed part of an annual festival competition. "It's well-known," she said. "People travel from all over Europe to see it."

I nodded, noting a particularly intricate white structure assembling a group of people in a line surrounded by a frame-like boundary that could have been a room or might have been a bus stop, but we passed too fast for me to make it out. Katharina pointed to several sculptured Disney figures, a spray-painted Mickey Mouse and Goofy, among others, talking to a Donald Duck and Pluto, but before we could comment on them Andrei turned off the road, followed a narrow drive, and pulled into what turned out to be the hospital grounds.

"This is it," Lee whispered, squeezing my hand.

Andrei parked, leaving the engine running, but Olga and Katharina got out, with Katharina leaning in again and smiling. "Come," she said, looking at both of us. "Meet your son."

"Will we be taking him with us?"

Yes, I had to ask that question.

"If you approve," Katharina said, frowning. "From that moment on he is yours."

"Perfect!" Lee smiled and left the car. I got out too and slowly followed the three women down the sidewalk.

25

Red brick gave way to gray and white institutional paint as Katharina, obviously in charge now, led us down a hallway and up a flight of stairs. I saw several children, in old sweaters and dirty sweat pants, standing around, talking as they looked at us. We crossed a room where two women in black and white striped hospital uniforms huddled together and, it seemed to me, tried not to stare. I smiled at them, nodding, and one embraced the other's shoulders. The embraced one raised her hands to her cheeks and lifted her foot.

"In here," Katharina said, beaming again. She opened a door, allowing Lee to enter first, then me, and finally Olga who had stood to the side to let us pass. We entered an office with a small couch, several chairs, and a desk, behind which sat a smiling gray-haired woman wearing a white lab coat with a stethoscope dangling from her pocket.

"Dr. Dugin, may I present the prospective parents of Mikhail Alexandrovich?"

The doctor nodded, rising to step around the desk and nervously motion us to the couch. I had the impression that much of this was new to her–as it seemed to Olga, I thought–and that the only confident person in the room (other than Lee) happened to be Katharina. She spoke a few words to the doctor, a few more to Olga–all in Russian–and Dr. Dugin sat back down at her desk. She asked about our trip, especially the flight from Moscow, and after smiling at my account of the seat-beltless stewardesses and passengers on the plane to Perm, asked us if we had questions about

26

Mikhail.

"Is he healthy?" I asked. "And ready for all these big changes?"

"He has had a few problems, but medically he is ready to begin his new life," Dr. Dugin said. "He should have little difficulty."

"Can we see him now?" Lee asked, interrupting my next question. "We want to see him for ourselves."

"Of course, that's natural," Katharina answered. "The doctor can send for him immediately."

She nodded at Dr. Dugin, who picked up her phone, said a few words into it, and then hung up. Lee went to the backpack I carried and took out diapers and clothes for the baby, several mobiles and games for the children of the hospital, and a dozen boxes of snack packs for kids and staff. She also brought out half-dozen pairs of pantyhose that had been suggested for nurses and others, and a pile of toddlers' pants and shirts.

She handed them to the doctor, who smiled gratefully but bashfully while placing them on her desk. Katharina grinned and said we were very generous. We sat in silence for several minutes, when suddenly the door beside the doctor's desk opened. A nurse stepped into the doctor's office, and then—while I held my breath—a second one followed, carrying a baby in her arms.

"Oh, there he is!" Lee murmured. She immediately reached out her arms, and the baby, in what must have been an automatic *frisson* of happiness (his first, I've always figured) beamed back at her, his

27

face flushing, his baby *goo-goo* absolutely joyful, his body lunging forward as his hands and arms stretched toward Lee.

"*Lyubov…* Misha," Lee said. "He's beautiful!"

I embraced her as the nurse let him lean into her arms, and Lee held him to her face and breast. I put my hand on his back and felt myself giggling and cooing uncontrollably while Misha smiled, cuddled with Lee, and then reached out to my hand. "Please, take a picture," I said, turning to Katharina and handing her the camera I had brought. She smiled, snapping the picture while Lee and I huddled around the boy. His fresh baby smell filled the room, and I felt the strength of his joy as he squeezed our fingers and pinched our hands.

"Uh, so …" Olga stammered. "Is the child … uh … satisfactory, then?"

We looked at her, giggling through our nervousness, not quite sure what she meant.

"The child. Is he…?"

"Oh, yes, yes, of course! He's more than satisfactory," Lee nearly shouted. "He's wonderful!"

Katharina nodded, motioned to the doctor with a large grin on her face, and, after we had signed several papers agreeing to the adoption, she led us, Misha, and Olga out of the office.

PART TWO:

BABEL

II.

So in that brief political, biological, ten minutes, after a few signed forms, a sudden gasp, that first photograph, and a quick change out of plain Russian swaddling into shiny throw away diapers, the three of us became a family — an American family.

"Transubstantiation," Lee used to joke. "It's the power of images."

Which accounts, she also said, though at a much later date, for Misha's obsession with theatrical costumes, masks, and eye-catching daily clothing. Since his second or third year, he has always loved Halloween, and for most of the many falls afterward, several days before and after October 31st, he would put on recent handmade costumes, once or twice the buckskin of an Indian brave that Lee had fashioned out of tan velour and leather fringes, occasionally the green and white space suit of a Buzz Lightyear clone (my construction: painted cardboard boxes, plastic helmet, vinyl gloves and boots), and in these later autumns, Misha's own Harry Potter variation, a Wizard-of-Oz-inspired mix of brainless scarecrow and brainy magician, with witch's cape, black hat, and blue overalls giving him a comic appearance of magical power.

"My son the showman," I tell people, when I show his picture.

Because of that, each year for at least the last five, I've pulled the car out of our garage on a gorgeous

30

end of October day, and as I've promised Misha for three or four weeks before, driven across New Jersey to the George Washington Bridge, parked on the Jersey side of the river in Fort Lee, and, thinking of Rip Van Winkle and Washington Irving, walked across the river into Fort Tryon Park, taking in the bruised and flowing water, the cruising boats, the boxy Palisades, and, with particular interest, the ever changing form of the glass and metallic skyline before us. Sometimes I've thought of Marsden Hartley as we walked, sometimes Joseph Stella or some other New York City painter, but always at the back of my mind my true master, Van Gogh, loomed, along with the Rhone and the bridges across it in southern France. The view of the Hudson valley, broad river, boats, and their watery energy seem like images Van Gogh might have appreciated. Misha loves them too, often pointing to buildings and sights he already knows from our many trips into the city–Riverside Church, the Chrysler Building, and of course the Empire State Building. About half way across on one recent visit, with the late October wind buffeting the three of us, he stopped, planted his hand on his hat, and, like a Dutch ship's figurehead, peered down river toward the narrows.

"I remember them still," he said. "Two aluminum boxes shining in the sun. One had a giant black aerial, and even with that I imagined them as polished salt and pepper shakers standing over the city." Lee smiled at the image, then pointed all the way past the memories to the distant bridge across the

31

narrows. We could barely make out an upraised arm and torch from the Statue of Liberty and, beyond that, a brownish Staten Island. Just below us a tug horn bellowed, pushing a trash barge upstream beneath our feet, and on our right a white sailboat tacked sharply away, toward the safety of the Jersey shore.

Misha had gone to school the day the towers fell, second grade. I attended a morning faculty meeting at work, and when word reached us through a cell phone text message to our department chair, we all stared out the window together at the clear blue sky (a gorgeous Provence sky, Lee and I might have said). A medevac helicopter raced across the horizon toward the hospital landing pad just beyond our campus, and we all abruptly, without the least nod toward Robert's Rules by our chair or anyone else, ended the meeting, whispered good-byes, and rushed from the building to go our separate ways.

Lee had left early for New York that morning, planning to attend shows in several SoHo galleries. She would then meet a friend for lunch at–you guessed it– the top of one of the towers.

I knew her plans and assumed that she had not arrived before the planes struck (about quarter to nine, you probably recall). But when I heard about the collapse of the towers, the clouds of ash, and people running, screaming in panic through the downtown streets, I worried, terribly. What about a second attack, I wondered–this could not be a one-shot deal, I figured– either from land or air? Where would she be? Where *could* she be?

She didn't answer her cell phone when I dialed, but Lee, like me in those days, rarely kept it on for incoming calls. Yet since she hadn't called to leave a reassuring message for me, I assumed that meant she couldn't, and because of that my worry deepened into a barely controlled panic. I called a friend in his office-studio on the Upper West Side but got a phone company recorded response advising me to try again later. I then called Misha's school here in New Jersey, relieved to hear a live human voice on the other end, but the hushed, frightened stammer of the principal's secretary increased my eerie feelings. "The children are fine," she said, with what I heard as trussed-up confidence. "We're in shut-down mode for now. We've locked all the doors and told them nothing. But many parents travel into New York for work, and we haven't been able to reach most of them. We're making plans to keep children here–with parents and teacher guardians–until we receive other directions."

"I'll pick up my son, Misha Alto, at the end of the day," I said. "And I'll be glad to take one or two kids in if they need a place. First, I've got to see about my wife. She's in New York, I think, but I'm not sure where."

The secretary stopped breathing. After a ponderous moment she barely whispered, "Have you seen those videos of people running and screaming? With the dust covering them, they look like zombies — or worse, ghosts."

"I haven't, and I don't think I want to," I told

33

her. "There'll be more than enough real ghosts to worry about, I'm afraid."

"Good luck finding Mrs. Alto," she answered, without a trace of sympathy. "We'll take good care of Mikhail if you need that."

I thanked her, hanging up after reminding her that I would pick up Misha at the end of the school day.

Lee and I had never planned much for emergencies. Like most married people, I bet, we assumed we'd be together if lightning struck or, should that not happen, then we knew each other well enough to figure out where the other would likely go, how the other would make contact, or make herself available for contact, and, finally, mutually took for granted that caring for Misha always had priority.

I called her cell phone again, left a message about picking up Misha at school, and then took the half hour drive home from my office to be near him should anything worse occur. Cars looked strangely ordinary on the road; drivers seemed unusually intent as they steered and, like me, very much tuned to something–not music, I knew–on the radio.

I figured Lee herself might be headed home right now, having joined the massive, hectic exodus from the city, and was speeding across New Jersey on Route 80 immediately before the bridge and tunnels closed. Intuition told me to believe that, but I couldn't quite keep the faith because she still hadn't called. I assumed a call or text would have been her first response once the planes hit–if nothing else, to ease my mind, as well as Misha's–and without one from her now I began to

34

imagine awful possibilities.

A second call to my Upper West Side painter friend went through, and his calm tone, the fact that he hadn't heard, or sensed, anything unusual as he took his dog for a morning walk in Riverside Park that morning, made me think Lee just wasn't aware of the attack or hadn't yet sensed its gravity.

"Just an ordinary day until some doorman on West End Avenue told me," my friend said. "All of a sudden I understood the quiet skies and the look on everyone's face. I'm at the TV now. Have you seen those bodies falling?"

"I'm trying to find Lee," I said. "And I don't want to think of her as falling. If you hear from her, tell her to call me immediately."

"Don't worry, pal. I'm sure she'll be alright, and she can always stay here if they won't let her out."

"Thanks. I'll leave your number on her cell."

"Do that. But I'm sure she's all right. It was way too early for lunch. She was probably in a chichi SoHo gallery and is now walking as quickly as possible uptown."

I agreed, but for the life of me I couldn't understand why she hadn't phoned. I couldn't imagine a harmless reason, of course, and there were scores of potentially painful ones filling — overfilling — my mind.

I said good-bye to my friend, called Lee's cell to leave his number, and, basically, begged her to call immediately once she received my message. I returned to the highway after hanging up and continued west across Jersey, noting the sky clear of both clouds and planes, and a sudden plenty of trooper cruisers on the road—more than a dozen from what I saw. At the halfway point toward Pennsylvania, I decided to make a phone call home on the outside chance that Lee had gone there before me. No one answered, my own mechanical New York voice projecting a false sense of optimism and well-being, although I'm proud to say I didn't wish the caller a nice day or happy week. In the end I left a message for Lee, hoping, desperately now, that she was well and virtually demanding that she dial my cell when she got home. With that I left my phone on the passenger seat, put both hands on the wheel, and forced myself to concentrate on driving.

Traffic slowed to a near stop at a couple of points, mostly because of congestion and merges, once because of road work then in progress. I watched the workers, usually one woman to a road crew, standing around and talking as they waved us by. For one of the few times in my life I didn't imagine their conversations to be useless or inconsequential. In fact, their work, I reasoned while driving by that morning, helped preserve an efficient emergency escape route. I noticed many of them looking eastward, as if they expected to see something there—or already had seen it. My mirrors showed me nothing but cars and trucks above the road surface, and so I assumed their glances reflected thought direction rather than actual sights. Their hard hats seemed pathetically comic and more useless than usual, primarily because the weight and power of events just a few miles away rendered them futile.

36

By the time I reached my exit, about fifty or sixty miles from the bridge and about ten miles from the Pennsylvania border, the road had emptied quite a bit and traffic moved ahead more swiftly. I got off in Blairstown, took some back roads north to avoid the center of town, and then turned on to our quiet country road where, I noticed, nothing seemed to register a dramatic event. A couple of new American flags hung limply above a pair of lawns, but apart from them this might have been an ordinary early fall day in suburbia: one man rode his mower, a woman placed pumpkins and pots of yellow mums on her front porch, and the farmer near the top of our road carried slop to his pigs, who wallowed and huddled at various places around his small pond.

I'd like to say these pleasant country scenes eased my mind, but in fact they had just the opposite effect. I felt sick at such normalcy; the blandness of it all brought a gag to my throat, as if I were seeing evil disguised as good. For the first, and so far only, time in my life I wished for a pistol or rifle, something to strike with at someone or something rushing toward me on the attack. I knew the pig farmer had a rifle and a shotgun, maybe more than one, and I knew that most of the men along the road kept weapons hidden somewhere up in their master bedrooms in case of a night-time invasion while they slept. "It's my family or them," one of my neighbors informed me. "I'll shoot first and ask obvious questions later. I'm going to defend my home until the very last breath in my body."

37

I had smiled and nodded ironically the last time a neighbor told me that, but on this sunny September morning as I motored home, I began to believe in a world where it must be the basic rule.

Our house, as I had feared, looked absolutely quiet and empty, without a light on or window open to let in air. And of course the TV screen looked dark, which on a day like this was a dead giveaway to lack of human occupants.

I parked the car in the garage, closed the overhead, and entered the house through our rec room where Misha kept games, Game Cube, a foosball table, and the family TV. Our dog, Vincent, ambled into the room as I entered, wagging his tail good-naturedly and stretching before plopping himself on his pillow again.

I turned on the TV, saw tapes of the buildings' collapse alternating with images of people running in panic away from them, and others, sickening, of people plunging to earth in deadpan silence while the networks very conscientiously repeated soundtracks of dead-weighted bodies thumping metal—car and truck metal, of course.

I went into the kitchen, saw no note from Lee as I had hoped, found no message from her on our phone, and no indication in any way that she had returned from leaving for New York after breakfast that morning. I have remained calm through most difficult events in my life since a troubled return I made from a two-year stay in France many years ago, but I admit I railed a lot internally, and on a regular basis, especially about negative possibilities. I was quite good at dismissing

38

those moods, however, reminding myself that many things — good and bad — are possible in life, and I have little power to influence them or make them change. But I tried. I made one more call to Lee's cell, receiving no answer again, no indication that she had attempted to leave a message for me.

"Damn it, Lee," I cursed at her voicemail. "I can't imagine why you haven't called. I hope, really hope and pray, you are fine and can retrieve this message. I love you, Sweetie. But I'm desperate to hear from you; please, please give me a call as soon as you get this."

I went upstairs to our computer to check my email. Apart from the usual spam about making a million, finding a mate, and speeding up my computer's ability to crunch such data, I found a couple of emails from colleagues, a note from a student saying she was not likely to come to class because of possible further attacks, and a reminder from the county library that several of the books Misha had borrowed last month would be due back on Friday. Not knowing what else to do while I waited, I fed Vincent his lunch-time meal and took him out for a walk in the nearby fields.

It is quiet in our neighborhood during the day, the main reason Lee and I moved here from the city. She has wonderful northern light in her studio at the back of the house; the turret-like study I work in has calming views of the Appalachian chain that threads through eastern Pennsylvania; and our country road, combined with the three-acre lot we own, guarantees horn-free, engine-free quiet both day and night. "Boring enough to

39

paint in any time," Lee likes to joke. "Other than an occasional deer, turkey, or bear, we've nothing to distract us from our hobbies."

"Except for a budding teenager," Misha used to add. "One who appreciates a loud TV."

Loud TV or not, I get out on the road with Vincent once or twice a day for walks that take me back to a civilized nature and away from the arcane mysteries of aesthetic theory and history. We usually walk down the road for half a mile, cross over to some woods spread out between and in back of two split-level houses, and then separate, me with leash in hand, Vincent with collar, and follow our noses anywhere from fifteen minutes to an hour or more. We see deer frequently, just about every bird on Audubon's northeastern lifetime list, and, maybe, two or three times a warm season, black bears that, luckily, always seem to be standing still just before walking away. A young pup, Vincent chased one once, but he was smart enough to stop short when I whisper-called him back to my side. Without a sound, the bear turned off the path in front of us, glanced an annoyed insult over his left shoulder, then plunged deeper into the woods, the rustle of grass and crack of tree limbs his only response.

We followed a similar pattern that terrible September afternoon but, to my relief and disappointment, we crossed no other animal's path. A military helicopter cruised overhead twice, pausing for a moment with blades whirring during the second pass to look down on me and Vincent before heading off toward the mountains. I knew that all aircraft had been grounded, so I assumed they were looking for unusual ground activity, something violent to be carried out on route 80, at a local shopping mall, perhaps at a State Troopers' barracks, or the local police station.

Vincent nosed among some ferns, peed on a rock or rotted fallen branch here and there, and eventually left a dump, our personal land-fill project, before trotting over and walking contentedly beside me again. Except for the helicopter, the day seemed extraordinarily quiet, ghostly, especially given the magnitude of events in New York, Washington, and western Pennsylvania. As we stood beside a stream flowing through the woods, where I could see the Delaware Water Gap off to the west, I tried to think of something to do other than wait for Lee — and worry. I'd pick up Misha at about 3:30, but that was nearly three hours away. I knew I wouldn't be able to work on anything difficult, but I dreaded the idea of watching TV, especially the repetitious images of buildings, dust, and people all a-crumble. So, at the house again, I turned on some music–a string quartet by Mozart, "Dissonance," seemed appropriate–and began to jot down notes for a critical article I wanted to write about suburban planning.

I worked for an hour, Googling journal articles on town layouts throughout the world, but when the Mozart finally wound to its dissonant end I had little energy to continue. I turned on the TV for more about developments in New York and Washington, but I could only study faces in crowd shots of New York City.

41

Lee's wasn't among them, and as I watched I realized how ridiculous it was to search. With all trains, tunnels, and bridges closed in or out of Manhattan, I realized she could only take the ferry to New Jersey or spend the night somewhere in the city. Either choice required a phone call home, and again I could not imagine why she had not yet made one.

Circling from room to room for a while, I entered Lee's studio again, hoping in some way it would bring us into closer communication. On her easel stood a landscape of the Delaware Water Gap gradually changing into autumn colors, and I admired the subtle way she had graded from dark blue and red at the bottom through pale green and yellow at the top with a patch of dark blue-green just above the yellow before the mountain gave way to the sky's transparent azure. She had painted the Gap frequently–four times annually since we moved here nearly seven years before–and I always admired the patterns and brushstrokes she used to make each canvas unique, with a slight change in angle, shape, or style so that the scene did not become repetitive.

"My Mont St. Victoire," Lee called it, "but I doubt I'll ever find the wonder Cézanne did."

She hadn't yet, at least to my eye, but who could? And somehow she always made the paintings moving, precisely because she brought the viewer close to the Gap rather than keep it at a mythic distance, with the result that she captured the range's fragility. "The mountain can change," Lee said. "It could be flattened, topped off, or simply blown apart. If it's a god, it's a god

42

that has to fear our power — wrath, ambition, the human rush to control and use up space."

None of that is obvious in the paintings I have seen, again at least to my eye. But it's very clear in each one that there is something larger, more explosive in the surrounding landscape. Occasionally, she shows it as a house, sometimes a stream or car on the highway in or out of Pennsylvania; sometimes it's a looming cloud cover that seems to threaten everything. Curiously, given the nature of that particular day's events, the absolute clarity of the sky, and the gorgeous blue this canvas managed to capture, I couldn't put much stock in the security of natural covers. At the same time I felt the irony and cold fear the picture projected for me when at last the phone rang, and I ran to the kitchen to answer it. It was Lee, of course, and, yes, I was relieved to hear her voice.

"Are you all right, Honey? I'm so happy you called. Are you still in the city?"

"I'm fine, Ben. I'm on my way home. I'm in New Jersey."

"80?–It must be loaded by now. How did you get out?–The bridges and tunnels..."

"I'm on Route 78, and I'll be coming up from the south. To be truthful, I never made it to New York."

"So you heard about it before you went in. How lucky." I flicked on the overhead light and stared out the window, thankful at last for that foreboding, now darkening blue sky.

"Not quite." She paused but then continued:

43

"Ben, I'll tell you about it when I get home. Right now I just want to drive."

"All right. I understand. I'll pick up Misha at the end of school. I'm not sure how to tell him about all this. Maybe I'll wait till you get home. The secretary said they haven't informed the kids at all."

There was a long period of silence. Lee seemed to sigh for a count of ten. Finally, she said, "It's probably for the best to let the parents tell them. I'll be home as soon as I can. We've got a lot to talk about."

"And to be thankful for," I added. "Drive carefully, my love. I'm really happy to hear from you. You can imagine what I was thinking. The worst part was what to say to Misha."

"I was thinking about that, too," Lee said. "It would be awful. In any case, I'll be home soon—if the traffic doesn't hold me up."

We hung up, and I mounted the stairs to my office, happy to write more notes for my article. I felt a mix of relief and privilege, seeing our family as lucky because Lee had been spared not only injury but inconvenience. I had imagined her, at best, stranded somewhere on the streets of the city for the night, her phone lost or not functioning, wallet gone, and, I assumed, no clear or easy means of finding shelter. I could not even think of her in the buildings or beneath them when the planes hit, or when the walls began to fold. Knowing she was on the road now, out of danger, and soon able to return to the life we had created together made me very confident. Without pausing to question why or what that meant, I sat at my desk and

44

continued to plan for an article that might become, eventually, a book.

I worked for another couple of hours, looking up definitions of suburbia and references to it through the 20th century, then thinking about a history that could include developments–or concepts of them before Levittown–I extended the search throughout civilized time, back to Greece and Rome, even before. I Googled outposts and settlements classical armies might have had, assuming their military and political grasps sent soldiers, ministers, businessmen, and priests out into the provinces, with artists following along to gain experience, material, and knowledge. People saw first light in those outposts, and they died, making only occasional visits to capital cities for entertainment and business, because life was hectic, maybe too dangerous, and just so inconvenient compared to the smaller community where everyone knew one another and cared.

I thought of that when I read about and participated in the nationwide outpouring of relief and support to New York City after September 11th that year. The event, shared on television and the internet everywhere, had at last made Marshal McLuhan's "global village" a reality to me. "Today we are all Americans," a French newspaper proclaimed, and when I read that I realized how well the suburban ideal fit us: a quiet community where people share the wish for a good home, a friendly neighborhood, and security against the outside world. Threaten anyone of those,

45

and you can count on neighbors to band together in opposition.

The message of the book hit me that day with a greater thematic clarity than I had ever experienced before, except, perhaps, for the year I painted in Paris as a young man. Of course, since I had allowed that artist's insight to drift, eventually spending itself in a quest for permanent work and material pleasures, I realized how little the flashy return of my youthful insight meant that September. Still, the freshness of it, the sheer physical pleasure I felt turning the impulse into written words excited me, despite an outside world burning to hell. By the time I left to pick up Misha from school, I had more than thirty pages of notes and a fairly detailed outline of what my book would say, what I needed to research, and where I should travel to find an on-site perspective for my theme. "Life is good," I said to myself as I started the car at three-thirty and drove the seven miles to Misha's school. "With all that is going on we have a lot to be thankful for. I can't let us ever forget the joy."

III.

I arrived at the school and parked in the lineup of cars, SUVs and vans mainly, driven by moms ready to head to soccer, dance lessons, or swim team. An occasional granddad or dad, like me, appeared, just ready for home and talk about the day, personal and public, or maybe tuning the TV for more news about events in Washington and New York. I remember thinking how a page had been turned and that I wouldn't be surprised to hear of fighter planes testing our air defenses, amphibious armies attempting landings on the Jersey shore, or enemy cruisers sailing from the Arctic to attack New England.

Not pleasant thoughts, of course, and I imagined Lee and me bringing up Misha in a world where planes flew low and loud overhead, bombs exploded all around us daily, and friends, family, and neighbors became more and more difficult to reach. Our own deaths didn't seem possible–strange, I know, even after spending much of the day watching images of people and buildings falling from great heights. But suddenly the idea of rubble, flames, and ash, let alone the inconvenient lack of water, electricity, heat, and light seemed imminently likely, yet never conclusive. I remembered seeing Vietnam villages destroyed, cities torn by bombs and constant military strife, its people devastated by a historical moment that seemed never to

47

end, even as their backbreaking labor in the rice paddies expressed the basic optimism of humans together with nature producing food.

When I saw Misha trudge out of the school door that afternoon, heavy backpack on his shoulders belying the huge grin on his face, I thought of how much I owed him. The simple confidence in his face, the happiness to see me waiting, threw off all my fatherly fears and brought me, along with a *sotto voce* note of warning, a fresh wave of inner contentment and happiness. I realized again why children, our own and those of others, carry such importance–biologically and emotionally.

"Hi, Dad. How are you? Did you hear what happened today?" He settled into the back seat and automatically attached his seatbelt.

"You mean in New York and Washington? The office secretary told me you wouldn't know anything about it."

"Hah! Mr. Moffitt told us about it–in class. Didn't those towers fall down?" He cringed, looking out the side window to the still perfect blue sky.

I cringed, too. I remembered how much Misha liked to look at the towers as we drove into the tunnel for New York City. "Yes, they came down alright," I said, "both of them."

"They wouldn't let us watch it on TV, for some dumb reason. But it seemed like every five minutes somebody came down the hall and told Mr. Moffitt something new."

"How could they not?–What did the kids have to

48

say? Were they scared?"

"Some of them didn't understand, Dad. I don't know. A couple of them said we'd drop the atom bomb on the bad guys. Mr. Moffitt didn't say anything. He looked kind of scared himself."

"Well, we're safe. No planes are in the air. All the police and soldiers are on alert. But I feel sorry for all those people caught in New York and Washington."

"Dad, where's Mom? Wasn't she going —?"

"She's fine, Misha, she's fine. Mom just called a while ago to tell me she's on her way home. She decided not to go into New York today."

"Dad, did people in the towers … die?"

I nodded, sadly; then I shook my head as if I had failed him somehow. "A lot of people died. I have a feeling it's more than we would guess. Maybe some of your schoolmates will lose family."

He said nothing, settling back in his seat and staring out the window. I heard a beep from the car behind, and with a wave of apology, I put the car in gear and drove quickly off the school grounds.

At home we fed Vincent, and I took him out for his afternoon walk while Misha ate a snack and watched TV. I felt sure I would see images of the Pentagon and New York on the screen as I glanced through the window and watched my son bury a taco chip in some salsa, but to my surprise Sponge Bob's underwater world glowed before him instead. Relieved at that, and slightly disappointed at the same time, I wondered how long the preference for cartoons would last, what it said

49

about him, and, of course, like all helicopter parents, whether I ought not encourage him to face the truth, no matter how gruesome the experience.

But it was early September, a gorgeous fall afternoon, and here I was walking a Retriever named after a suicidal painter of sunshine and brilliant, though dying, flowers. I envied Misha's ability to deny the ugly, and I wished — on this day especially — for more of the child's ability to dismiss it myself. It's no ordinary afternoon in our lives, I thought. But we have to get homework done, take care of Vincent, welcome Lee from a difficult daytrip, make dinner, go to bed, and rise in time for work and school again tomorrow. Our world, for the moment at least, is still intact.

As Vincent and I walked down the road toward the woods, I noticed how everyone else in the neighborhood seemed to follow the same plan. One neighbor mowed his lawn, earplugs in place as if to keep out all dangerous noise. Another hung sheets and towels on a line to take advantage of the sun's late summer heat. A third climbed a ladder to continue work on green window shutters he had been cleaning through the weekend; and a fourth, a woman, airily and lightly fed her daughter basketball after basketball as she circled the periphery of her driveway and bombarded the hoop with her jump shot.

At our turn-around spot near some sugar maples, where we often surprised a lone deer, a shrieking hawk, or a rafter of prowling turkeys, Vincent wagged his tail, pulled up into his working crouch, and dumped the residue of his day's eating. I petted him

50

happily, he rubbed his ears lovingly against my knees, and we headed back at a trot on the mile return home. Letting Vincent off his leash when we reached our driveway, I waved at Misha through the window, and he, glancing up for the moment, chomped on a taco chip and stuck up his thumb. I saw Lee's car in the garage when we entered the back door, and I must say that the day's events, both public and private, faded immediately. The three of us were home together, safe, at last, despite everything that had occurred in the world. Food waited in the refrigerator, water ran freely and cleanly in the pipes, the walls and roof of our house remained intact. We had a life to share and, by God, despite everything we would have a peaceful family dinner, talk about our day's activities, then share some fruit, a little music or TV, and sleep.

I left the kitchen and went out back to see Lee in her studio. She had placed her camera, plus a small shoulder bag full of equipment, on the floor next to her easel and studied her painting of the Gap as well as the view outside her window. I embraced her from behind, turned her toward me, and kissed her lips immediately as I pulled her close.

"I can't tell you how relieved I am to see you. I thought–"

I stopped because I saw tears rolling from her eyes and knew the tension of the day had got to her. I asked how close she had been to driving in, and she just shook her head and looked away.

"I'm sorry. It must have been awful. Did you see

51

anything from the Jersey side?"

She said nothing, made no motion that I could read, but I felt the tension and sorrow seeping from her limbs and shoulders into mine. I stood taller, inched closer, letting her emotion fill me as I looked past her dark hair to the world outside, where a lone military plane crossed the horizon, looking, I imagined, for possible problems hidden among the pines.

"I saw nothing," she said, "until I turned on the radio and heard the news. It seemed unreal; I still can't believe it wasn't a doctored video I watched through a window."

"You saw it? Were you in the car?"

Lee said nothing. She pressed closer to me so our bodies touched from head to toe. She lowered her chin to my chest. Her shoulders and back shuddered suddenly, and when I looked at her face I saw that she cried uncontrollably now. "It was the most miserable feeling I've ever had," she said. "It was worse–worse–than losing our babies because I went through it and felt alone. I never thought I could have a worse day than that."

The military plane had disappeared by now, leaving the scene as innocent as before, and I closed my eyes, trying to nudge the calm of the view out of my mind down to my arms and legs so it might find its way back into Lee.

"Honey, I love you. I can't tell you how glad I am to have you home."

She sobbed, loudly, pulled my face to hers and, with tears pouring down her cheeks, kissed me heavily,

52

passionately, for a long, long time. At the same time we heard a sound at the door. We looked up to see Misha just outside the room, staring. "Excuse me, I just wanted to tell you I'm going to do homework. Don't want to break up anything important."

He grinned, shyly, but with a sense of precocity as well–as if he knew he surprised us with his sophistication. "You're not breaking anything up, Misha. Mom's feeling bad and needs a hug. Come join it–we all need a hug for the family."

He smiled, crossed the room, and smacked into my side. I felt his arms about my waist, saw him reach for Lee's, then she and I put our hands on his shoulders and pulled him closer. We stood quietly, breathing together–in unison–but not by plan. I can't describe the relief I felt, the sheer feeling of strength and safety no matter how fleeting. Lee sniffled; Misha looked up and saw the tears on her cheeks, and tightened his grip on both of us, his fingers digging into the loose flesh on my left side.

"We love you, my boy."

"I love you unequivocally," Lee said. "And I don't want us to part."

Fresh tears came to her eyes, but she laughed in embarrassment now, breaking the embrace to go for a tissue on her desk. Her hair hung in a braid low on her back, and when she stood to blow her nose and wipe her eyes, I saw the serious, sorrowful expression return to her face.

"It's been an awful day," Misha said, looking at

her. "But I feel so safe being home with you."

I took his hand and, as I often do, thought of him wrapped in his swaddling clothes on the day we met him in Russia. We left the room with Lee between us. It seemed important to remain together, so while Misha sat at the kitchen table and began his homework, Lee and I went to the refrigerator and stove to start dinner. Light poured in through the windows, turning the maple floor golden, providing an uncalled for sense of light and cheer to our movements. Lee put a Boccherini CD in the Bose, and the sprightly guitar music turned the preparations into a retro family dance. I watched Misha tapping his foot and pencil, followed Lee in a complicated two-step from sink to refrigerator to stove, and hopped over or around Vincent as he searched for scraps we providentially let fall to the floor before him. In less than an hour dinner was on the table on the screened-in portion of the deck. We sat to it, just smiling at each other and our good fortune, then reaching out to hold hands together in a circle.

"Thanks," I said, looking up at the ceiling. "For everything."

"For letting us remain together," Lee added.

"And for letting us eat again." Misha loosened his grip on my hand, let go of Lee's, and turned to the food on his plate. "*Bon appétit,* everybody," he called, his mouth already full. Lee and I smiled at each other, looked down at our plates, and began dinner, too.

IV.

Later that evening, with Misha already in bed, Lee and I went to her studio and talked over a cup of tea while she painted and I leafed through the daily paper, no item of which seemed relevant to what it would contain tomorrow. Lee didn't go back to the Gap landscape. Instead she put up a new square stretcher and, with a palette of acrylic, began to slap and dab a formless variety of colors on the canvas it contained. From time to time, I glanced to see where she intended to go with it, but after half an hour I saw no pattern or direction emerge.

"Is this something you're imagining," I said. "Or one of those whatevers?"

"It's confusion, pure and simple." Lee laughed, slapping some red into the lower background. "Exactly what I'm feeling."

I nodded, turning over a page of the daily arts section, where I had noticed an announcement for a new exhibition of local artists at a nearby gallery. I wondered if Lee had been invited to show there and, of course, whether that caused the confusion I saw spreading in her paint.

"Like Misha said, it's been an awful day. It's kind of hard to keep your mind on work. I guess that's just free painting," I said.

"Hmm." Lee brushed some ochre and orange

55

into the top right hand corner of the canvas and nodded. It could have been the sun she was painting or, more sinister (and appropriate, I had to admit), a threatening ball of fire.

"Did you see anything over there–on the horizon, before or after the impact?"

She shook her head, silently concentrating on the orange and ochre blob she had created. "The radio let me know," she said. "I didn't stop to look. I didn't want to. I just went back to the car and started home."

I watched her fill in the space around the orange ball with a dark blue and gray square form and a few elevated needle-like triangles that seemed unmistakable to me, though they were primitively, unevenly, drawn. "You didn't see anything from New Jersey?" I asked. "Even at the entrance to the tunnel?"

She shook her head and sobbed, her shoulders slumped forward, her mouth and nose pointing toward her shoes as she took one or two deep breaths. "I never got that far, I'm afraid. Not even close to the tunnel."

"Where were you? Did you see any planes go over?"

"Ben, I saw nothing. I'm telling you I wasn't anywhere near New York–or even on the way. This is very hard for me to tell you."

The slumped shoulders squared themselves, the downturned face did too, with an angry, impatient expression taking the place of her sorrow. I decided to keep quiet, but then I remembered that she had come home from the south and added, "Were you going to the Jersey shore?"

"No, not the shore, Ben. Bed," she said, frowning. "Bed with your friend Jean-Luc."

I laughed, thinking at first that she had made a silly joke. Jean-Luc is a gallery owner in New York to whom I showed Lee's pictures when she was my student. As a result of that meeting he had given Lee her first New York gallery show. Certainly not my best friend, but pretty damn close I have to say, especially when we were younger. He was a means of bringing Lee and me together, and for that I'd always been grateful. "You went to his gallery?" I said. "But that's–"

"In SoHo. Of course. But I never went there, and in fact I didn't intend to. I was driving to meet him ... in Philadelphia."

I said nothing. I tried, in fact, to show nothing on my face as the realization of what she was actually saying sunk in. Lee's own facial expression, her dark, narrowed eyes, her tone of voice, the mix of annoyance and guilt I thought I heard from her, told me everything. Need I say that Jean-Luc is my age, maybe a year or two younger, but eminently better connected, more sophisticated, and, yes, wealthier and more handsome, too?

"Philadelphia?–"

"He owns a brownstone there, near the Art Institute. We've spent several pleasant afternoons at the place."

"Pleasant?–"

"Yes."

"Really?"

57

"What do you want?–Something graphic?"

I said nothing again, probably the only appropriate response, given all that we had experienced that day, and all that we had gone through in our married life. I studied Lee as she turned back to the easel and slapped more red onto the lower half of the canvas, spreading it like blood. The obvious questions– How long? How important? How often, or when? And, of course, how about us?–didn't seem to be worth asking. I looked out the window, watched an orange glow settle behind the hills of the Gap, and then, as if the last ten minutes had never occurred, turned another page of the day's meaningless paper.

I pretended to read an article, ridiculous as that felt, and in reality glanced at headlines and photo captions. There was one about a pack of Cub Scouts collecting money for a trip to the Statue of Liberty and another about a high school group selling raffle tickets to a Broadway show. Both would be cancelled, I guessed, along with dozens of other potentially educational trips for kids in school and their parents. Education, along with our family life, had suddenly become less carefree.

"It's been more than six months," Lee said into my silence. "Since last spring, as a matter of fact, when you went to that conference in Los Angeles."

I nodded, afraid to say anything because it would have come out as aggressive anger. Finally, I mustered the self-control to let my head—physically, at least—do the talking. I nodded a second time.

"I visited the gallery. We had coffee, and when

58

you flew out to deliver your paper... I had coffee again."

She shrugged and went back to the canvas, a study of red, orange, yellow, and black by now. She picked a brush with a fine point and started to draw in action lines: things falling from the top, wavering lines of movement across the red, some hectic traces left and right, as well as up, throughout the middle. To me it looked like news imagined against a background of reality. Maybe the news was inside the color.

"I know you wanted me to go with you," she said. "But I really didn't feel the need. Art history doesn't interest me anymore. I need to paint, not research. I need to look at things being done around me—now."

"So you went to Jean-Luc's."

She looked at me, steadily. "Yes, but from his gallery to something more."

I smiled, despite everything. I knew it wasn't a comforting one, to Lee or me, but nothing else seemed possible at that moment. Looking back now, I can say the smile covered a cold rush of anguish and fear. That day I would have said I was trying to breathe. "Are you-?" I couldn't finish the question. Lee saw my hesitation and answered the next one instead.

"I was going to leave you, today. I was going to spend the next few days or weeks with Jean-Luc in Philadelphia because I knew you could stay home with Misha. I wanted to see if it would work, at least temporarily."

"Work?" I barely made the word audible

because my voice seemed to be caught at the base of my throat.

"Between Jean-Luc and me," she said. "But then, when we were talking in his living room, the news came over the Temple Public Radio station. It changed everything."

Again, I could say nothing. The trap at the base of my throat seemed to bite deeper into the howl it had swallowed there.

"I left, almost immediately, but then I couldn't decide to come home. I went back to Jean-Luc's, and we watched the events unfold together on his TV. The one solace I had was that nothing seemed to have happened up here. At least you and Misha were all right."

"But you didn't call. I worried about you, terribly."

"Ben, I couldn't talk. I needed to see you. The phone just wasn't the right way."

I folded the newspaper and dropped it to the floor.

"You mean if... If all that hadn't happened, you would have called to tell me? Or would you have left us–Misha and me–in the dark?"

Lee shook her head. "I was very confused. I would have told you something. I'm not sure what."

"Another lie," I said, feeling my teeth bite against my cheek. When she nodded, turning back to the canvas so that her slumped, rounded shoulders seemed to close around any words she might utter, I picked up my tea and stood beside her. I stared, not at the canvas, not out the window, but at her. "You were

60

going to leave a second grade boy alone, one we flew to Moscow to give a family to? And me?"

"You," she said. "Not Misha."

I felt hot tears roll down my face and bathe the corners of my mouth. The heat and salt seemed to paralyze me, and for a short while all my lips could do was tremble as I stared at her.

"I would have called," Lee said. "I would have told you something. In the long run I would have made sure that he saw both of us, regularly and often."

"For Jean-Luc!" I shouted. "You would have given all this up for him–as well as ruined your son's life." I gulped the tea, tasteless but for the contrast it provided to my salty tears.

"For God's sake, Ben. I wouldn't have ruined anything. At least that wasn't my intention. I knew you would care for him. I knew we could share his time until he went out on his own. And I knew you could handle all that."

"Handle it?"

"You're reasonable. We both are. But that's exactly why I wanted to try something new–*needed* to try something new, in fact."

There it is, I thought, the ax of connubial boredom. Yes, and when that ax comes at your neck, man or woman, you have no defense. Your head will roll, and life will go on as before–for everyone but you.

"Well, I guess that clears everything up," I said — reasonably, I thought. "But tell me, what made you decide to come home?"

"The horror," Lee said, without hesitation. "And what might come next. I couldn't bear the thought of separation. Not now. I'd miss you–*you*, I mean–and Misha, of course."

"Despite the boredom, you'd miss me? Why —?"

Lee frowned. "You don't have to be nasty, Ben. I know this can't go down very easily." Then her voice shook. "At least I'm holding nothing back."

"Neither am I!"

I shrugged, allowing a look of doubt mixed, I'm sure, with intense indignation to cross my face. At the same time I felt pretty damn stupid.

"I love you," she said. "I felt it when I was in Jean-Luc's living room watching TV."

I laughed, though not with any joy or humor. Lee turned, put her hands on my shoulders and looked into my eyes. I've been a sucker for such soulful looks most of my life, not from arousal, although that can happen, too, but from deep emotional sub-verbal attachment. Automatically, I put my arms around her and drew her close. There wasn't much more I could do–or say–than that, but it was enough, I guess, because I could feel her own anger and frustration ooze from her arms, and then her legs and chest, not exactly bathing me, but somehow washing both of us clean. Everything from that awful day seemed to run off during that embrace, and when I looked through the window into the orange and purple sky of the evening's sunset, all my fears, public and private, began to fade. Lee put down her brushes, took a sip of my tea before I finished it, and together we left the room to go up to bed.

PART THREE:

BEFORE THE FALL

V.

Anne-Marie: not a women's magazine or hair product, but a real woman. It has been years, and yet, to my secret embarrassment, I still see her in carved stone or painted images: burnished skin on her long legs and arms, a cascade of strawberry hair and shining eyes that lent bright fire to her head and shoulders. Once, when she returned from a family vacation in Spain, where she had spent days on a topless and bottomless Atlantic beach, I saw her nude figure in my Paris apartment when I returned from work one afternoon: I opened the door, saw her stand expectantly with a glass of wine in each hand, and sank helplessly to my knees before her.

"I must have you," I blurted, heat and blood rising instantly to my face.

She fell to her knees beside me, giggling, placing the glasses on the floor near our legs. Flattered by my obvious pleasure, she took me, lovingly, in her arms. "It's all for you, my love," she whispered, her tone motherly as she pulled my head to her breasts. "This is all for you, no one else."

More than thirty years have passed since that day, and to my astonishment I still feel it—the bald, in fact brutal, combination of emotional and sensual longing. It was not our first intimate moment, and it certainly wouldn't be our last, but I hadn't seen her in weeks, and I still go back to that meeting for a lightening-like feeling of perfect happiness and comfort. Anne-Marie shared herself with me as she never had before and, I'm sorry to say, never would as fully again. The pure confidence we felt from her naked beauty satisfied both our dreams. Next morning, when, finally, we had to dress and prepare for work—I to a class in English, she to a magazine she helped edit—we drank coffee, kissed, and parted at the Metro station near my apartment in a pure emotional glow.

"It was wonderful," Anne-Marie said, "a perfect joy. I thought of moments like these all the time on the beach. The ocean whispered to me only of you."

"Up here it was the river talking. I heard you on every single *quai*."

We embraced and kissed again, her smile revealing the memory of many secret joys as we held hands for a moment and turned toward our trains, hers heading east toward the suburbs on the Marne, mine north toward the Marais above the Seine.

Because of Anne-Marie, especially on those two particular days, my thoughts about French life always come filtered through the recall of warm and soulful afternoons. It is why I love the country, I think, and feel at home there. At the risk of unintentional humor, let me emphasize the gentle affection Anne-Marie and I felt toward each other. *Lust* Lee would call it, though her own affection had a very questionable outcome on that awful September morning in 2001; *romance* others might say, with a nod toward some teenage heart-stopper film. But I think of it differently: as physical harmony and emotional joy, its deeper colors evoking some mythic

65

spiritual order. I'm a bookish art critic, I know, but to me, with all its bizarre immigrant politics, the shame of the anti-Semitic Vichy regime, the *Charlie Hebdo* massacre, the patriotic egos battling over culture and language, along with food, there's still something grand about France, Paris, and now—especially in recent years—the south, especially Provence.

Beauty.

From an airplane window French landscape offers a mind-stopping message, particularly after crossing the ocean through the night and passing over Spain in the early morning hours. I see more than Pyrenees and fields in the sunrise; I feel the land's softness and heat as we cruise over farmlands and valleys. Then I inhale the country's rosemary, lavender scented breath and hear its quiet, fulfilling murmur when I step out of the terminal into the sun: not Anne-Marie in the flesh, certainly, but every wonderful thing that reminds me of my time with her. The language, spontaneous on my lips and tongue now, brings back the gasp and greeting, the full embrace with the afternoon's first welcoming kiss on our knees.

Sketches I drew of Anne-Marie that afternoon still hold my attention, as well as one large oil of her in the nude on my bed. Although she and I would eventually split up, and I left my apartment and Paris for another, more possible life, her land and people have always pulled me back, claiming me as if I were a lover or son. I return often, speak the language easily, defend the country during every attack from freedom-fry lovers back home, and always, *always* feel as if I have entered another life–the real one I left for academic criticism and art history in the United States so many years ago.

Now, with a wife and a son, both of whom I love, along with many more years of regret than a man with such memories should count, I return regularly–for short visits, summer vacations, an occasional conference or sabbatical year–to harmonize two important parts of my soul.

The process usually starts just after the winter holidays: the lights of Christmas dim; the gloom of a new year descends into dark, bitterly freezing western Jersey nights, and at some point I get an idea for an article or book–or Lee, blessedly, will decide she needs the climate of France to re-inspire her painting.

"There's a nice house for rent in the Ardeche," she'll say. Or, "Near Vic there's a real Count who wants to rent his family villa."

I frown, shake my head, then think about the light around Arles or Avignon, and ask about St. Rémy de Provence.

"Too expensive there, too *chichi*," Lee will say. "If we want to spend the whole summer, we'll need to find something affordable."

"It's tax deductible–if I write something from it."

"Or I sell a painting."

Lee smiles, sadly. For me as well as herself because she always wishes–matching a secret desire of my own–that I would make time to go back to painting. It's her means of making our life together whole, even though she knows she is not of that earlier part.

"You do the painting," I say. "Leave the

67

evaluative work to me. That's what I changed my stuffy career for."

And so the yearly process starts. In our spare time Lee and I search the internet for decent airfares and car rentals, interesting places to visit or return to, and then we start the phoning and emailing to make it all come true. This year I have a real project, a book-length essay about the life and times of people in Roman suburbs during the glory days of Julius and Augustus and how that life extends to us today—especially through Provence. I have an idea that Roman suburbs-their distance from the center along with their accessibility to it, as in "All roads lead to Rome"-are central to the development of our present life. We-and I mean ordinary family people like you and me-are always outside looking in, but our presence makes that center, the one in Rome, say, hold.

As a result this past winter Lee and I planned a sort of trans-Alpine tour: Rome to Siena; up the coast to Liguria; through the Maritime Alps to Nice; and then westward to St. Rémy de Provence, Montpelier, and Spain-most likely Barcelona, where we'd turn around and retrace our steps to Rome. I wanted to register for myself and my readers the feel of the journey from center to periphery and back again, and emphasize the role of St. Rémy, which has always been a comfortable spot for Lee and me, as well as a historic one with the suburban Roman town of Glanum lying beneath it, the influence of the Troubadours in nearby Les Baux, and the intense visits of people like Thomas Jefferson and my artistic idol, Vincent Van Gogh.

A modern suburb, St. Rémy emphasizes commerce, the surrounding roads providing efficient means to transport goods and, therefore, easing and making more efficient their distribution. Rome codified and unified the political world, but perhaps more important for people like you and me, it spread its economy widely, increasing the distribution of items and money among the people living on the edges. Glanum was a stopover for transport across the French mountains and the harsh desert landscape of the Crau. The street of shops I dimly imagine in the rubble there, like the shops more clearly outlined in the distant city of Vaison-la-Romaine and the port of Ostia outside Rome, show how sophisticated classical shopping practices were–in fact, much like our own.

So, the town of St. Rémy de Provence loomed large in the book as I planned it that winter. It had personal resonance too, because I still remember my first visit there with Lee many years ago, and a morning, a Saturday I believe, when I walked from our hotel, The Nostradamus, into the circle, wearing a straw sun hat I had bought in Venice and a gray spring jacket in which I usually walked and, occasionally, played golf. As I toured the circle, I saw most of the shops open, people lining the streets, and Gendarmes directing automobile traffic onto the side roads. I saw a flower stand on one corner and, passing it, I walked to the newspaper store where I bought copies of the *International Herald Tribune* and *La Provence* and then continued around the *périphérique.*

The breeze braced me, the temperature, sun, and

69

cloudless sky were perfect. Buoyed by the elements on this first anniversary of our marriage, I decided to let the day develop on its own. I lifted a bouquet of roses in my hands at the flower stand, held the newspapers under my left arm, and felt, or saw, a wonderful premonition of happy days extending before Lee and me without end. I don't think I've ever experienced a more confident life-moment, even with Anne-Marie. There have been times when seeing an artwork in a certain light, or sharing an intimate hour or two with someone, or seeing happiness light the face of Lee or Misha, has made me feel as wonderful, but always with the sense that time passed inexorably and the happy moment must inevitably end.

Yet that morning (and that bouquet of flowers, along with the town itself) caught me off-guard, rubbing my face in the intense optimism of a moment as if to teach me a larger lesson: I would be a successful husband; Lee and I would forge a happy marriage; our life together would produce endlessly beautiful moments like this one, each serving to eradicate the idea of time passing, moments ending, and change leading into inevitable decay. Spirit would win out.

We still have photographs of those pink roses–and ourselves–from that day. The health of the flowers and the freshness of our complexions belie the cheap camera we used to capture the image and the mood, as if the pale blossoms and our faces somehow held the true significance of that morning. Each time we've returned to the town, especially on the *périphérique*, I feel the impulse of the moment I lifted those flowers, their

70

stems wrapped in crackling cellophane, and inhaled their fragrance as I started back to the hotel and Lee. She feels it when she sees the plane trees arching over a perfectly straight road just outside town or notices the showers of lavender at various corner gardens and plazas. It is as if we held hands together for the first time, gasping at the fresh wind they call the mistral, and dived into a cool, sky-blue pool–again and again — after a long time away.

We didn't fly to Provence the previous spring and summer, partially because we had other plans, partially because of health. But we read about it — arson-set fires decimating the landscape around Fréjus, young men and women rioting in cities throughout the country — and wondered about the complexities of actually living there: the day-to-day aridity, the beautiful, yet bruised and brutal, landscape. We thought of friends there–the Feiges, the Gorets, and the Bernards–and wondered how dramatically their lives were affected by the events, as they did about ours when they saw live images from the World Trade Center, the Pentagon, and Western Pennsylvania in 2001.

We saw televised images of forests in flames, smoke rising darkly above the southern French mountains, and thought about the history of the place, the mysterious power it still holds over the two of us. In memory, it easily placed us in a car on the Autoroute du Soleil as we stared at mountains of exposed red rock, white granite mounds dotted with blue pine, abandoned stone houses, and small, ochre towns struggling, yet lovely beneath the heat. We've always felt we are a part of it.

Van Gogh's paintings of Arles and St. Rémy revel in that feeling, gaining power, it seems to me, by showing the mystery arched over humans and landscape in swirls of dark blue clouds, pinwheels of light breaking through them, and the generally boxy sense of strength and ominous weight he invested in hills, trees, and boulders. A somber couple walks in the underbrush in one such painting, but even his bright, sunlit oils reveal a sense of foreboding, giving the golden glow of sun overwhelming power and heat, placing it burning behind a sower of seeds or infusing the figures of a father, child, and mother coming together in a dried-out, sterile garden. Van Gogh journeyed there to find fresh light and paint it against his memories of a gloomy north, but my guess is he also missed the human comforts of Paris, Flanders, and Amsterdam while he stayed in the south–the urban night life, the cities' emphasis on human community, which I think he dearly valued. It made the rupture with Gauguin, a man of intelligence as well as paint, that much more violent. So, he demonized the landscape, infusing it with ambiguous soul and power through color, line, and form.

That's my thesis, anyway, and I believe the history of Provence carries the interpretation. Ancient as well as modern armies have marauded here, brigands of many races and creeds have operated freely (some say they still do), individuals fought, stabbed, punched, and ground each other into the powdered earth. Yet the sowed fields of lavender, the cultivated olives and grapes, the abbeys and churches, the organized mill towns and farmers' markets testify daily–along with paint, stone, and clay–to a possible easier world of love, friendship, warmth, and trade, exactly my feelings for the place in memory despite Van Gogh.

I still remember walking into my apartment to see Anne-Marie that Parisian afternoon, only the Rhone is my river of reverie now, not the Seine. I see and feel her soft reddish hair, the pale lavender of her dress draped on a wooden chair, and the eager smile with which she greeted my surprise at her complete, earthy tan. Thinking of it now, her body image shines so vividly in my mind that the emotion brims in my eyes. Somewhere I have read that beauty provides a glimpse of the eternal, and that glimpse causes the hint of sadness and tears we fight back before a work of art. We know instinctively that our pleasure lasts just a very brief moment.

I lived a moment like that during my time in Paris — two years swelling with daily nostalgia because I knew it would have to end. As you might imagine, the figure of Anne-Marie that afternoon rises above the rest of the time, though I fiercely, and protectively, treasure it all. Cézanne had his Mont St. Victoire, Van Gogh his brilliant sun and starlit nights, Petrarch his Laura of the antiquities, and I have Anne-Marie — images from life evoking an experience that is almost magical.

I told Anne-Marie about that once, on a less than beautiful day as we waited for a bus near Parc Monceau in Montmartre. It was near the end of our time together, a cool fall or early winter afternoon after we had walked through the district, visited an obscure museum, strolled through Père Lachaise, stopped to listen to buskers, and stared out over the roofs of Paris. We listened to American songs from the 60s in various French impersonations and then descended the steps beneath the Sacre Coeur to take a bus back to my neighborhood, just south of Denfert-Rochereau and the Catacombs. I perceived an unusual coolness in Anne-Marie that day, a reluctance to spend more time than was necessary on this, our special afternoon and night out together. I felt let down. In truth she lived with another man at this time, and while she shared the intense emotion I felt toward her while we were together, she openly refused to leave him for me.

I always regretted her reluctance, but I sensed that somehow she felt I wasn't *settled* enough, that for me art held more importance than life–at least life with a family–and she sensed that my ties to France and to her, while strong and a product of genuine love, had very little practical substance behind them. Eventually, she thought, I would leave her and her country to find work and substance back home.

I have no idea how right she was, what would have happened should she and I have lived together, but I do know that at the time Paris, Provence, and France seemed to be the absolute center of the world, a linguistic, artistic, and cultural tradition I ached (as much as I ached for her) to make my own. After two years I thought and dreamed French, I taught English at a private school and wrote reviews for a couple of

English/French language publications, as well as painting daily for myself. I felt committed to the country and the city, yet I must admit I never seriously thought, except in my relationship with Anne-Marie, of giving myself over permanently and completely to the life. The way I saw it, a half year in New York, a half year in Paris would probably be ideal. But then there was Italy—Florence, Siena, Rome, and my family heritage in the south—all that other art and life to experience. Raised in a suburb of Paris, Anne-Marie would never have been able to share tri-nationality with me, and she must have known—despite her intrigue with my Americanness, my foreignness, as she saw it—that I would never really be planted in true French earth.

The subject came up clearly that afternoon. I don't quite remember how, but I'm sure it arose from the coolness and reluctance I sensed in her as we were leaving Montmartre. At the bus stop we chatted about the buskers and the cemetery, with several famous American writers and singers lying there, and the finality of the burial places came through to me–dimly at first, then with increasing urgency as I considered what that meant about a life—and, yes, ours.

"Where would you want to be buried?" I asked. "In Paris or somewhere else?"

She shrugged, laughing, clearly not eager for additional heaviness on this gray afternoon. "I can't think about that yet," she said. "I'm not ready to think about any kind of ending, especially death. Certainly it can't be important to you."

The look in her eyes warned me not to go

further. Still, I could not let the challenge pass. "We'll remember this moment, this day, one way or another," I said to her. "At least I will. And that will be its permanence, though we may not make much of it in the long run."

I saw the look again, and certainty—even as she smiled softly—her mute enthusiasm a reminder of that once-in-a-lifetime afternoon in my apartment. "Cemeteries. Roots. They're a matter of accident, not choices," she answered, finally. "Wherever we land. What should we make of them?"

I shook my head. "Flesh and blood is what we make of them, if we're lucky."

She looked away, frowning, and I admit something collapsed inside because of her indifference.

"We can go beyond place," I said, "if we give new life a chance. It's the best thing we have against an ending."

The smile again, but with an even cooler cast to her eyes. Clearly Anne-Marie had some private thoughts—you know, second thoughts—and at the moment I didn't want to hear them. Still, they came. "I can't live with you, if that's what you're getting at," she said, turning away. "Or have children. I don't want to, Ben–either in New York or Paris. I couldn't be happy, although I know for both of us the afternoons and evenings this year have defined happiness itself."

After a long pause, I managed to choke out, "We can extend those afternoons, can't we? I want to."

Anne-Marie turned back to me, sad again as our bus pulled up to the curb. "Afternoons are not a life," she said, her forehead wrinkling as the doors opened. "Just happy thoughts—exciting moments—that you can't make real flesh-and-blood life grow from."

VI.

I said nothing to that, not immediately. Looking deeply into her eyes before we mounted the bus I could think of nothing but the obvious: Children, family, a life we could make for each other and whoever followed. But I saw that was not at all a road that she would take with me. I'm not sure about my own thoughts, but I know that at that moment our affair, the real possibilities behind it, ended. Our mutual silence on the subject cut us free. The bus started moving. We popped our orange transit cards into the fare machine and walked toward the back as the driver turned from the curb.

"This has been a very important moment," I said as we sat. "We can continue it if we really try."

"That's crazy," Anne-Marie said. "Real people give birth, raise families, die. No one's *trying*, as you say. It's just life."

I flinched, looking up at the Sacre Coeur as the bus, in traffic now, inched further down the block. "But ours is passing. Our youth..."

Anne-Marie frowned, turned to the road ahead, and just shrugged. As I write these words today, I realize that I had just let her down, disappointed her, and the disappointment changed everything between us. In her own way, she had asked for a simple human feeling—unselfishness, hope, a future—and I had offered nothing but silly profundity about getting old.

Our afternoons did not end immediately; but they cooled down considerably, I must say, becoming less frequent, with occasional flashes that made us both wonder if love could start again. It didn't—not in any meaningful way. We could never bridge the expectations that divided those afternoons, find a place where nights, days, months, and years became comfortable for us. To be honest, we could not endure each other for longer periods of time from then on, and our passion, what was left of it, seemed to yield to haste.

Perhaps I bore most of the fault, but Anne-Marie obviously had issues, too, and during that time we began to doubt the sexual interest that brought us together. We persisted for a while, with three-day weekends in London, Belle Isle, and Brittany, visits south to Provence and the nude beaches in Spain or the Cote d'Azur. Finally, I decided to return to America and jumpstart my career, while Anne-Marie chose to remain in Paris and make a life. My paintings did not catch on in New York, but I kept plugging away, finally compromising the art by taking courses in history and criticism until I had enough credits (and a conscious intention) to begin writing a Ph.D. dissertation. While I was writing it, Anne-Marie flew over from Paris once or twice, stayed with me for a few weeks in the city, and although those New York afternoons stretched into nights and weeks, we could not build them to any type of lifetime premise. In June that year, I accompanied her by subway and bus to Kennedy Airport, walked her through customs, and with a shudder of heart and

79

mind, watched her cool facial expression as we embraced and she disappeared down the hallway through the doors to an Air France plane.

It was the last time I saw her for many years–until one recent summer morning, when Lee and I drove down a plane tree-lined route in search of adventure, light, and Provence's many natural ghosts.

By then I had earned my degree in art history, writing a dissertation on the obscure, mostly non-existent social liberalism of the post-Impressionists. For a variety of reasons, mostly biographical, I had centered my study on Van Gogh. I referred to his religious family, the sacrificial attempts he made to preach in the coalmines (yielding his first great painting, "The Potato Eaters"), his relationship with the prostitute Sein and her daughter, the baby she carried when he lived with her. I also discussed his important friendship with the liberal postman Joseph Roulin and his suicide upon learning that his brother Theo's growing brood made it difficult to support Vincent's painting. It all revealed what I described in my thesis as a liberal, socialist bias in favor of working class families and life. I pointed to additional evidence: Van Gogh's love of Zola, his admiration for Millet's "The Man with a Hoe," and finally his wish to paint pictures for ordinary people's walls, cheerful, decorative canvases with a somber weight to them that, while never selling in his lifetime, hang everywhere today as printed copies, reminders that nature hides something fearful as well as sentimental behind its beauty.

"Never one to understand capitalistic forces," I

wrote, "Vincent Van Gogh nonetheless possessed marketing savvy far ahead of his time. His audience would never be aristocratic or culturally sophisticated. Rather he reached the working and middle classes, most likely religious people searching for evidence of God's grace and force in nature, while, of course, wanting nice homes with beautiful images of gardens, woods, and pastures in their rooms. Socially, and perhaps economically, ahead of his time, Van Gogh merely lacked the technology to make his visions ubiquitous. Yet he was the first painter to decorate suburban houses."

Quite a torturous academic mouthful, I know, but the language worked back in the 70s with my dissertation chair and his committee, all radical intellectuals who liked to think of artists as allied with laborers and viewed the spread of pop culture through print and electronics as an easy way to revolutionize the world. I received a minimum of challenges to my ideas, was asked to change only a word or two and a punctuation mark here and there, and with the offer of some help to choose illustrations for the text, my chair pointed me to an editor who liked political views on art. I had a published volume in just under a year, and with that, teaching and curating at small artsy universities and museums sustained my own capitalistic needs, although I rarely, if ever, picked up a brush to paint something of my own. I had succeeded in one way, of course, but I failed in the one that—to me at the time—had truly mattered.

I worked for years that way, in and out of New

York and New England, building a modest, yet solid reputation in art history and criticism. Occasional paid trips to Paris, Rome, Florence, and Milan provided icing on my career cake, and then the meeting with Lee at one of my universities created a sustainable private life. Lee attended one of my art criticism classes, wrote several impressive papers about 20th century French art, and one day came to my office in paint-spattered jeans and denim shirt to invite me to her studio, which also happened to be her apartment.

She lived and painted in a small loft just south of Houston Street in New York City, the apartment above a storage garage filled with large wood crates and white metal chemical drums that I had to weave in and out of before reaching the stairway to the second floor. She had no bell, so I hammered at the steel plate on her door till she opened it and led me to the large space–easily fifty feet by fifty feet–that she occupied.

"I apologize. It's a mess," Lee said, her jet-black hair braided and reaching down to her low cut jeans. "But I must say your office is almost as bad."

She smiled, walking through a curtain at the end of a small foyer, and when I followed her through, my eyes felt the glare of six large glass windows facing north with a view of the Empire State Building through one of them.

"Very nice," I said. "You must like to do large projects."

She pointed to a corner, and there they were, several landscapes of varied shapes and sizes, one or two vertical, two square, and the remainder a set of blue, mauve, and pearl-colored rectangles easily twenty feet wide and eight to ten feet high. She had made of a sky above some body of water an abstract reflection of Monet's Water Lilly pond, so that the image seemed to be above your head, even as you gazed down upon it near your feet. Sunset or dawn, maybe somewhere mysterious in the beyond.

I said nothing, although I felt an inner shake at the sheer daring of her images, her willingness to attempt a fresh look at an Impressionistic cliché: just light and color on water with a step back from the famous technique to make the image more bland, almost as if it were painted on richly textured plaster instead of canvas.

"Nice," I said. "Professional. I had no idea you had this kind of ambition."

"That's the art historian in me showing off in paint. You do it with words."

She glanced into my eyes, performed a little elusive toss of her braid, and laughed, saying it wasn't ambition as much as desire to prove she could make something beautiful and intellectually interesting at the same time. "At least it's attractive. I'm not so sure I've reached the interesting part," she said.

"It rivets *my* eye. Have you shown these to others?"

She shook her head. "There are galleries around I thought I'd show them to, but..."

"Galleries?"

"For the money," she said. "I need it for bills and some of my tuition. Do you have any suggestions?"

83

Lee was twenty-five at the time, raised in Central Jersey, which I, a Dago from the Midwest, condescendingly thought of as an artistic wasteland. I envisioned suburbs with little to offer but malls, highways, checkerboard subdivisions with split-level houses pushing and hopping over one another as if they, like the car in every driveway, had important places to go. So the New York chutzpah at this moment startled me. In jeans, embroidered denim shirts, and wooden clogs, Lee presented an attractive image, a young, smart woman with energy to spare–as well as wholesome sexiness that given the right conditions might be fun to experience. Yet I had never thought of her as ambitious, let alone wanting her work hung in public, and I must say that something about her hopeful face, her willingness to ask my help, and the reflection of my own youthful ambitions in her eyes touched my heart.

"I know one or two people," I said, nodding. "If you like, I can take a couple with me to show around."

"Take this one," she said immediately, pointing to a small, pearly gray canvas with just a hint of white sun behind a cloud. "And choose another–perhaps with more color."

I took a square one—a hint of mauve as its principal shade—and that along with the small pearl-gray made a nice pair to carry down to my friend Jean-Luc Guichet, *patron* of one of my favorite galleries just off lower Broadway. A naturalized American born in the southwest of France near Spain, Jan-Luc retained his swarthy Catalan good looks along with his accent. He held marathon readings of French classics at his gallery twice a year, and I had spent one or two New Year's Eves drinking his good French champagne, listening, and then reading passages–once from *Madame Bovary* and another time from Stendhal's *La Chartreuse de Parme*. I hoped to meet other Francophiles there, especially women, and make some new Parisian contacts, but while I did find a few new acquaintances, Jean-Luc had become the only real friend.

"They have possibilities," he said to me, staring at the two canvases I propped before him next afternoon. "In a couple of months I'll sponsor a show for new French artists. Perhaps I can include her because of the references."

He smiled, but I wasn't sure if he genuinely saw something in the pictures or hoped to do me a favor.

"So, you like them? Do you think they have something?"

"Oh, they have something, all right." He leaned back on his heels, hands in his pockets, and closed his right eye. "They look young–derivative, but still fresh. So, where does she go from here?"

I shrugged. "Damned if I know. But I'm pretty sure she's ambitious."

"They all are," he said with a knowing wink. "You don't push canvases like this unless you want to go somewhere with them. Or on them."

Jean-Luc was probably right, I had to admit— along with another shrug—and in a month I brought Lee down to his gallery with seven or eight of her landscapes in tow. He looked her over more than her paintings, I thought, but chose two–a yellow and aqua sky along with the pearl-gray reflection of the Water Lilies–and hung them in a show called "Vernissage: Fresh Faces and French," for most of the following month.

In a few days Lee went to his gallery and, with Jean-Luc's help, installed her two paintings among the others. She invited me to the show's opening, and I was surprised to see how simply and directly she and Jean-Luc spoke to each other. I was also surprised and pleased to see how well Lee's two paintings stood up to the others. Within a week and a half she had sold one for just under $3000, and at the end of the show's run she sold the other, the only artist to sell more than one painting in that time. An interior decorator bought them for two of his clients, telling her he admired the way she added depth as well as subtle color to small rooms.

Jean-Luc felt satisfied. Lee's face bloomed with pleasure, and I, of course, shared both their feelings as well as some vindication for having trucked the pictures down lower Broadway in the first place. I treated the three of us to lunch at a good restaurant around the corner from the gallery, and a week or two later Lee invited us up to her loft for dinner. Jean-Luc sent regrets, and so I went on my own to spend the evening. It was an interesting Provençal-style dinner–lavender-stuffed chicken, a juicy vegetarian terrine, with paté and cheeses that were impeccably chosen. I brought along two lovely bottles of my favorite Cote du Rhone, and Lee and I, suitably impressed by one another's taste, began the affair that ended with our marriage.

We set up house in my apartment. Just south of Columbia on Riverside Drive, we had corner rooms with a view of the G.W. looking north, and a tidy, if uninspiring view of New Jersey toward the west. Dawns were peaceful, the sparkle of windows lighting the buildings across the river, and sunsets complemented mornings with a spectacular fire.

Lee kept her loft for about six months as a kind of escape valve and as a place to work, but by the following winter, though she had turned out more than a dozen paintings since the exhibition at Jean-Luc's, she gave it all up—loft and canvases—for me. At the time I felt flattered, but wondered if she had made a mistake.

I encouraged her to continue painting, ceding her the small office area in one of our two bedrooms, but she said she wanted money, was tired of waitressing work to make up for her art, and wanted to have a more stable professional life, like me. So she continued taking Art History courses, studied Latin, French, and Italian as I had, and finally earned her Ph.D. with a dissertation on Horace's Epistles and Van Gogh's letters, which, together, she called "the most comprehensive and eloquent collection of comments on artistic value, and the value of the artist's life, since Plato and Aristotle."

She was right—I had to agree. But to Lee's (and my) regret, the dissertation was never published, and so she spent the next several years breaking it down into smaller, more publishable segments that several philosophic and art history journals accepted for their pages, especially with illustrations of prints from Van Gogh's paintings. She taught art history in the same department as I did, offering courses on aesthetic theories from Cro-Magnon Cavemen till the present, and eventually specialized in courses on women artists whose gender—because of bias—had worked against deserved public recognition. Those courses, and the crowded classrooms for her lectures, earned her a tenured spot in our department.

We experienced some jealous or competitive professional tensions, I admit. But she tried, earnestly, not to say I was lucky I'm a male. I strove to encourage her new work, although I felt Van Gogh's suffering—along with the nearly absolute lack of sales during his and Theo's lifetimes—argued effectively that gender wasn't the sole determining factor in public success or failure.

Together we made yearly trips to Europe—the artistic holy grails of France and Italy, especially—and for years those summer sojourns defined our lives, essentially placing us in a trans-Atlantic grouping where neither America nor Europe functioned as true home. "Living on a hyphen," I joked, finding work in both places, although the work in France and Italy always satisfied me more fully and happily than anything I found at home. Finally, after nearly a decade of sharing the Riverside Drive apartment and various hotel rooms, *gites*, and *agriturismos* in other countries, we decided to marry, traveled to Ireland, Greece, and Italy for our honeymoon, then returned to New York to do, as we said, "something totally different," create a life.

VII.

Ah, but easier said than done, as any childless older couple will tell you. To our surprise, after ten years of worrying about an unwanted pregnancy (much more if you count our pre-significant-other days) we now had to worry about a wanted pregnancy. We had assumed a month or two, read that six months to a year, of trying was about average for married couples, but after two years of not even achieving a maybe, we tried to be methodical. After another year we decided to seek professional help. My sperm was low in count and energy; Lee's egg productions were irregular and poorly shaped. I thought back to my days in Paris and before — in college — and laughed at the memory of all those worrisome days when a rubber broke, a missing pill was found, and a period arrived late or — horror of horrors — skipped an entire month.

"What god is this?" I wondered aloud, trying to laugh.

"One with a bad sense of humor," Lee answered.

I gave her injections, watched absurdly pornographic videos, "produced" sperm, as the doctor said, and sat in cold, fluorescent clinic waiting rooms while my lethargic sperm were juiced up chemically before filling a tube and then descending a plastic conduit past Lee's cervix.

"I can make you pregnant," one doctor had

89

assured us, godlike. Talk about a bad sense of humor, he said that without the slightest hint of a smile. And after two years of monthly "dates" (his choice of words) in the laboratory, he achieved nothing. We gave up on him and, as if a hand from above extended to touch our fingers, three months later Lee missed her period. We smiled and laughed at ourselves, of course, yet, nervous in our sophistication, we waited a month to visit our doctor's clinic for a pregnancy test. The rabbit, as they said in those days, died, and we found ourselves afloat in a warm sea of unexpected joy. I found myself running around the Central Park Reservoir or up and down the walkway along the river in Riverside Park, and imagining one of those three-wheeled running strollers rolling in front of me, our daughter (Daisy might be her name) smiling up at *Dah-dah* as he jogged and pushed her from behind. We had already chosen a school to send her to and fixed up our second bedroom as a nursery. Lee filled every surface of the room with painted cartoon characters, her Snow White and the many-colored Seven Dwarfs forming a frieze just under the ceiling molding on all four walls. She looked full-bloomed and confident as she worked, her flushed happiness reminding me of our first year together. But one night, when I returned from a late class and entered the room to help paint, I found Lee — eyes closed — lying on her back at the base of the ladder. Her hands rested on her abdomen, her knees and lower legs were propped on the third or fourth rung.

"Lee, are you all right? Did you fall?"

She said nothing, but her eyes opened a moment

as she looked at me. Slowly, she lifted her hand and reached for mine. I felt something sink as she squeezed my fingers, hard.

"Something doesn't feel right down there. I'm afraid."

She had descended the ladder awkwardly when the sensation occurred, lain that way for an hour, fearing the slightest movement would start the bleeding. I gave her a pillow, pulled out several books we had recently bought, studied, and read aloud sections on miscarriages. We decided together that, even with necessary movement, bed would be a safer place. After gently lowering her legs to the floor, I raised her to her feet, sat her in a desk chair with rollers, and wheeled her across the hall into our room. At three o'clock next morning, sick at heart, I walked out to the Drive, hailed a cab, and the three of us—rapidly about to be two again—rode to the hospital.

It was an awful night, one I will never forget, although I would like to. The OB-GYN on duty was surprisingly sympathetic given the lateness of the hour. He had already endured one alcoholic birth and two miscarriages through the evening, the nurse told me, and his tolerance for life's arbitrary biological decisions was wearing thin. Pale, unshaven, and obviously tired, he still managed to look like he cared, even whispering to me that Lee looked too nice for this to be happening to.

"We've tried to be careful," I said, "with diet, exercise, and all the rest."

"You can only do your best," he whispered.

91

Then he waved his hand as he helped Lee into the gynecological stirrups and scrubbed his hands. I stood at the table, holding her hands and trying to comfort her. In the fluorescent light, the doctor donned his surgical mask, bent to peer between her legs, and with a shake of his head began the scraping procedure as Lee shivered and cried out. I squeezed her hand as hard as I could, embracing her as she moaned in pain. In a few minutes, the doctor carried the extracted matter to the sink to examine it. Looking at him, I was about to ask, "Is it all right?" but the absurdity of the question silenced me.

"Not advanced enough to know the sex," he said angrily, then put a bloody mass in a plastic bag before dropping it in a pail. He turned to the table, took both our hands, and held them. "You'll do better next time. You're both healthy. Just don't get discouraged."

We didn't get discouraged, but I've always thought that something between us altered that night, something fundamental that returned me for a moment to that day in Montmartre with Anne-Marie. And like that afternoon, the change, though immediately evident in my reflections as well as the woman I was with, manifested itself very gradually. The bloom slowly left Lee's face. My belief in physical and emotional happiness sank into an absolute lack of faith. Lee and I both soldiered on, but with obvious new weight on our shoulders. Instead of pushing Daisy in front of me on the Reservoir jogs, I pushed a carriage full of doubt and—for a while—absolute metaphysical despair.

Some people say that a crisis can test a

92

relationship and, if it's strong, bring two people closer together. I'm not sure about that, as I'm not sure what brings two people close together in the first place. Certainly for Lee and me there was a shared, if unspoken, quality to our dreams and intellectual interests that made us partners without much effort. Sex was good, if somewhat perfunctory, the spark that movie critics write about only rarely arcing between us in or out of bed. But we had real fun at museums, conferences, movies, and concert halls. We shared great enthusiasm for French, Italian, and South East Asian food. We both loved to read or paint, and we often spent whole evenings seated across from one another with a book in each of our laps, or an unfinished canvas on an easel before us. Better than a TV to stare at, I always thought.

We enjoyed travel, exercise (I jogged, she took aerobics classes), attending operas, visits to downtown galleries like Jean-Luc's, disdainfully bragging to friends that we never turned on the television, even with a tape or DVD running. In the beginning I thought sex would get better between us, the embers expanding to a nice controllable fire, as I envisioned it, instead of suddenly bursting forth into an unsustainable blaze as had happened to me and Anne-Marie in Paris. It worked that way for a little while. There were afternoons of laughter and passion in Florence, a day or two of intense feeling during week-long winter breaks at home, a six-month series of nights when, to be frank, we came pretty close to blazing, but then work–on one of Lee's articles or canvases and a Gauguin monograph I had agreed to write–suddenly doused the fire.

We studied and wrote side by side until we finished and then, for some reason couldn't find the warmth again–or develop it. I thought of my age, time passing without writing the one great book I had in me, and, regretfully, journeyed back to my years in Paris as the turning point in my life as well as my career. Had I stayed, I told myself, I would still be painting, not writing, and the age-old French tradition of supporting and admiring the artist no matter what his success or background would have sustained me. Here I had (by choice, I admitted) descended into the world of getting and spending and, with a comfortable, if unexciting, life ahead of me, had to invent ways to keep myself entertained. That doesn't make for an ecstatic marriage but an outwardly stable one. Our shared interest in writing and travel worked for a little while, but eventually both Lee and I felt the repetition. As we walked in Riverside Park or along the pathways toward the Metropolitan Museum on Sundays, we looked at kids riding tricycles, women and men pushing baby carriages, and the next necessary move in our life together became evident.

"Cute," Lee said about a young toddler with blond curls who stumbled across the pavement before us one day. "What would you say if he were ours?"

I smiled, nodding. "That the conception must have been immaculate–at least from his looks."

She glanced down at the pavement and then, with a hopeful expression, stopped and turned. Her hands came to my chest, her chin went to her hands, and then she raised her eyes and, like a little Daisy, looked up at me. "It's time," she said. "It's definitely time."

I knew what she meant, but I wanted her to say it. "Time for what?"

"It's time for us to have a child, no matter how."

After our miscarriage and about six months of biding our time, the sex began again, especially earnestly in the week or two when Lee was most fertile. After six months boredom returned and, amazed at that feeling, I began to look back at our first months together. Lee had always been reserved, careful about her expressiveness until the very last moments of our love-making, as if she wanted to save all her emotions for an explosion of feeling along with her orgasm. Trouble was that, for a variety of reasons, those orgasms occurred less frequently now, and instead of the relaxed glow I remember feeling in her downtown loft, a cool lack of fulfillment and lonesomeness came between us. Where Lee used to rest her head on my shoulder and laugh or talk about our lovemaking, she now rolled to the opposite side of the mattress and said nothing. Then one of us, brooding and always silent, would get dressed and go to what had been the baby's room—once again an office.

Other things had changed as well, I remember thinking. Lee's carefree, bohemian artfulness had been, in appearance and behavior, her most attractive youthful feature, but it had disappeared now under a veil of professionalism, academic seriousness, and an intolerant, predetermined view of aesthetic, moral, and political value. In certain ways I bore the responsibility because I had introduced her to that academic world, but I had never hoped, or envisioned, that she would take it more seriously than I ever did.

I have no idea what she saw in me in those days, but I was sure that now she had begun to regard me as a little careless, a less than serious teacher, a man whose cynicism about the world in general and art in particular made him unable to commit to anything–painting or a cause–and certainly not a family. Of course, the fact that I saw it as her perception meant I at least partly agreed with her, but at the same time it contradicted everything I had felt about Lee in our beginning.

I had begun to age, and to mellow; I had begun to lose confidence in any sort of important future–as a painter or a critic–and although I tried not to be bitter, my lack of prominence weighed on me, not as directly as the miscarriage, but in a general sense as a malaise that weakened my limbs, making movement, mental as well as physical, difficult though never quite impossible. My hair thinned and began to turn gray, my energy departed and arrived as capriciously as a flighty animal, my gloom made our home life–in or out of bed–a very somber affair.

I began to remember, fondly, my days of solitude as a single man, the hours I could spend in communication with paint and canvas, and the opportunities I felt for something shocking and life-changing to occur. But some memory inside me cast doubt on all those possibilities again, and my commitment to the goodness I perceived in Lee, her belief that in trying she could make life happy and even beautiful kept me close to her. I have no idea what kept her close to me, but when, after six months of effort, we had achieved no second pregnancy, she began to talk of an adoption. I demurred at first, felt doubt about the effort and possibility, but on a trip to Italy and France that spring an accidental fall down a flight of stairs changed my mind completely.

VIII.

We were in St. Rémy de Provence again, the small tourist town where Van Gogh had rehabilitated after cutting off his ear and delivering it to a bordello—his mystifying response to an argument with Gauguin and Gauguin's projected leaving of their yellow house in Arles. Lee and I arrived one spring day after two weeks of driving the length of Italy, from the Swiss Alps to the instep in Basilicata and then back to France, in a cheap car rental with no air conditioning during one of the hottest European summers on record. We wanted something quiet and cool, and as we left Nice and headed northwest, the chain of mountains on the horizon seemed to invite us back to one of our favorite spots.

"St. Rémy," Lee said, looking at a map. "I feel it pulling us."

I looked at her, grinning. Despite the heat, we had enjoyed ourselves in Italy, passing romantic nights and afternoons in Ravello, near the Bay of Naples, Santa Margherita, beside the Ligurian Sea, and one memorable night overlooking the Piazza Signoria in Florence. Lee hadn't menstruated since before we left New York, making her more than two months overdue, and we felt giddy with certainty that the heat and romance of southern Europe had profoundly affected our lives.

We circled the center of town by riding the *périphérique*, found the St. Rémy tourist office again, and took down the names of one or two places with studio apartments for rent. We followed the road toward Avignon, found one or two disappointing places near Frederick Mistral's hometown, Mailane, and then, as we drove back toward town for the Tourist Office, we followed a shady road lined with old, gnarled plane trees that formed an absolutely straight lane between two fields of lavender, wheat, and beans. The speckled light danced on the blue overhang of shade and triggered some kind of perfect feeling for lost summer days that, I'm sure, never really existed. Still, the image moved us–as it had before and would often afterward–and we thought, on a whim, to follow it to the end.

The trees led us toward town, brought us to a traffic circle beside an athletic field, and the circle took us to a road that passed a school. We crossed over a small canal, ascended a modest hill, and found ourselves near a grove of umbrella pines and poplars. A rooster crowed from among the umbrella pines ahead of us, a flock of sheep and goats moved toward us, their bells, bleats, and smells mixing with the voices of the shepherd and his dog.

"This is absolutely beautiful." I pointed to the blue Alpilles ahead of us and a vineyard with a red-tiled roof and stone walled house in the middle lying before them.

"Let's try it," Lee said. "We don't have to be in town."

I shook my head, thinking she had meant to try

99

the house in the vineyard, but she was looking at a sign on the road beside us instead: *"Maison au Crau: Chambres d'Hote; Gites."* We saw a large stone house, beside it a line of four smaller buildings, and beyond them a mix of building materials, grapevines, and another magnificent view of the mountains with the light from the sun turning them aqua-green.

"Looks a little unfinished," I said. "But the setting can't be beat. I'll bet the sunsets are wonderful."

Lee nodded, and we pulled into the drive.

Two shaggy dogs leaped from the patio before the house and attacked the car. We drove slowly over bumpy gravel as they ran on either side of us and, barking, leaped at the open car windows. I parked near a small stone house beside a pool, and we sat in the car while the dogs–sheepdogs apparently, their gray, tan hair matted with dried mud and pine twigs–barked and jumped, making us hope someone would come from the house to calm them.

Finally, I pushed open the door and stood outside. Both dogs came at me, growling, one of them nudging at my knees as if to provoke a fight. I remained still, hands deep in my pockets, and looked around. Blue wooden shutters covered the windows of the house, gray shutters swung open before the doors of the four smaller buildings beside it—rentals, I assumed. Telling Lee to stay in the car, I walked to the house, heard the voice of a French announcer calling a soccer match, and knocked on one of the blue shutters. No one answered. I knocked several more times, and at last I heard someone open an inner door and push open the shutters in front of me.

"*Oui?*" An older woman stepped out, lovely, fair-skinned, and tall. I liked her face immediately and with no hesitation or doubt inquired about a place to stay for the next two weeks. She was polite, seemed very intelligent, and showed an absolutely honest, well-intentioned expression on her face.

She showed us two places, one large, on the corner, with a loft that spanned the back wall of the house, and when Lee and I saw the view of a distant mountain ("*Mont Ventoux*," the woman said. "Petrarch's mountain."), we decided to take it, putting a deposit down immediately. We moved in our bags, put on our bathing suits, and, cautioning each other all the way, walked carefully down the narrow, polished steps from the loft to the ground floor.

The dogs followed us to the pool, barking and whining as we swam and splashed, then lay down peacefully between our chairs as we sat to dry, staring out over the vineyard toward the looming Alpilles. Needless to say we felt wonderful, the swim combining with the clear blue sky, the dry air, and the deep sense of age and civilization that lay heavily on the landscape to make us feel young and at the same time settled, even accomplished.

"This is it," Lee said. "I want to bring up babies here."

I laughed, but in fact the same thought had crossed my mind a moment before. I could see a son or daughter–or a son *and* daughter–playing beneath these umbrella pines, camping in a tent near the vineyard, playing with our own dogs amid a herd of *baa*-ing sheep. There was the school we passed down the road, another, a music school we soon discovered named after the composer Charles Gounod, and the culture and history of two-thousand European years dotting the landscape in nearby towns and cities.

We spent the next week touring those places, seeing Glanum and its two Roman monuments on the outskirts of town, the medieval city of Les Baux, Roman Arles and medieval Avignon, then beyond them to the Vaison-la-Romaine and the vineyards of Châteauneuf-du-Pape. We visited Nimes and Aix—more Rome and more plane trees—and picnicked at several spots along the Rhone. We loved the area and, without doubt, had we the resources and a plan, we would have bought something there to live in.

But we had other things on our minds, and the anticipation of our return home and the six or seven exciting months we envisioned following it kept us from doing any serious looking. The proprietors, Madame and Monsieur Bernard, worked constantly on the grounds, the rental properties, and their own house, painting windows and shutters, pruning trees, hanging wash on the line or beating carpets. M. Bernard stopped at our patio occasionally to talk and told us that they had come down from Annecy–near Geneva–some ten years before and had found the property by chance, almost exactly as we had found it. "It pulls," he said. "There's something mysterious about this plot of land, and it will make you stay."

He and his wife passed us newsletters from time

to time, telling us they contained "the truth," although they had no religious affiliation, and when I mentioned Nostradamus, who was born in St. Rémy in the early 16th century, they smiled knowingly, saying he held more of the truth in him than any man of his time, and most men since.

Monsieur Bernard had fought with the *maquis* during the German occupation. Madame Bernard had helped the *maquis* out, and together they had found an astrologist who, back in the 1940s, had pointed them toward their shared destiny. They had settled in Annecy, built a business out of printing and selling religious books from Geneva through Alsace, and then ten years ago had felt the pull of the Crau outside of St. Rémy. "The mountains," Monsieur Bernard often said, "at night you can hear them speak."

He had spent several months here during the war years, fighting the Vichy government, and he looked at the mountains and surrounding brush with infinite respect. "We lived on insects and snails we found on the ground," he said, and he and his companions raided many a vineyard and private garden for vegetables and fruit. He told us of one vivid moonlit night when they marched for miles along the crest of the Alpilles so they could ambush a German caravan moving down through Provence toward the sea. "Up there," he said, pointing to the mountains. "We felt Caesar's army among us. I assure you, it was not a dream. We heard the clash of their armor as we moved in perfect silence through the trees."

Once the men broke free of those trees, they

gazed into the valley of the Durance River. "To a man," Bernard said, "to a man, I tell you, we gasped to see the glint of spears and shields in the moonlit passage below us."

They ambled down the mountain quietly, gathering strength from the companionship of Roman ghosts. "In brief," Bernard said, "we planted mines, blew them as the Germans passed, and killed or drove out those invaders as if we, too, were Gauls fighting Caesar's army."

I complimented him on his courageous past, and he nodded but said he had never found the same sense of right and purpose since. "A wife, children, my portion of Paradise on this land have been my reward– my sole compensation. They have made it all worthwhile, and yet ..." He waved and let his voice trail off to a whisper.

I smiled, recognizing the life adjustment he had admitted to, and wondered how I would regard my own rewards: compensation for art, study, and career? Or would it be a minor substitute for adventure, risking all I possessed for faith, hope – and belief – in myself?

"You, too," Monsieur Bernard said to me. "You, too, must find something here that holds you. I can see it in your eyes."

I don't know what he saw, but I had to admit I did feel an attraction. During moonlit nights Lee and I would take a bottle of local wine, walk to the pool, lie back in a couple of loungers, and stare through the overhanging pines at the mountains beyond the vineyard. The breeze was cool, shuffling the limbs above us and, together with the murmuring *cigales*, created a song and a sound I have always associated with the Crau. Occasionally it carried a distant lowing of sheep and goats, which added another layer to the music, but apart from that and an occasional howl from the Bernard dogs, everything else was quiet.

Lee and I held hands, sipped wine, and let the evening voices speak to us. We said little ourselves, filled with a shared sense of deep contentment. I have always been a bit edgy with such feelings, seeing them as an invitation to certain, perhaps deserved, disaster, but the moon and the ghosts of the mountains lulled that all to sleep. The experience filled me that much, and when we finished the last of the wine, we carried the two glasses and the bottle with us past the construction project, back to our *gite*, and prepared for bed. Next morning it might rain, but we didn't care. Provence rain would be beautiful. That's how we felt, anyway, but one of those mornings, about nine days after we arrived, Lee, carrying a half-drunk glass of orange juice, fell down the stairway from the apartment loft to the stone floor at the bottom.

Groggy from a restless night, she missed the center of the third or fourth narrow step. She cried out as her foot slipped on the edge; her back and head smacked the polished landing hard, and then she slid to the terra-cotta floor—quickly, one sharp bump after another. Before I could rush across the fifteen feet from the bed, I saw her on her back at the bottom of the stairs, the glass, emptied, resting in her outstretched hand. Her eyes blinked at me once then remained closed. As I ran

105

down two or three steps–careful not to slip and fall on top of her–I saw her head roll to the side away from me. I retrieved a pillow from our bed, went down the stairs very consciously, and placed it beneath her neck. Her eyes opened again, but she hardly seemed to see me.

"Lee, are you okay?"

She said no, handing me the glass.

"Did you hit your head?"

She nodded and then seemed to black out, her eyes open yet somehow dead. Her hands dropped to her abdomen, and, rhythmically, without saying words, she began to moan. I lifted her to her feet, half-carried, half-walked with her to the bath, and there she collapsed into my arms. I lowered her to the floor, and went to the stairway again for the pillow. When I returned, she was mumbling to herself, and listening closely, I heard Lee say that she had "lost it." Of course I knew what she meant.

"Sweetie, it's all right. We'll do it again. It'll happen. I'm sure."

Her eyes opened, and although she seemed to look in my eyes, recognizing me as if from a distance, I wouldn't say she was really conscious.

"Do you want anything—for pain? Do you want to go to a doctor?"

She shook her head, and I–stupidly–assumed that she was probably right. I sat near her for about half an hour and then brought her some water. She sat up, sipped it, and then lay down again, saying she couldn't stand on her feet because of fear.

"Don't sell yourself short, Sweetie. I think you're

very brave."

"I lost it," she said. "Again."

"Lee, you don't ..."

"I've started to bleed."

I can't tell you how much hearing those words took my breath away. I sank to my knees, held her head in my lap, and almost as if she were a corpse, began to rock and keen. I still wonder about the loss I felt and the regret over one more missed chance. Yet, as I've said, I hadn't been that eager to have a child, hadn't staked my life or future happiness on one. I was-or so I thought-simply acquiescing to Lee's desires for something to fill our lives, to make up for an increasingly ordinary academic marriage: papers to grade, conferences to attend, occasional forays into the larger world with published articles that very few people-including our colleagues-ever read.

I had been swept up by more than redemption from all that, more than the lavender perfume and moonlit clarity of our pool side nights. Something human had taken me, closing deep synapsial circuits that connected, probably, to genetic wiring from hundreds, perhaps thousands, or millions, of ancestors living before. I wanted a child to pass on to this world-a mind and soul like mine (flawed though they might be), with values, thoughts, and imagination that Lee and I could share—with movements and memory close to ours. Sure, we attempted that with students in every class, but we knew that they had arrived before the lectern already formed. I wanted daily contact, intimacy, a shared sense of goals and achievements. Some of that

occurred from time to time with students–as it certainly
had with Lee and me many years before–but none of it
with the total commitment and emotion that a child–I
was sure–inevitably would bring to our life. As I knelt
next to Lee on the washroom floor, still keening, I
realized that what we had lost in her menstrual flow
that morning was a dream of the future, a material way
to combat the forward rush of an indomitable
destroyer–time.

      We did little more that day: breakfast, clean-up,
the sad reappearance of the box of tampons in the
bathroom cabinet. Then we got in the car and drove
toward Aix and Nimes, talking little but hoping a
change of scene and some old Roman monuments
would pick up our mood.

      Strange, that impulse to soldier on in those
moments, as if all we can do is turn a page to begin
again–a new chapter, a fresh book, a poem. But all the
while that last line on the previous page stays with us,
hovering near our shoulders, forcing us to continue
going back.

      We headed out to our favorite road–the straight
one with the plane trees on both sides–and tried to find
some cheer in the dance of sunlight through the
overhanging leaves. We reached the autoroute heading
west toward Spain and drove for about an hour with the
hot sun seeming to burn the arid landscape on either
side. The wind held still. Fields of lavender and
vineyards didn't move but sent us their perfume. There
had been times when that view exerted magic for us,
but that day we could only see and smell its arid,

burning textures as a sign of our own inability to reproduce.

We exited at Aix, drove the local routes into the town center, and parked in an underground lot near the *Cours Mirabeau*. The weight of trees, fountains, and traffic felt like burdens instead of invitations to pleasure. We strolled the length of the *Cours* in silence, sat in one of its famous cafes, but feeling neither the beauty nor the excitement of the atmosphere, we returned to the car and drove further on to Nimes. With lunchtime traffic streaming around us, we stood before its famous Roman temple, looked at each other, nodding sadly, then, without a word, walked hand in hand to the underground lot and drove back to St. Rémy.

At the *Maison au Crau* I knocked on the Bernards' door and told Madame that we had to leave. "But you have paid for five more days," she said. "Is something not pleasing?–Something in your cabin?"

I shook my head. "A change of plans." I mumbled the phrase and, to my surprise, felt tears brimming from my eyes.

Madame Bernard looked at me, nodded, then entered the house and returned with money to cover the next five days and handed me one of her truth-conveying sheets. "Life:" its headline said, "Everlasting and Beautiful." I thanked her, gave half the money back to cover any loss she might have incurred and, with truth in hand and a sad smile on my face, went back to the cabin and Lee.

IX.

There's very little to tell about our movements after that. We headed west again, past Aix and Montpellier, spent nights in Carcassonne and Perpignan before heading up the Atlantic coast and then across the middle of France (over the *Massif Centrale*) toward Lyons and farther east toward Annecy. During our last day in France, we spent the night in Ferny-Voltaire, where Voltaire lived and wrote for twenty years in a château he bought. We went to visit the château in the afternoon before our flight home but, finding it closed to the public, we sat on a bench outside and stared out over a farmer's nearby pasture, trying to console ourselves with pastoral beauty and the sense that genius had once walked this very land and seen this field. But we felt no consolation. Instead we heard a black and white cow lowing miserably in the field, and when we looked we saw that she had very recently given birth to a calf. It lay on the ground beneath her, enveloped in membrane. For nearly an hour, it didn't move, did not seem to breathe, and, to our biased eyes at least, appeared dead, making the cow's lowing particularly mournful to hear.

Fighting back our own mournful bitterness, we drove to a wooden house at the opposite end of the pasture. Assuming it belonged to the owner of the cow, we knocked on the door several times, hoping to find

110

someone home. No one answered our knock or our calls, and upon looking through windows we saw no signs of anyone home. Finally, I climbed through the pasture fence and stumbled toward the cow through high grass, still not seeing any evidence of life from her newborn. The cow turned, stamped her feet, then stared at me and snorted. Raised in a Midwestern city, I knew little about cows or their habits (still don't), and as I moved closer I became more aware of the horns protruding from her head.

"Could that be a bull?" I called back to Lee. "Look at those horns." I fought the urge to run, mostly out of fear. What if it came after me?

"A bull wouldn't stay close to a baby like that. Besides, we've seen lots of black and white cows with horns like that."

"On females?"

She nodded. "I think it's part of the breed."

"Maternal instincts can turn aggressive," I muttered.

The cow moaned as I turned toward it again. The calf still hadn't moved, but then the cow stepped toward me, leaning forward like a yoked ox, as if she were pulling a heavy weight.

"It's still attached," Lee called out to me. "Poor thing. Poor baby, too."

I stepped forward, watching the cow lower its head and suddenly lurch in my direction. Freezing, I saw the last bit of membrane and hoof fall free from the cow's underside as she stumbled toward me–two or three steps. Scared, I ran to the fence where Lee stood

111

and with a little cry slid between two rails to her side.

"It's finished now," Lee said, laughing. "You could have helped with the delivery."

The calf still hadn't moved, and the mother, trudging groggily toward us, paid it no attention. I looked at Lee, happy to hear her mocking humor, even at my expense, but I saw tears also, rolling from her eyes. I embraced her, tightly. There was nothing more to do.

The flight home went smoothly, uneventfully, that night, but the following year changed all our expectations. Although several doctors–specialists in fertility and authors of well-known books on conception and parturition–virtually assured us over and over (and over) that we could and would get pregnant, that we could almost certainly deliver a baby successfully–Lee and I considered our ages, added them, and calculated that not only biological time was waning. In fact adoption, our alternative plan, had chronological limits as well. Most important, some states and countries put limits on the combined ages of adoptive parents or on the age of one parent. Since I was now in my late forties, and Lee rapidly–too rapidly, we both thought–now approached forty, we soon would be aged out of the adoption market, either by biological parents' preferences for youth or the official, legal ones established by legislators.

At the same time adoption horror stories began to hit the news channels, recounting cases where biological parents, male or female, having renounced a child and not contacted it for years, would express a change of heart and income, sue in court to regain custody of the child, and to our dismay have judges solemnly decide in their favor over the expressed preferences of the adopted children and the adults who raised them. We heard and read of such cases in two or three states, felt heartbroken by them, and decided we needed to protect ourselves.

After countless meetings and evaluation, scores of frustrating phone calls and, yes, annoying sales-marketing pitches, we decided to work with an agency just outside of Washington, D.C. They specialized in international adoptions from the Caribbean and South America where, with weak economic prospects for so many people, we thought it unlikely that parents would change their minds. We filled out forms, got police and F.B.I. clearances, searched for original birth and marriage certificates, wrote heartfelt autobiographies, presented exhaustive financial information, submitted to evaluations by local social workers, paid fees to lawyers and an uncountable number of agencies, and passed through it all with colors defiantly flying. In the end we chose to adopt from either Costa Rica or Brazil and felt energized and eager to be placed on a waiting list for each country–"Right at the top," the adoption agency said. When, three months later, we hadn't heard from either country about a prospective child, we called the agency for a progress report and were told for the first time that the waiting period for Central and South American adoptions was now two years.

"Two years!" I remember crying out, internally counting and getting closer to fifty than I ever wanted to be. "But I thought it was a matter of months."

"It might be," the voice on the other end said, "though it's not likely now."

"I'm going to be ancient!–I want to be around for my child. See her–or him–grow up, go to college–get married and..."

"Oh, you're not *that* old," the voice said, laughing. "But perhaps–with our new Russian program it's likely to be shorter–maybe a few months."

"Months?–Is that true?"

"Of course, I can't guarantee anything because this is new for us–you would be our first or, maybe, second Russian adoption, and we're told they are ready to move immediately."

"Russia, is it?" Lee said, with a smile.

I remembered cold war emotions, fears of nuclear attacks, lost Olympic events, and frenzied races into space. In my elementary school we had monthly practice diving under desks or burrowing under blankets at the first sight of a mushroom cloud. "The Russian bear," I had called it in one of my essays on painters under Communism. Could a country that had expelled Nabokov, forced Tchaikovsky to suicide, and tried to arm Fidel Castro at the risk of nuclear war that would destroy us all, maybe wipe out Manhattan's towers, give birth to a loving son or daughter to complete our family life?

"Maybe," Lee said. "Babies don't know history, so let's keep an open mind. The agency says we still have the options of Costa Rica and Brazil. Walls have come down. The world is changing — for the better."

"Better?" I said, as we filled out forms for the Russian adoption program.

"Absolutely," Lee said. "No question."

"Absolutely," I repeated, though with many, many secret doubts.

X.

"*I sat on the couch in my living room. My hands covered my face because I could not bear to watch. At least twenty years have passed–no? Yet I still remember the afternoon vividly: you and I leaving the elevator, stepping on to the roof, and looking down upon the world. Meanwhile, I felt your arms around me and, as if we stood on an airplane wing, I braced myself against the wind, feeling it lift us higher for a moment as we looked left and right toward the two rivers flowing toward the bay. Maybe it was the height, maybe it was the strength of the surrounding elements, but I never felt more naked or more intimate with you than I did during that half hour up there. And then ... To think it all has turned to ashes and dust.*"

I stared at the screen before me, not quite sure I lived or dreamed at that moment because the name beneath the email said, "*Anne-Marie.*" Yes, and the experience she described brought me back to an emotion I had not revisited in years. It added even greater poignancy to the attacks and collapse of the two buildings just a short week before.

"*I hope you continue to be well and have lost no one dear to you,*" she wrote. I read the words with complete selfishness instead of sorrow. Sure, no one I knew and loved had died or been inside the buildings as they collapsed–thank God. Emails from several students referred to lost relatives or friends, but I had seen, felt, and heard nothing personally until I turned on the television that awful afternoon and saw the images while hearing the screams.

Now in my safe New Jersey home, with Misha at school and Lee away at work, I felt the old mix of emotions again with Anne-Marie's note in front of me. But the mournful sense of loss, along with my still-smoldering resentment of Lee and Jean-Luc, made our break complete, referring to another life, another self, in fact, when I felt stronger, and, at least for the time on top of the building that spring afternoon, very much in command.

"I am fine, Anne-Marie," I wrote back. "Wife and child and other family members were all safely distant from Lower Manhattan when the planes struck. Others I know who worked there had the luck to be out of the building at the time. I have lost no one close, no one ..." I paused, took a breath and deliberately typed the last two words, *I love,* feeling a mix of joy and improbability that placed Anne-Marie's face squarely before me. I stared at the screen and clicked on *send.*

I had asked Anne-Marie to marry me that day on top of the towers. With the bright sun shining on the buildings all around us, with the two of us seeming to float above the horizon and its gray-blue waters on three sides, with Anne-Marie warm and lovely in my arms, I simply could not let the moment go, although I knew my very impulse would make it fade.

"I'm so glad you came," I had said, nuzzling her neck and feeling her weight lift lightly in my arms. "You make me live again–in our lovely Paris days as well as this one."

She stood on tip-toe, and I felt her left thigh tight against mine. We turned and stared uptown over the spires of the Empire State Building and the Chrysler Building, seeing the rectangular carpet of green that formed Central Park. She smiled and, as we looked up, opened her mouth and turned toward me, pressing my lips and body as we seemed to meld. Our days together in Paris came flooding back.

I had never felt this physical union with another woman and, hard to explain, I have never felt it with equal intensity since, even though others, especially Lee, have brought an emotional closeness that Anne-Marie never did. I have never understood the attraction we had for one another, probably never will because, beautiful as she was to me at the time, there was something more than visual between us–something magnetic. I have thought about it and analyzed it from every personal, social, and psychological angle, and the most appropriate theory I have comes from the old Greek myth about the separation of the sexes: At one point humans were whole; the gods felt jealous and cut them in two, condemning all of us to spend our lives unfulfilled until we found our wandering other halves.

Which is the way I felt about Anne-Marie for almost twenty-five years: Despite different countries, languages, ages, and sex, we were two halves of one physical whole yearning for completion, and that accounted for the way we lit each other up. On that spring day in New York, seeming to float above the clouds beside her, I felt the rush of current between us as we embraced like never before. Both of us on our

118

toes, both of us breast to breast and mouth to mouth, I leaned back to breathe and look at her with the East River and the Sound beyond.

"I want to get married," I announced. "I don't want you alone in Paris with me alone over here. It's not right."

She opened her eyes and stared at me, seriously. As her emotion rose, I felt her breasts rest against me as she buried her face in my shoulder. Her body went slack and, gradually, I realized her head shaking side to side–ever so slightly.

"No," she whispered. "I can't do it. It will swallow me up."

Words came to my throat, but I squeezed them back. Later, I would tell myself that she hadn't turned *me* down; she had turned *us* down, and there was little I could do or say to allay her fears since I felt similar ones myself. Still ... I hated it, I have to admit.

In the end I said nothing, though for weeks afterward I wondered practically every hour if my silence had been a mistake. Do you give up joy and happiness in the pure, physical sense for a comfortable self? Does duty to some unknown future life cancel the intensity of the present–which may, after all, last longer than this particular moment? Aeneas thought so when he left Dido to her funeral pyre. Absent Rome's grandeur, was this a message Anne-Marie and I should heed?–If not, what should we do?

Our next few days in New York passed under a cloud of emotional regret that never let us regain the intimacy of our moment above the city rooftops. Days brought clear, crisp, sunny weather; evenings provided active and full nights with friends, theater, or music. But sooner than I or she wanted, Anne-Marie had to return to Paris, and the morning she left arrived quietly, undramatically, and, I should add, with an aura of sad inevitability infusing it. We knew that a certain part of life—for each of us—had ended.

I accompanied her to Kennedy, shuffled with her through baggage, passport, and ticket control, and then when we arrived at the door that only passengers could pass through, we looked at each other hurriedly, smiled self-consciously, and, without further eye or physical contact, not even a French style double-cheeked kiss, waved good-bye.

I assumed I would never see her again, and through more than twenty years we didn't, despite occasional birthday wishes, Christmas greetings, or post cards from our own, regrettably separate, travel destinations. Once she wrote to me about an article I had written that she had seen translated into French in some Paris art journal, and once or twice I wrote to her about my life and career changes: taking a job in New York, marrying Lee, adopting Misha. At one point Anne-Marie wrote about visiting Amsterdam and seeing the Van Gogh museum there. At another she wrote about spending time with her parents (whom I had never met) in the south of France and touring several spots that Van Gogh had visited near Arles.

But that was all until that email message arrived. After the attacks of September 2001, she had found the address through our university's web-page and wrote to commiserate and hear some news. In the next few weeks I found out that she had indeed married, had a child now–a girl about fourteen years old–and then separated from her husband, moving with her daughter to the south, just outside of St. Rémy, near her parents' home.

That intrigued me. Interspersed with discussions about Al-Qaeda and the coming war in Afghanistan, I found that she and her daughter lived in a house with a beautiful view of the Alpilles, that she made a living by cleaning rental houses and caring for sickly elderly people, and that her parents were now estranged from her because of a man she now saw, an African-American musician who had been born in the Caribbean and raised in Philadelphia when his parents emigrated.

"They don't like his skin-color or his profession," she wrote to me. "They don't want him to live in this house–which they bought for me–or influence my daughter, Celestine."

My heart stopped and then went out to her although, when I heard about the jazz musician's beliefs–a sort of Rastafarian belief in magic and his own fated return to Paradise in Africa–I admit I also sympathized with her parents. To be honest, I also wondered–yes, after years and a wonderful wife and now an adopted son (also wonderful)–how Anne-Marie, given all our naked intimacy in the past, could have turned *us* down and taken up with *them*–a French businessman, she told me, who had dumped her for a younger woman during a trip to Switzerland, and then a musician who might leave her at any moment for

Africa and a new Messiah.

By November of that year, we had exchanged nearly one hundred messages–some banal, Facebook-like accounts of daily life, some larger, emotional comments on world events, travel, French-American sympathies, and the funny difficulties of raising children. Seeing her name among my email messages so frequently still sent emotional charges through me, and writing to her brought out a daring, youthful quality to my French prose that reminded me how far I had evolved from the young man she had known with a paintbrush in his hand. The emotional charges made me read those emails for clues about her changes, but I confess I saw little that was different except an absence of passion and a new maternal concern for her daughter and lover.

Still when winter arrived and the holiday season passed, I began to think even more fondly of a return to Europe, and especially St. Rémy. I had no real thought of taking up with Anne-Marie again, but I felt curious about seeing her and wondered–with, alright, I contradict myself, a *frisson* of sexual curiosity–what I would feel standing next to her after all these years. How much current would flow between us? Would I still see (and feel) her beauty? What would she think of this middle-aged man, a gray-bearded professor of art, who traveled with a younger woman and an even younger son, yet couldn't hide his slowing, potentially arthritic, gait?

Lee, of course, felt eager to go, especially as an opportunity for Misha to see the south of France and some of Italy with us. I began to work on my book project more fully, and the idea of Provence as an Ur-suburb fired my imagination. If I could portray it as a vital, yet distant part of Rome's Golden Age, illustrate some of the commercial and aesthetic energy it added to the central city's luster, and recreate somehow the harmony and beauty of its daily life, I would contribute something to increase our understanding not only of Roman grandeur, but also of human civilization itself. We build great cities for comfort and security, but at some point we need to leave them as well to seek harmony between ourselves and the earth we occupy.

We booked a flight to Rome and reserved rooms in our favorite places near Siena and in Liguria. We telephoned the Bernards at the *Maison au Crau* in St. Rémy and reserved our old cabin for most of a month. With that done, Christmas and its festive reminiscence of Russia and the meeting with Misha now past us, winter seemed to loosen its grip, and our daily tasks, in addition to work and family things, turned to preparations for our summer journey.

I had written to Anne-Marie about my book project and our trip, but she did not reply for several weeks. In March she responded that she would remain at home most of the summer, making it likely we would see each other. The news lent fresh enthusiasm to my plans, and throughout that spring I did a lot of research on St. Rémy, Provence, Roman antiquities in Provence, Nostradamus, and other subjects. Anne-Marie sent me a 19th century history of St. Rémy and told me there had been some construction changes around the ruins of

Glanum as well as the presentation of information around St. Paul de Mausole, the hospital Van Gogh had stayed in after his breakdown.

I finished course work in May, wrote a couple of reviews of current New York exhibitions, and at the very beginning of June, just before our wedding anniversary, Lee and I drove out to Kennedy with Misha and took an Alitalia flight to Rome. We landed very early in the morning, picked up our rental car and, after a tour of the magnificent ruins of Ostia, drove two hours north and stopped in Umbria, about thirty miles south of Siena. We stayed at the Simonellis, on their Agritourismo farm, with the ruins of its 11th century castello overlooking the countryside of the Val D'Orcia, a natural basket of wheat, olive trees, hay, and many vegetables.

Adriana Simonelli, tall, angular, sweet, whose family owned a principal house in nearby San Quirico, greeted us with a warm smile when we arrived, pointing to a distant field below us where her husband, Carlo, rode on a tractor plow.

She held Misha to her breast, cried *"Ciao, Bello!"* as we found many Italians do when they see a young boy, and immediately took him to her office to give him candy and a toy soccer ball. Meanwhile, we emptied the car and carried bags up the flight of stairs to the apartment Adriana rented to us. As usual, we marveled at the light through the windows and the views of the countryside, a vision of dark green, yellow, and tan, the fields in square or rectangular patches, like an old country quilt.

We spent a week at the Agritourismo, driving out to Montalcino for wine, and for views and food to Pienza, one of our favorite little Italian towns, a small city designed to be perfect by Pope Pius II.

At the end of the week we turned north toward the Alps, following the sea into Liguria where we stayed in small coastal towns, threading through mountains like huge granite stones on an antique necklace. We regretted leaving Italy, but at the same time Lee and I felt the pull of France, eager to enter the more primitive and, to us, rooted life of Provence for painting pictures and writing words.

"Home," Lee said, smiling when we crossed the border at Ventimiglia, coasting down valleys and fields toward the autoroute.

We followed signs toward Spain, bypassed Nice, Aix, and Marseilles along the way, and finally found the route for Avignon. Near Cavaillon we left the highway, and after one more time on that perfectly straight tree-lined road, we followed side routes into St. Rémy's center. We turned at the sign toward Les Baux once more, and after two *carrefours*, we found ourselves on the dust-filled dirt road ascending toward the Bernards'.

The dogs greeted us as we pulled in. Monsieur and Madame Bernard walked out of the house, hands raised to greet us, and after hugs, kisses, and handshakes, they motioned us down the row of *gites* to our usual: "Number four." Misha hopped from the car, excited about the visit, claiming to remember the tree stump in front of the house as well as the metal table on the cabin's veranda, although he knew he had never been here before. As we unpacked the car, we saw the Bernards' daughter, Rebecca, along with their granddaughter, Claudine, who waved and walked across the yard for cheek to cheek greetings. Rebecca pointed to her house, which we had seen as a construction site a few years before.

"Complete," she said, "and just a year old now. You must come see it before you leave."

We stayed at the Bernards' for the next week, swimming and taking long evening walks on the Crau. West of the house on a joggers' lane behind a thick row of oak and umbrella pine, we found a view of St. Martin's Church as in one of Van Gogh's "Starry Night" paintings, its yellow bell tower lifting a crooked finger toward the darkening sky. Other times we walked northward, following the uneven line of the Alpilles toward the snow-capped Mont Ventoux that Petrarch climbed in 1336, always, I imagined, dreaming of Laura. Misha loved the shepherds and their flocks on the crau, talking to one of them about his dog and wooden flute, and listening each day for the muffled rattle of the herd's bells along with their incessant *baa*-ing as they circled trees and vines, leaving dents head-to-shoulder high in any vegetation standing in their path.

We hoped to find a nearby house eventually, for more living space and privacy since we planned to stay the rest of the summer. In town we checked real estate office windows and bulletin boards for rentals. One or two places interested us, but one day Rebecca told us about a house several towns away–in Châteaurenard – where a friend of hers cleaned rentals. We drove there several days later, finding an old, refurbished *mas* in a little farming community about ten miles from St. Rémy. The setting intrigued us. A narrow irrigation ditch ran along the street, and every house in the area had a large family vegetable garden. The owner of the *mas*, a retired professor from the university in Avignon, spoke excellent English and was happy to have an American colleague doing research in his house. He sat us at a table beneath a huge chestnut tree, brought out a bottle of local wine along with nuts and crackers, and basically begged us to stay in his house because he and his lovely wife wanted company.

"Frankly, we are lonely," he said. "We love it here–the house, the garden, our agrarian neighbors, but we miss spirited conversation."

They lived in the house next door, with a garden gate and fence separating the two properties. At first Lee and I worried they might be intrusive in their loneliness, but at the same time they seemed aware of that possibility themselves. "The house is yours," Monsieur Lelande told us. "You can be sure that gate won't open without your permission."

Lee and I smiled. When Madame Lelande promised to have a maid come in weekly at no extra charge, we both nodded in agreement that this would be our summer place. With an upright piano to play, a powerful laptop with an English keyboard at my disposal, and a lovely garden to paint and eat in, we could hardly see ourselves going wrong.

We finished the week at the Bernards', and at the beginning of the next cleaned our *gite* and threw clothes,

127

toys, and other belongings into our car. With a fond farewell from everyone, we drove down the short highway road to Châteaurenard, turned down a small country road with three houses on it, and crossed the irrigation ditch in front of the Lelandes' house.

Leaving the car beneath a poplar tree, we went to the back door, found the key in the lock and pushed it open. Lee carried an armful of groceries into the kitchen, and Misha and I unpacked toys and other equipment from the car. The garden spread out behind the house, and Misha decided to explore it as I brought things inside. I felt pleased by the quiet. An occasional birdcall or rustle of wind-driven leaves made the only intrusions on the garden's silence. I saw someone briefly in the second floor window as I dragged a couple of bags across the shale stones around our car and was surprised upon returning to see Lee standing in the kitchen on the ground floor.

"Is that Madame Lelande upstairs?"

Lee smiled. "I think so, and she's doing a wonderful job. Look how spotless the kitchen is."

I nodded, running my finger along the counter and observing the neat stack of magazines on a table in the sitting area near the entrance. I also noted the clean windows overlooking the six pear trees in the center of the garden.

"Nice," I said, looking out and seeing Misha staring up at one of them. "Very nice."

Lee opened the refrigerator door, pointing to the dry, clean interior with a few unopened bottles of Evian standing in the door shelf. I entered the living room through a small alcove off the kitchen and admired the spinet in the corner as well as the two or three framed paintings that Monsieur Lelande, a talented amateur painter, had done years before. One was a red, white, and green still life, and the other two–in blue, amber, and tawny brown–captured a pair of my favorite buildings in St. Rémy. Light glowed across the dark wooden floor from the glass garden doors and, after glancing through them, I turned to mount the stairs. Calling out to Lee to let her know I was carrying bags to the second floor, I heard a flurry of footsteps, and looked up at the dark landing. With mops and feather dusters trailing behind her, a woman leaned forward above me.

"May I help you with those?" she said, reaching for the *minuterie*.

"No, thank you, Madame Lelande. I can handle them."

The stairway light clicked on. I looked up and, wrestling with the luggage, drew in my breath. About to re-introduce myself to Madame Lelande, I saw that the woman standing above me was Anne-Marie.

XI.

Not much happened after that. Not that first morning. We acknowledged each other briefly, hardly smiling, and because Misha charged into the living room, stumbling on a coffee table and crying out as he fell to the floor, our attention turned immediately to him.

"Dad," Misha said, taking the slightly trembling hand that I held out to him. "Come quickly–into the garden. I want to show you something cool."

With a nod and a glance back at Anne-Marie, I let him pull me through the glass doors into the garden out back. We walked around a hedge, past beds of beans, squash, peppers, and a large variety of tomatoes– till we came to a small grove of fruit trees, apples, pears, and cherries. Misha stopped, pointing to the gnarled base of a cherry tree, and I felt my hand go slack in his as I saw a gray tabby cat on her side, nursing six kittens.

"She's not afraid," Misha said. "She let me get real close to them. You see her nipples?"

"Misha, you give her room. You don't want her to feel threatened."

"Aw, she knows I only want to pet them." Misha fell to his knees, and the gray tabby raised her head and claws, but with a sleepy slowness. Misha inched closer.

"Misha, I want you to stay back. She'll want to protect her young."

130

As if in response, he raised his hand, and the mother hissed, lashing her claws at him, just nicking his fingers as he pulled back. Misha sat on his haunches, silently licking at his thumb and middle finger.

"Oh, she always does that," a voice behind us said—in French, and then I saw Anne-Marie slip around the trunk of an apple tree to look at Misha's hand.

"Just a scratch," she said, in English this time with a better accent than I remembered. She brought his hand to her lips very briefly. "My daughter carries several wounds from her."

Anne-Marie smiled, looking closely at Misha's fingers, and took a Band-Aid out of her blue smock pocket to cover the scratches.

"Some ice?" Misha said. "That will make it feel better. I'll go ask Mom."

Anne-Marie looked at the door to the kitchen and nodded. She handed Misha two Band-Aids. "Just wash your hands–carefully. Then put these on. You'll be fine in a little while."

Misha nodded. After a quick look at me, he ran toward the house. I followed, slowly, and, once inside, continued carrying the luggage to the second floor.

Lee and I unpacked, carrying clothes to a walk-in closet in our room, then placing Misha's things in a huge walnut armoire in the room next to ours. The door opened with a loud screech that set our teeth on edge–Misha loved to tease us with it every morning as he dressed–but the armoire carried lots of shelf space, plenty of hanging room, and half-dozen or so drawers for socks, underwear, and the various rocks, shells, and

131

pine cones he had begun to collect.

Later, as I returned to the car to check for things left in the trunk, I saw Anne-Marie talking to him again with a couple of pine cones in her hand. She showed him how to get at the pine nuts, extracting them with a spoon or her finger, and then popping them in his mouth. She had not changed much, I noticed, now that the shock of seeing her after so many years had passed. Her hair shone less, though it still possessed a warm, reddish-blonde tone, but her skin looked less smooth than I remembered. And her body–especially her arms and legs–seemed more wiry than full. She glanced at me as I walked by, and my hand went automatically to my head (covered by a cap, as it never had been in the past) and brushed through the gray at temples and chin, as if to cover it. I thought immediately of a photograph taken many years before, when Anne-Marie and I spent a day poolside in a suburb of Paris. She had taken a photo of me with my feet dangling in the pool, very brief bikini-style trunks covering my groin, and a huge, dark aureole of beard and curly Sicilian-Afro covering my head. I kept it on my office wall. When Misha was five and looked at it one day, he turned to me in complete innocence and asked, "Who's that, Dad?"

I laughed. "Don't I look familiar?"

He stared at the photograph and then looked back at me, eyes wide. "You were that young?" he said.

"I was." I nodded, not grinning quite as widely. "And a different person."

He turned and hugged me, burying his face in my hip. I've always seen that as the moment Misha realized our separateness, and that the separateness was not simply a matter of biology. As I strode past him during his conversation with Anne-Marie, I saw with a little tug of sadness that he was just as interested and intense with her as he usually was with me or Lee. As if to confirm that, he turned toward me in surprise and came running toward me–not for another hug, as he might have years earlier, but to pick up a little black kitten that had followed me from the house.

"*Charbon,*" Anne-Marie called it. "It just appeared one day to play with the other kittens, and it's never left."

Charbon stayed at the house with us that whole summer. Misha left it bowls of milk daily, along with some dry cat food from the bag Anne-Marie showed us in the laundry room. He called it "Charcoal," for its American name, and the cat, rather quickly, I thought, adopted us and our language, hanging around while we ate in the shade of the garden chestnut tree, walking and pouncing on a fluttering leaf or feather at a distance, and eventually lying in Misha's bed at night while he read himself to sleep. My job, or Lee's, just before sleep was to lift the purring kitten from Misha's side and carry it downstairs to the garden before locking the door.

Sure enough, in the morning it stood crouched and waiting when I drove into town for bread, and by the time I returned it would be purring and licking milk from a bowl in Misha's outstretched hand.

"He likes me, Dad," Misha said as I strode past him into the kitchen, placing fresh bread and a newspaper on the counter.

"That's great, my boy. But, then again, why shouldn't he?"

I pushed the start button on the coffee-maker and went upstairs to wake Lee, who enjoyed late mornings with no school or studio work pressing her. The three of us ate in the garden, Charcoal on Misha's lap, the paper on the table before me, and the warm sun raising a gold color on Lee's face as she leaned back and closed her eyes.

At about half past eight I drove Misha through St. Rémy and Les Baux to Mouriès, where he'd spend a day in camp, and then I returned home, either to pick up Lee and tour some archeological sites, or sit at the desk near the piano in the living room to gaze out at the garden and write. Anne-Marie came around twice a week to take care of linens and any other household laundry; and the Lelandes themselves, we soon found out, left for the sea, not to return until late August. So much for loneliness.

My writing went well, mainly because each day's sighting of an archeological monument increased my sense of Rome as the center of a huge urban sprawl, with Provence its principal suburban legacy. All of modern life—its emphasis on ease of communication, organized utilities, and centralized (though highly debated) political power—seemed to descend from the time of the Caesars. For whatever reason, history had never appreciated them in quite that light: Julius as creator, Augustus as facilitator. When Rome collapsed in the centuries after Augustus, Europe lost not only

134

civilized power and aesthetic eminence, but also a way of life that marked itself as especially human. The decayed yet still magnificent buildings and structures our family now saw in Provence marked a beauty and history that the world had permanently lost but would in its genes (and souls) forever aspire to. Thus our love–romantic and Platonic–for the wonderful combination of shattered gray buildings and blooming natural colors that marked passing time in the suburbs, particularly in Provence.

Often on my way back from Misha's camp, I stopped at the ruins of Glanum to walk on its streets and imagine life there when buildings stood whole beneath the rock quarry. Markets functioned, merchants rode through the gates, and soldiers and women mingled within and without the walls of houses. From Glanum I drove into St. Rémy itself and did a little shopping on my own–either in the large Wednesday street market, or in the many boutiques dotting the *périphérique*. I usually stopped in one of the cafés around the bend from St. Martin's, ordered a croissant, and over several *cafés au lait*, took notes or wrote chapters for my book.

There was a Vietnamese restaurant I knew from eating there regularly with Lee and Misha, and frequently I'd see the owner-chef walk by on his way to open it in the morning. His name was Gilles. He had been born in Saigon, then adopted by a French couple as a baby back in the early sixties and had a special feeling for Misha and us. He'd thread his way through café tables to smile, shake my hand, inquire about "the

135

family," as he called us, and, occasionally, ask permission to sit down for a café himself. We discussed my book and his restaurant, his sister, a French Caucasian woman living in Washington, D.C., and general things concerning St. Rémy, the war in Iraq, even local politics. Gilles occasionally introduced me to other passersby, and one morning one of them happened to be Anne-Marie.

"You like jazz?" Gilles said to me as he stood and called her to us. "Her guy—her old man, really—Zach, is an absolutely fabulous bass player–the best I've ever heard."

Anne-Marie blushed on hearing that as she approached the table, but she sat at it quietly and allowed Gilles to order her a coffee. I felt awkward, but Gilles led us through an animated, affable discussion of musical and social styles since the sixties–when he had arrived in France–and by the time he excused himself to continue to the restaurant to prepare for lunch, Anne-Marie and I had no obvious reason to part.

Still, there was a long silence afterward. We hadn't talked much alone since Lee, Misha, and I arrived at the Lelandes'–things like the weather, the sufficiency of towels and sheets, how we were feeling–so our first few moments alone that day felt strained. She smiled warmly enough, seeming quite willing to talk if I broke the ice. Trouble was I could think of nothing, not with images and moments from twenty years or more crowding the present.

"Marketing?" I asked finally, just to break the silence. "Or just out having a stroll?"

"Neither." She smiled—nervously, I thought. "I have several apartments I care for in town. In the center here, there are some lovely old buildings that go far back. People like to rent them."

I nodded, testing my old disdain for landlords and private property–an attitude I held firmly when we were together in the seventies–against my current desire to think positively, especially about her. "You keep busy, I see. I admire your energy after all these years."

"Energy? I'm exhausted."

She laughed, surprised I think, but also a little hostile. I was conscious of how girlish–or at least young–she still seemed, how her stride when I watched her out at the Lelandes' and here at the café as she came toward Gilles and me from the sidewalk contained the same long-legged spring that used to carry her beside me as we walked around Paris. The very thought of it–although making me feel old–rekindled my desire to touch her.

"So, what do *you* do in France," she asked me, "apart from providing a bright light for that marvelous boy of yours?"

I shrugged, annoyed, a little, at the change of subject; but I felt delighted by it, too. "Not much. As I think you know, I write now. That's what I'm doing here this summer."

"I gathered... But the painting–?"

I shook my head. "Not for profit in any case. And not even for fun anymore. I'm ashamed to say it, but I let Lee do the painting for me."

Sinking, I stared across the street at a hotel front

137

undergoing renovation. It was a scarred two-hundred year old building, clearly from the Haussmann era, with gray blocks of weathered stone turned bluish-black from soot and exhaust. Van Gogh had painted on this street during one or two excursions from the clinic of St. Paul de Mausole, and the thought of him struggling through all his depression and pain on the street in front of me just to show human forms against the dark background of that building sent me into a deeper funk of my own. As I tell Lee and Misha, sometimes you just have to grind through your pain—like Van Gogh.

"You had such desire," Anne-Marie said, shaking her head. "To paint and think about painting seemed to be all you wanted from life."

I nodded, knowing that had been true until I met her.

"I just think about it now. My son tells me I look like a dark Vincent sometimes, because of the beard and hair. I tell him I wish I could paint like him instead, although I want nothing of his sadness."

Ashamed, I added, "At some point I wanted other things, too. You know, normal things: a job. Children. Some sense of permanent comfort to make up for losses."

"And a wife, which the real Vincent never had, I believe." Anne-Marie chuckled mockingly, although I couldn't tell if she was jealous or having fun. Fun, I decided.

"With a woman who wants to be my wife," I said. I looked into her eyes, but Anne-Marie turned away to stare at the hotel across the street.

"And what about you, my friend? I know about your divorce and your daughter, but you have also re-married, I think."

She shook her head, looking directly at me again. "Zach is not my husband. I live with him."

I shrugged. "According to Gilles ... Well, perhaps he misjudged my English. Or I misjudged his."

"I doubt it." She shook her head and smiled. "Gilles likes to tell interesting stories."

"Is he as good a bass player as Gilles says?"

Anne-Marie pursed her lips. "Some say Zach is the best in France—or was. Here, they compare him to great Americans–Percy Heath, Jimmy Garrison–he's played with Phil Woods, Lester Young, even Coltrane."

I nodded, impressed. I don't follow jazz anymore, but at one time it was the only music for me. "I'd like to hear him some time. Are your parents— about him, I mean—still unhappy?"

She nodded, biting her lip. Then she looked away. I had no idea where to go from there, so I thought of what we still could share.

"And your daughter, Celestine?" I smiled grimly, but Anne-Marie's firm mouth discouraged even that. For a moment her eyes watered and, rather than embarrass her, I turned to the battered hotel front across the way.

"We are estranged," Anne-Marie said. "My parents have taken Celestine from me. Or rather, she has chosen to live with them instead."

"Chosen...?"

"Because of Zach," she spit out. "They–and

Celestine–think he has cast a spell over me. My parents want to preserve her soul."

I saw the awful irony on her face, the amazed smile and grim anger, but in her eyes I recognized nothing but weariness and pain. "I'm sorry," I muttered after a moment. "I find it hard to believe they could legally do that."

"A black man? A musician with dreadknots and some 'interesting' spiritual ideas?–In France we have our prejudices, too."

I said nothing for several moments. Staring at the cars and motorbikes streaming between us and the hotel, I remembered how much Anne-Marie loved music–all kinds, but especially American–when we were together. That love had clashed with my profound admiration for French art, and at the same time, like blood, we admitted, it bound us together. The singing of Louis Armstrong or Stevie Wonder, and the guitar strings of Django Reinhardt and Steely Dan evoked sunlit landscapes for both of us. Meanwhile, the landscapes we walked through back then–in Paris or outside it–along with the ones I studied by the Impressionists or tried to recreate in sketch books, seemed to lie before us under the sound of a melody from home. And now Provence…

"Don't they respect his artistry?" I asked. "That must say something."

"They don't think about it–neither my parents nor Celestine. They see him as a gypsy–or a witch doctor, believe it or not–the complete bourgeois fear without having talked to him or heard him play."

Her anger flushed her face. I thought of our own disagreements–petty compared to what distressed her now, and a lot more laughable. I confess a pang of jealousy pushed through my chest over so much love and loss.

"Celestine has never talked to him either?"

She smiled, slightly. "Not as a father–or care taker. She says she hates him."

I said nothing. Celestine obviously carried her mother's stubbornness in her blood. I wondered if she also had her mother's wonderful capacity for warmth, which could lead to something positive. Anne-Marie's tenderness toward Misha at the Lelandes' struck me powerfully, and of course I still remembered our own youthful feelings. No woman, including Lee, I might add, had matched her caring since.

"That may change," I said. "A young girl, she'll..."

"A very stubborn young girl. She doesn't like when Zach takes up my time. She wants me for herself–exclusively."

"At fourteen?"

"At nearly fifteen."

I had no reply. Like all children, I guess, Misha had shown such jealous traits, and like most parents Lee and I struggled to balance his desires and genuine needs with our own. Most of the time we failed, because just as soon as we thought we could devote some time to each other, a lace would break on his shoe, a friend would ignore him at school, or worse, something would darken his mood that not even Misha could explain.

141

"They're our future," I said, shrugging. "We have to spend time to shape them–make them happy."

"And spoiling them!–Zach, my love, is dying— dying! And my daughter can't stand that I try to give him hope as the end comes. His music is all he has; his best playing has hardly been recorded."

"He's dying?" I whispered the question, not sure if it was sympathy for her or the man who inspired its passing between us.

Anne-Marie bit her lower lip very hard. "He has cancer. It has stolen his music and will slowly destroy his ability to breathe. I am trying to preserve his spirit."

"Lungs." I shook my head.

"And the esophagus. He is thinner than I have ever seen. He can barely eat, let alone play his instrument. He spends his days listening to tapes of his live concerts. He needs to talk, but no one, except me, ever finds time to see him."

XII.

It was an opening of sorts, as I understand it now–I mean Anne-Marie's statement as well as the whole conversation. We saw each other more frequently after that morning, either at the Lelande house, where she occasionally stayed with Misha while Lee and I ran errands, or at the café on days I brought him to camp. Despite her description of Zach's illness, he still worked occasionally, traveling to clubs in Marseilles, St. Tropez, and Juan-Les-Pins, although he functioned more as MC than as a performer. "Very faint," Anne-Marie said, to describe the sounds his instrument made of late, and even with a microphone his voice rose barely above a whisper. But audiences loved him, and musicians asked him to make appearances.

They lived outside of St. Rémy, near a side road on the route toward Mouriès, where we met from time to time in the shade of the café on the tree-lined main street. I'm not sure what kept those meetings going: my sentimental desire or Anne-Marie's emotional need. I know I felt comfortable with her again, as if a lost, dearly central part of my life had returned, and I could go back to certain essences I once craved. But I doubt she shared the feeling, even though she never missed a proposed meeting and even suggested additional ones now and then.

Once or twice she invited me to her house, a

small, two-floor *mas* on an agricultural plane with mountains in the distance and a surround of lavender, spinach, and bean fields with irrigation stanchions dotting them. I admired the quiet there, the rocky isolation that bespoke toughness and beauty. I could hardly wonder that Anne-Marie lived there, given her interest in plants and soil, but what about her lover? What would a jazz musician, a Rastafarian from Philadelphia, let alone a man dying, find amid all that quiet Mediterranean growth?

"Our love," Anne-Marie told me at one point. "It's all that gives this sad time meaning."

The walls were white, enlivened by photographs of Zach, a smiling, heavy-lidded black man with curls like electronic coils, pointing in all directions from his head, and muscular arms and torso that, as he aged, looked in the photographs thinner and more boney. They had pictures of Celestine as well, a sort of darker, smaller version of her mother, with brown hair and gently rounded features seeming to belie any anger she expressed toward Anne-Marie or Zach.

The furniture lay about like old country animals–solid, functional, nothing particularly beautiful — with bold grain of oak and pine taking earthy, reddish glow from the combined gleam of floor and sun. They had a wall of books–mostly French titles about music and art–that formed a backdrop to a long pine farmer's table and a sophisticated-looking CD, tape, and vinyl music center in one corner, with recordings by famous jazz groups and tapes of Zach playing solo lying all about. The corner also featured a heavily textured oil painting of a black man, bow in hand, playing his bass.

"So… This has to be Zach."

"In healthier days," Anne-Marie said.

The room looked much like her Paris studio, as I remembered it, and the feel of the place, so unlike the bookish, formal suburban home that Lee and I inhabited, made me see the different paths our lives had followed. I studied her face, saw the deep sadness there, and admired the simple perseverance she had shown. Plainly, Anne-Marie did not live grandly; whatever romance and excitement she had experienced with Zach was slowly winding down; and yet she maintained a warmth, really an optimism, that shone in the ready smiles on her face and the energetic motions of her walk. I, on the other hand, felt glum, in her presence or not.

"He's away now?" I said, the first time I saw that painting of him at her house. She nodded, her firm expression warning me not to make awkward assumptions.

"I miss him," she said, "but I'm happy he still enjoys the road, even when he's not really playing."

I put myself in his place, a man with supreme musical skill no longer able to perform, and I wondered how he bore the torture of watching–and applauding–others. I myself still felt bad that I didn't paint, and secretly I felt worse each time I entered an exhibition to write about it rather than participate.

"He wants to earn some money for me and Celestine," Anne-Marie said. "So he goes when he's invited and they offer him a fee. He has a dream of Celestine attending college in America–with me there as her chaperone."

She smiled–warmly–at the idea, especially, I'm sure, for me, the man with whom she had shared so many important moments of her youth. "I'm not sure I'll be qualified for the job—not with my experience." She nodded, going into the kitchen to make some coffee.

I felt little tension or overt desire for Anne-Marie during that time although she still, obviously, remained an attractive woman. My relationship with Lee felt relatively secure again, especially during this settled European summer of 2002, with the presence of Misha, still new and exotic for us, and really so satisfying in his demands, somehow shifting the terrain of my own needs from love and sex to fatherhood. I've read a bit about that sort of mature switch in men (except where it's absent—and shameful), but the longer we had Misha in our life, the more certain I felt it to be natural. Normal. I remembered that Van Gogh had shot himself just after learning that his brother Theo's wife was pregnant, and that Theo's financial support of Vincent's painting would be compromised; and I remembered the bitter time Gauguin spent living with his son in poverty while he tried to begin his painting career. I had experienced the conflicts of art and life in my own career, but before Misha I had never fully understood the genuine sacrifice of human joys some artists have made.

I reveled in showing Misha new places, teaching him languages, and especially revealing to him in

146

museums and exhibits the rich combination of art and history surrounding us. Often we stood before a canvas together, wondering what the paint was doing, how the painter had manipulated it, and why consequently we now found ourselves so strongly responding to it. Misha astonished me sometimes with detailed comments about what he liked in a certain part of the painting: a face hanging in a pile of skin in Michelangelo's Last Judgment, a certain curve in the petal of an iris by Van Gogh, the color and shape of a design on a dress of a woman memorialized by Matisse.

I felt proud of our family, formed not by biology or shared education, but by our shared experience of life; and the mere sight of this young boy–my magnificent son–responding seriously to thick dabbles of pigment made me perceive the natural pull of beauty and the ability of humans, no matter what their background or intelligence, to try to understand the mechanics of that appeal. So art, rather than blood and genes, tied Misha and me together as father and son–and as Lee loved it too, held together the three of us as a family.

At the same time, I found it hard to understand what held Anne-Marie together with Zach. I confess a side of me still needed to know why she hadn't stayed with me, and I could not imagine–on that first visit to her home, at least–what she had found with a renowned, but not so financially stable, musician to make her risk so much–the loss of parents, her daughter, and her own career ambitions.

At one time Anne-Marie wanted to write. I

147

remembered exquisite poems and stories, many turning on some moral or psychological blindness, that she had published in the small literary journals and tabloids that constantly sprang up in Paris during our time together. I had illustrated one or two of them, and we had actually collaborated on a literary gathering to celebrate the first number of a little magazine we had both contributed to. I spotted her at a table, poured some Bordeaux into her empty glass, admired the poem she had on page ten, and the rest, as we used to say, became our professional history.

We joined our separate arts in about half-dozen publications after that and always made that long, pleasant walk down Boulevard St. Germain to look at them in the windows or on the shelves of bookstores before stopping at Deux Magots for coffee and a little self-conscious preening with copies of them in our hands.

Looking back, I guess I thought we were going somewhere together–as artists and as a couple. Sartre and Simon de Beauvoir lived and worked as ideals for us, a couple who blended together politically, loved each other with all the anti-bourgeois freedoms we desired, and turned out separate, impressive bodies of writing that allowed them individual reputations even as it held them together in the world's eyes.

Anne-Marie and I envisioned collaborating on illustrated volumes of her poems, essays, and stories that would join our aesthetic points of view. We thought of ourselves as embodying a new Franco-American relationship that combined classical food, culture, and language with a new, modern efficiency that spanned the ocean and made contemporary life less alienating than it had been. It all happened, we thought, because of the natural bonding of our lives through love and, yes, sex!

Recalling all that now, especially with my recent image of the older Anne-Marie in her house in Provence, it all seems terribly stupid—and sad. I can only say we felt it, felt it in an absolute, innocent way that carried–especially in those heady early post-modernism years–the weight of absolute truth: this was not the way life could be; this was the way, inevitably, it had to be. Bodies connect through affection, new worlds of custom and taste are born. Founded on that basic affection, these worlds had somehow always existed, crossing geographical, political, and even temporal boundaries. And, of course, with all that so sure, Anne-Marie and I felt destined to remain together. It was a faith that I clung to despite some real-world doubt, and here, close to her again in magical Provence, I confess I still felt its draw.

We drank coffee as we talked. Seated on her couch, with the smooth, thoughtful sounds of Zach's bowed bass playing some Satie and Poulenc along with a small trio behind him, we somehow found the strength to break down some of the barriers time and her sound system put between us. I confessed a long period of remorse after she left me in New York; she spoke of constant remorse and an almost hourly change of mind about hopping on a plane and flying across the ocean to stay with me.

149

"Then why didn't you call," I asked, "at least to let me know what you were thinking?"

Anne-Marie shook her head, laughing–at herself, not me. I had the distinct impression that she saw her long-ago self as a complete stranger, perhaps more foreign than my own earlier self had been.

"I couldn't do it," she said. "I was afraid."

"Of me?–I adored you. Maybe–"

"I adored you, too, but that was my fear."

"Maybe..." But I hesitated because she was clearly in mid-thought.

"If I came to live with you in New York, I would have left too much behind. Who, or what, would I become? I was just too frightened; I'm sorry."

I nodded, acknowledging to myself that she carried something grand inside–at least in her potential–a daily life more rich with meaning than I could have given. Yet I could not say why she would not have achieved that potential with me. A glance up at the portrait of Zach, thick with the live energy of paint— and exploding with an unheard sound you could actually sense in color and lines—made me wonder if I was destined to live on a lower plane somehow.

"Why didn't you ask me to come stay with you in France?" I asked. "I was ready to live here, make my peace with teaching English and painting on the weekends. I just needed to know you wanted that, too. I never got that feeling."

She shook her head again, not particularly in regret, I thought, but in resignation. We had become two very different people, yet we stared back at a shared dream that dwarfed the two real individuals it had become. I remembered picking up the phone often in the months after she left New York, even dialing once or twice, but no one ever answered. A combination of pride and fear–in the two of us, probably–simply could not overcome circumstance.

"And here we are," I muttered, after a long moment's thought, "not much wiser after all these years."

Anne-Marie blushed. We sat for a bit, listening to the slow soothing lift of *Trois Gymnopédies*. Zach drew it out in a clear, surprisingly light melodic line for a bass. I leaned against the back of the couch and, noticing Anne-Marie's hand next to my thigh, took it and held it against my heart for the full remaining minutes of the piece. As it ended, I turned and, moved beyond embarrassment and meaningful words, kissed her softly on the lips. The silence that followed, unrelieved by Zach's playing since the CD had come to a full stop, demanded that we both stand and separate before something more awkward occurred.

"I have to drive back to Châteaurenard. I promised Misha to take him fishing this afternoon."

Anne-Marie nodded, smoothing her blouse and picking up the coffee cups. Wordless, and with that gesture, we parted–she to her kitchen, I to the car to drive back home.

We didn't see each other for several days. Anne-Marie managed to come to the house when the three of us were driving somewhere, or when I was doing research, or out fishing with Misha. The Durance River

151

flowed near the house. One of the longest, most powerful rivers in France, it hurtled from the base of the Alps and sputtered through nearby fields in Châteaurenard as a stream of less than twenty yards' width. Misha and I would take poles, a can or two of worms freshly dug from the garden behind the house, and bicycle past a couple of farms to an unpaved road cutting through a bamboo field. We stopped at a wooden bridge, leaned our bikes against the rail, and trudged through the green bamboo plants to a bare spot on the bank where we sat on a rock or fallen tree trunk to cast our lines.

We spent hours there, smelling manure from the nearby farms and soaking up sun. Misha had learned to cast with an expert flip of his wrists that spring and loved to do it over and over, more for his joy than catching an occasional trout or perch. Sometimes we read to each other: one fishing while the other (usually me) secured his pole under a rock and recited passages from a favorite book. I was big on poets that year, while Misha leaned toward an early Harry Potter.

Whenever he caught something, he'd stun it, then place it on a rock for study. He admired the look of a fish, its lines, eyes, and markings, and made a mental note of its size for later comparison. He could never eat them, however, more out of a sense of shame and fear than taste, I believe. He simply felt guilty to have killed something, although it did not hinder in any way his joy in a graceful cast of the line, completed, of course, by a successful hauling in of aquatic treasure.

Misha and I felt close on those afternoons,

confirmed for me by the huge smile he gave as we packed to go home. And I felt more committed and loved when, as we trudged through bamboo to our bikes again, he would suddenly throw his arms about my waist, pull my head down, and kiss me on the forehead. "Thanks, Dad," he'd say. "That's absolutely the funnest thing we can do, exactly what I needed."

Occasionally, Lee would join us, standing straw-hatted among the bamboo, or amid fruit and vegetables in a nearby field–with the familiar wooden easel and canvas she had standing before her. She loved to paint the bridge, or one of the ochre stone buildings we passed on the way to the Durance, but she always liked to smother those man-made structures with a colorful overhang of trees or a sudden burst of fruit or flower, the shades of which glowed against the earthier colors of wood and soil.

These were incredibly happy times, family days and hours that I could imagine Misha remembering for the rest of his life and passing on to his children as stories from his happy childhood, paintings from his mom, and the lofty, knowing image of a father who turned them all into essays about an important, appealing form of physical life: Provence.

And despite all that—my joy in our family and the world we had settled into that summer—I could not escape my continual longing for something else: Anne-Marie. I recognized it as an aberration, a critical weakness from my youth, a desire to relive and remake something I really had no right or ability to revisit. I saw that, felt it very strongly in my gut, and assumed Anne-

153

Marie saw and felt the reluctance too. Yet we met more frequently (for longer periods of time) and one day later that summer, at the café in Mouriès, I could not resist the impulse, nor did she. We stepped into each other's arms upon meeting, not bothering to order coffee. We drove to her house instead, where she led me, running, up the stairs past a wall of photographs of Zach in concert, and into the bedroom where we started immediately to pull at each other's clothes.

"I love you," she said. "Now... I've said it."

"I've never stopped loving you," I answered. "I know that now, even though I've spent the last twenty years with a woman I also love."

"Differently," she said.

I nodded, grateful that she had already closed the drapes as we fell onto her bed.

"I feel the same way with Zach. I've never understood the impulse of this love. Our love."

Not long afterward, with what I thought of as lack of real satisfaction, we pulled away from each other, lying naked side-by-side in our confusion. I felt very young, younger and more naive than during our real youth in Paris. As I remember it now, my life's future seemed absolutely open, my place in the world unfixed, the possibilities ahead so large and, yes, exciting that they erupted well beyond the comfortably known.

"Here I am," I said to her that afternoon, "in my fifties, freshly in love–but with someone from my twenties–and no idea of where to go next, or how to hold it all together."

"I assure you I'm no better," Anne-Marie said.

Then we turned away from each other, almost in shame.

It would be nice, I think, to say we made love again, relaxed and with greater joy that afternoon, but in fact the walls around our separate lives would not come down so easily, and we couldn't. Zach's music drifted around us, emanating from the photographs and painting, without a sound device in the house turned on. And I heard Misha's voice calling out for my attention, even as Lee's silent, knowing gaze of awareness could not hide the hurt and disappointment I imagined in her eyes. I knew Zach's music, Anne-Marie knew Lee's and Misha's characters, and the knowledge brought all three into our bodies as well as part of the surrounding air.

We dressed quickly, eyes averted as if we had been seen exposing ourselves in public. The old sixties and seventies issues of flaunting inhibitions, proudly doing it in the road, and defending the innocence of naked flesh seemed wildly, I would even say, horribly, inappropriate. Without so much as a shake of Anne-Marie's hand, I said good-bye. She led me down the stairs and unceremoniously opened the door. I left quickly. As I started my car and drove away, I wondered regretfully if I would ever see her again. Certainly, the romance that had filled my memories of her and our time together had evaporated, blown away in the storm of our brief half hour in bed.

I drove back through the bauxite hills toward St. Rémy, pulled into the parking lot across from Glanum and St. Paul de Mausole, and spent the rest of the afternoon on the grounds of both places. It was hot and dusty, with the Sirocco picking up piles of dust and blowing it in every visitor's face. Men held hats, one woman lost a hair piece, and everyone had trouble with the sheets of paper guiding them along walkways–either to see the sites of Van Gogh's paintings or view the principal ruins of the Glanum community. The rock quarry, the barren surrounding plain, the blue rise of the Alpilles toward Les Baux, along with the eroded grandeur of the old Roman suburb reflected and weighed down on my mood. Caesar had fought and defeated Gauls near here, Van Gogh had tramped the earth covering the ruins and, with paint and brush, tried to escape his personal pain. I fought my own internal wars as I thought about these things and tried, like Van Gogh, to see clarity and order in the world about me even as my own hope in the future crumbled.

Van Gogh had died–shooting himself in the heart, as almost everyone knows–less than three months after leaving the asylum near St. Rémy. "Cured," the principal doctor wrote in his final report, although Van Gogh had attempted to poison himself several times during his year there and still fought bouts of deep despondency regularly. As I've said, his brother and patron, Theo, had begun to raise a family, making funds for Vincent's art less likely to continue; his canvases found no customers, providing no hope of gaining a permanent patron; and his friend, Gauguin, had left the south a year before after nearly falling victim to Vincent's knife one night in Arles.

156

The gloom of those days is rarely seen in Van Gogh's St. Rémy work–especially from the outdoors–yet for me the profound grandeur he paints–in the sky and poplars on a starry night, in the sun so yellow it seems to burn a sower's seeds before they touch the ground, and in the immense pleasure of a child with parents in a dry corner of a garden–reveals a certain emptiness within, as if the viewer–that is to say Vincent Van Gogh–cannot see beyond the surface of images.

I say that not to fault a great painter, but to wonder about the possible depths of things, especially at moments in time when we think we understand them fully. Here beside a road in St. Rémy, I wandered a field and saw a dead Roman city that Van Gogh never dreamed of–at least never painted or mentioned in his letters. As he gazed at the colors of the sky or the forms and shades that filled a garden, did he wonder who had walked already in the gray, pale dust beneath his feet, or did the past assert itself through his living things, like the deadly lushness of irises and drying straw he loved to paint?

When I thought of my previous hour with Anne-Marie that day, I wondered how much we saw, and how much had asserted itself without our knowledge. We clearly wanted something from each other, and our wishes derived from another, quite distant, pair of selves, in another time and city. Yet I felt the weight of this particular place where time somehow drove us to the bed we had shared fitfully, no matter how briefly, that day.

"Excuses," I whispered to myself as I glanced

157

over a standing bathhouse in Glanum. "You betrayed
Lee and Misha. New York towers have fallen, but the
rocks in this place haven't budged although they've
suffered sun and wind and rain for thousands of years."

Our time together on her bed had been fitful,
guilt-ridden, not joyful, I realized. Yet I knew that if
ever I saw Anne-Marie again, no matter where, I would
have to run to her. Yes, and I would eagerly take her in
my arms.

XIII.

Despite all this thumping of head and heart, I found the strength (*chutzpah*, Lee would call it) to continue things as they were: morning commutes to Misha's camp, visits to ruins, libraries, and museums, note-taking and writing in some café (but not in Mouriès), and, in the late afternoons, lots of what I hoped Misha would remember as warm family time.

Lee painted several canvases of the Durance and the Crau, green, gray, and ochre images that managed to convey abundant fertility in a dry, stone-littered landscape. She registered a rich impression of life that managed to be Provence and something grander at the same time, a panorama of earth where humans were just one product of its forces. Misha and I seemed small, fishing on the bamboo banks she put us on. With the clouds and the pace of the Durance current merely forming a backdrop to our life's concerns, the house, high in the far left corner, downstream and across the road from the Durance, carried meaningful texture in its stones and earthen tile.

"It looks like a church, Mom," Misha said on the afternoon she finished it. "Is that a cross you put there on the roof?"

"It's a weathervane, Munchkin, a rooster. Look at the house the next time we go past. You'll see it."

Meanwhile, the Alpilles out on the Crau

embodied electric energy in Lee's aqua-blue washes, as if in these renderings she saw mythic animals stalking human forms, bent over plants or rock, populating the dry, chalky earthen floor. I have to say I felt very proud.

"It's nice to see your imagination on fire here," I said to her. "It certainly brings back other times."

Lee smiled, earnest as she saw me study her work so seriously. Misha shrugged beneath her embrace, and I felt myself grow warm—partially from embarrassment— when she hugged me, too.

"You ought to do some of this, too, Ben. It will relax you; maybe help keep the writing fresh."

Absolutely true, I thought, and learned from her own less-wrenching visit to another time, one we had shared during our first meetings in New York. In fact, Lee did not know me much as a practicing artist because I had been teaching and writing for a couple of years when we met. But I had let her know how much I regretted my failed calling, how, before I met her, a part of me had died during the years after Paris, and how I regretted as fully as mine her turn from painting to teaching and criticism during the years of our work on marriage and family.

In a certain sense my current interest in suburbs and my idea of portraying them as basic to human culture was both a reassertion of my creativity and a defense of my career turn for the more-traveled road. So, Rome, its civilization, its logistical control that could build highways to span a known world and make all its citizens feel connected, seemed to make art in all its forms, but particularly in images, a mere superficial

160

addition to the engineer's skill and the politician's social one. But here, in St. Rémy, I could not escape the ghost of another past: Van Gogh, who had trumped Roman engineering in ignorance, never even sketching the monuments he had to see daily across from St. Paul de Mausole. He had given up everything I personally wanted–love, comfort, career, belief in God, and even his life–for colorful canvases, without having made one significant sale of a painting!

My vision, as I liked to think of it in relation to the book, was my personal contribution to the development of the individual spirit, something that might put me, as a writer, on the same plateau as a great painter. I wanted to be light, but incisive. I wanted to give real joy, but combine it with meaning. Although I knew a book could never be hung as a source of pride and joy the way a painting could, I wanted to produce a work that the reader would be proud to own and show, perhaps even pass on, to his children. Yes, in the end it was like framing a painting for Misha.

So, the publisher in New York and I made plans for beautiful photographs and sketches, along with a typeface and layout that would allow someone to browse and turn pages as well as read. I knew it was a supermarket approach, sort of like seeing Van Gogh's irises as prints in a dentist's office, but at the same time I felt I could make something to inspire people as they went through their ordinary days. Be proud, I wanted to say to my readers, you are the foundation of all these wonders. Life is great because people like you will it–and make appropriate sacrifices.

It was romantic, I told my editor, a philosophy that allowed forgiveness for the most persistent failures, so long as they weren't due to complete indifference. We are human, I told her, and so we want things. But most important, we want to earn those things, do something to deserve them, and that is the most basic human drive.

"You mean," she wrote back one day, not trying to conceal her cynicism, "humans want to turn the weight of their endeavors into gold."

"No," I replied. "We just want to be a part of a force for good."

Eventually, she decided someone would take pictures and make sketches. Lee and I could do that, I told the editor, but in a somewhat condescending tone, she said she preferred that I stick to the writing. I didn't argue much. Lee enjoyed painting nature alive rather than *morte,* as she referred to the ruins, and neither of us had a great appreciation for the camera as a tool of art. Besides, the editor said that she could see the graphics growing out of the writing, making them second in importance to the words which, of course, flattered my wish to put myself on a level with the masters.

I worked hard on the writing after that, read a lot and thought a lot in search of special insights. As the summer progressed, I felt the book grow larger, contributing something, I hoped, to the triumph of Rome as well as its tragedy. Its civilization created something important, an idea of world as community, sprawling, but united by roadways and aqueducts so that all people could feel part of it. Those who didn't, or

162

resisted, risked attack, but those who did feel comfortable as citizens enjoyed wide opportunity for travel, commerce, comfort, and culture. Virgil's *Georgics* give us the pastoral feel of the Empire, just as Caesar's monuments of block and stone provide an image of its urban force.

I wrote feverishly with those ideas in mind and, for a while, gave up on Van Gogh and his isolation. I also managed to keep my secret longing for Anne-Marie distant, and our afternoon together just beyond my mental vision. Through some arrangement, either with the Lelandes or Lee–though Lee did not mention it– Anne-Marie continued to visit and service our rented house, but never when I was there. And although I worked in the same café in St. Rémy daily, I never once saw her walk by the entrance again. Misha mentioned her occasionally when we strolled through the garden in back of the house. Lee took note of the neatness and cleanliness of the house. But I, although I sometimes ached to, never saw Anne-Marie and certainly did not ask.

Then, one day as I wrote about Glanum and its commercial past, I looked at the empty hotel across the street and noticed my Vietnamese friend, Gilles, threading his way through the tables toward me. He smiled, giving a little wave, and turned at the same time toward a skinny black man walking uncertainly behind him. His dreadlocks were a giveaway, along with his beard. I recognized immediately that he was Zach.

"Well, well, well, the American at his office. How are you?"

Gilles shook my hand, one sharp pump in the French manner, and turned around to guide Zach toward the table. "Zach Douglas," he said. "This is my American friend, Ben Alto, a writer."

I shrugged, taking Zach's hand, softer, less direct than Gilles' although he looked me squarely in the eye — as if we shared something, I thought.

"Châteaurenard," he said, more Philadelphia bop than Caribbean lilt in his voice. "You live in that house out there."

"For the summer. I'm sorry to say it's not our permanent home."

"Anne-Marie told me about it."

He smiled, and for a very brief moment I wondered what he meant. His eyes showed nothing except friendly recognition, and so I invited them both to join me for a coffee. Gilles pulled a chair from the neighboring table, Zach took the one across from me, and I ordered three more coffees from the passing waiter. We sat for a bit, admiring the bright day until the coffees arrived, and then Gilles once again brought up Zach's music.

"The best," Gilles said, patting Zach's shoulder. "No one in France, not even Europe, plays the bass like him. It's like a violin!"

"I've heard some," I said, smiling, "on CD. The Satie and Debussy are great."

Zach nodded, sighing a little, and to my surprise lit up an unfiltered *Gitane Mais* to go with the coffee. Gilles declined the package pushed toward him, as I did. "Anne-Marie would kill me," Zach said, staring at

164

me. "You guys have great self-control."

I nodded, still ready for any hidden accusation, but, honestly, I heard none. Zach's voice, rough and gravelly, barely rose above the sounds of passing traffic, and I found it hard to read anything sinister. Of course, I wondered. He raised a slim, almost trembling hand to his lips and inhaled before blowing out a cloud of bluish smoke—right in my face. His eyes stayed on me as Gilles sipped at his cup and smiled. "Words and music," Gilles said, proudly, "but because of my poor English I can only understand the music."

I nodded. Zach muttered, saying nothing really, just a long, whispered hum of contemplation. After another long drag he added, "You top us both, my friend. Food reaches everyone."

"And where it counts," I added.

Gilles grinned. The three of us turned toward the street, where a young, beautiful blonde boy and girl, dressed in embroidered shirt and blue jeans, walked swiftly past. We all stared in silence until Zach glanced down at my opened notebook and asked what I was working on. I outlined my Roman suburb idea, a little uneasy before his intent, respectful stare, and suddenly felt how weak the whole project was. But he listened carefully, asked a couple of sympathetic questions and said that for him all the arts belonged to rural communities. "They're less commercial there," he said, "and more human." He talked about that for a while, how in rural and suburban communities life gives work time to ripen. "Almost any important artist you can think of has had to get away from the pavements to

165

survive," Zach said, "either by drink or drugs, or retreating into the country."

I nodded but said nothing. Of course, I also thought of Van Gogh.

The three of us sipped coffee, and in a few minutes Gilles left to prepare the restaurant for lunch. I thought Zach would leave with him, but he very politely asked if I minded his company, again nodding at my notebook. Of course, I said I didn't, pushing aside my notebook and pen. But I must say I wondered if he expected Anne-Marie to join him, which I wasn't sure I could handle.

"Your wife and boy are here," he said, "at the house in Châteaurenard."

I nodded. As would often happen that summer, I felt myself move backward while he kept a step ahead of me.

"Yes, she paints. He fishes, feeds the cats, and takes care of the garden."

"The boy." Zach nodded. "Does he like it here?"

"He says he does." I shrugged. "We're hoping he learns to speak some French, but it's not happening as fast as we had hoped."

Zach smiled and laughed a loud, broad guffaw that had other patrons looking at him. "Anne-Marie's daughter has a horse–a present from her grandparents. I don't know where she's going with that since she hardly even looks at it, except to ride. On the other hand, I played my first music on tin cans and clay jugs in the south side of Philly. I was twenty before I owned a real musical instrument–a clarinet."

166

"You learned something," I said. "And fast."

"Just hanging out and listening." He shook his head. "I never had a formal lesson in my life. We left the Caribbean, landed in New Orleans, then my aunt took us in up in Philly, and somehow music and musicians became part of my life."

"Do you read it—music?"

"Badly." He laughed. "My aunt would say I'm blessed. I have an ear that seems to go directly to my arms and fingers. Always has—which helps with the kind of music I play."

I nodded my head in appreciation. My best quality seemed to be doggedness, I admitted. That–and real desire–moved me, yet at some point I recognized it wasn't enough. In fact, the harder I plugged away, the more lifeless my canvases appeared. In each painting I saw a section that revealed something–but never a whole painting that lived, that embodied me or what I felt.

"You're very lucky," I said after a pause, not even close to thinking about his cancer or the mess his body was in.

"Let's say blessed," he said, smiling. "But it's very hard to live up to. I often wonder if that's why artists need to withdraw."

"You mean from the pressure?"

He nodded. "The fear that the world will squeeze it out of them."

"Crush it, you mean." I nodded, too.

Zach laughed. "That's why Miles and Coltrane turned their backs. It was all for themselves. The hell

167

with the people out front."

I sat in silence, glancing down at my closed notebook. I had always wanted to say something to the really smart people of the world–at first through painted canvas, then through words and paper. Sitting quietly in my room — or at this table in a French café — and writing or sketching solely for myself had never been an option. Lee loved to paint for the pure pleasure of seeing the canvases hanging on our walls, but I could never accept that sort of reserve. When it became fairly certain that I would rarely, if ever, make it in a New York gallery show, I turned to art history and criticism. Lee turned to that as well, of course, but she had never abandoned the pure joy of the work itself, the act of painting as an expression of life.

"Are you still playing?" I asked. "Gilles says you occasionally go on tour."

Zach said nothing. Just a slight tilt of the head told me I had touched a tender spot. "I get up on the stand. I introduce guys–longtime friends, mostly. Then I start them with a downbeat and step aside. Strength is just gone from the arms."

He held them up — thin, really fragile — and I looked across the street again.

"I feel great emptiness," Zach told me, pointing to his chest. "But it doesn't stop me from remembering the thrill. That's why I go out there now. I still yearn for the life. And no one can take that away."

I forced a smile. I imagine that as a young man he had pictured himself dying with an instrument in his hands–never believing he would give it up while he still

168

breathed. I remembered similar thoughts concerning brushes and paint. Neighbors would find me no longer breathing, but the spirit I had left would throb to life continually in the undiscovered canvases all about my body.

"It's a special life," I told him. "I imagine it's very hard not to continue trying."

He shook his head and then, with half a smile, changed the subject. "Does your son have any interest in painting–or music?"

I shook my head now. "He likes animals and plants; and loves to read. He also likes to look at paintings. Very little talk."

Zach's eyebrows rose. "Not bad. Bring him out to the house some time–after camp."

I glanced at him and said nothing, although by now I guessed that he and Anne-Marie had spoken of me. In the end I agreed to bring Misha out, but of course I wondered about his motives–how much he knew. He hadn't shown one hint of anger–or jealousy; yet from what I knew of Anne-Marie, and what I sensed about Zach, I gathered she had already told him about our recent afternoon. I couldn't imagine her keeping anything from him. In a certain way, I doubted I could. Yet why would he invite me to his house after I had gone with his lover into their bed?

"Sounds good," I said, finally. "Misha might enjoy it."

"It'll do Anne-Marie good to see him. She misses her daughter."

I nodded again, *very* uncomfortable, and

169

gathered my notebook and pen. Zach looked a little disappointed when I said I had to leave, but he said nothing to stop me. I paid for the coffees and ordered him another before walking out of the café and turning toward St. Rémy's interior to visit a gallery I knew.

I strolled past St. Martin's Church, hearing an organ player practicing, and walked toward the *mairie*, where I turned a corner toward the gallery and saw Anne-Marie, head to the side, striding toward me. Glancing in a store window, she didn't notice me at first, but she looked up as I approached, and her face turned pale. "Hi," she said, extending her hand and offering friendly kisses to my two cheeks.

"Hi, yourself," I answered. "You'll never guess who I just had a coffee with."

PART FOUR:

A FUTURE WITHOUT WALLS

XIV.

"It doesn't get any better than this," Misha shouted, above a loud sax that for a moment sounded like a monster growl. I opened my eyes, centering them on Anne-Marie's face, and we both, without a signal, suddenly let out a yelp.

The music began to fade in an increasingly rapid descent with a last barely audible whisper from Zach's mournful bowed bass, as if to say something wonderful had just passed through us. When the note died, Anne-Marie pushed the pause button, and the three of us stopped at once, trying, I think, to hold on to that final note for an even longer time.

"Amazing! It works so beautifully."

"It makes my heart sink when I hear those last few bars," Anne-Marie said, looking at Zach. She leaned against the wall giving her full love and admiration. He nodded his head and smiled. "You worked so hard on that final line–just holding it steady."

"Weeks," Zach said. "We were spinning wheels, spinning, and then that final bar came, the classic dying fall."

I said nothing, breathless while I went over the gradual fadeout again and realized it had surprised us all as if by accident—even Zach. Whatever produced such a sneaky exclamation point at the same time it slowed and faded into silence struck me–in my jealousy, I admit–like a feat of showy magic, as if it were not quite

172

honest.

To complicate things, I looked at Misha and for a brief, uncomfortable moment, saw the admiration fill his eyes, too. On his instrument Zach could do something Misha's Dad couldn't come close to, and I confess to a fear all fathers must feel at some time or another, but what must be worse for adoptive ones: somebody else might make a better, stronger, cooler dad.

"Awesome," my son said. "I could feel that music in the ends of my toes. How do you do it?"

Anne-Marie smiled, and Zach put up his hand to receive Misha's high five. We had just listened to one of Zach's live performance tapes—in Juan-Les-Pins, when he was in his "prime," as he said.

"It's in the jaws of that big wooden Albatross I carry around my neck," he told Misha, pointing to a bass in the corner. "With a lot of hard practice and, I guess, muscular control."

He sawed his right arm across his body, and I watched Misha's eyes widen. At the time Lee and I thought he might be musically gifted–at least as a listener–but he had balked at taking lessons on any instrument, even drums. "Boring," he'd tell us, although he surrendered to any instrument's sound completely, as if it set up spontaneous rhythms in his muscles.

"Can you play some for us now, live?" he asked. "I'd love to watch you."

"Not now, Misha. Zach needs rest," I said, intercepting the regret on Anne-Marie's face. Zach

173

himself showed nothing.

"Can't do it anymore," he said, wheezing and tapping on his chest. "My heart is ready, but the chamber holding it doesn't have the strength."

His voice fell into a hoarse whisper, but he smiled and showed none of Anne-Marie's sadness, certainly no self-doubt. Instead he walked to the corner of the living room and released the pause button on the sound system so that the silence of his last sustained note now segued into another upbeat melody. Misha turned to Anne-Marie to begin another dance, but she backed off and turned toward the kitchen. Misha followed, and they returned in a few minutes with trays of food and drinks that we carried out onto their patio.

The sun shone clear in a bright blue sky that afternoon, illuminating the Alpilles and the white bauxite hills surrounding us. I've seen hundreds, maybe thousands, of those skies during our visits to southern France, but the clarity of the light never ceases to produce an inner high. I saw Anne-Marie's contented gaze and turned to catch a similar expression on Zach. The fact that they lived with that scene daily brought on another level of envy to me. Lee and I had read all the fashionable books about buying a Provençal house and turning it into a home, but lack of money had stopped us then, and now, with Misha, it seemed too upsetting to change his world and language yet again. So, that summer we returned with a stronger, more complete feeling for the place, a more heart-felt tie for both of us, but at the same time we sensed the life-long dream of it slipping away.

As the four of us stood and looked toward the distant mountains, Misha came upon a cat that had wandered onto the patio. Anne-Marie put down a small bowl of milk, and she nodded when Misha asked to feed it bread and nuts. It was tabby-colored, with clean white paws, and a sweet, mincing way of chewing that struck us all as feminine. Anne-Marie said it lived with a tribe of cats in an abandoned barn behind some pine about a hundred meters down the road. It wandered into their garden frequently–probably tracking birds at first, but now welcoming more civilized stuff.

They lived on a grazing plain, as the Bernards did near St. Rémy. Rich with wild grass, bushes, and uncultivated flowers, it provided the shepherds food for their flocks three seasons of the year. In the beginning of June, usually on Pentecost weekend, they drove the sheep and goats by truck and van into the cooler, plusher mountains. That's when the cats started coming into Anne-Marie's garden in search of food.

"She's a cute one," said Misha. "Does she have a name?"

"*Chat*," Zach said. "That's all. She doesn't really belong to us or anyone else."

Misha tossed a nut about ten feet from the table and laughed as the kitten pounced on it. He launched another in a higher arc that landed another five feet out, and we all watched as the cat lifted its head to follow the flight then leaped and landed on it within an instant of the peanut's fall. She chewed mincingly, on her haunches, and then waited for another flight.

"Throw her a cracker," Zach said, and when Misha let it sail, the cat eyed it, took two steps along with a right-paw swat, and knocked it to the ground. "Cat Kong," Zach said, grinning. "She murders butterflies."

We each took turns throwing after that, attempting to make the cat perform a fancy maneuver. Gradually, it moved farther from the table, and at one point while we paused to admire a passing hawk, something caught the cat's eye, and it dove into a hedge surrounding the garden. Later, after we finished the drinks and left in our car, Misha pointed to it walking calmly down the road. We followed a bit, beeped as we passed, and watched it recede as we turned toward Châteaurenard.

"Nice afternoon?" Lee said, after we parked under the large pine at the end of our driveway. She stood beyond the hedge in the garden, laying on the red and yellow colors of gardenias and stretching the thin skeletal lines of the pear tree across a canvas.

"Not bad," I said. "It was nice for Misha to meet Anne-Marie's husband, and..."

"Husband?"

"Lover. Significant Other." I raised my fingers into quotes as Misha left to enter the house. "Sometimes, though, I wonder..."

Lee brushed on some dark green blotches, along with strokes of black and brown invoking pear leaves. "Wonder what?" she asked, stepping back to gauge the effect of the paint. "Wonder if they're lovers?—Of course they are."

176

"But what it would be..."

I paused. I really couldn't think of what to say.

"What it would be like to be with her — here?" She smiled, slyly, a look that I found annoying at first, although I admit there was a genuine touch of humor in it. I had told her very little about Anne-Marie up to that moment, but sometimes she seemed to know the story already. Or at least sensed it.

"The whole package, really. A house here, the life of art, a-"

"And a beautiful French chick." Lee added, "Along with a dissatisfied daughter and no family continuity. Poor Ben." Her smile had no real friendliness now. "Feeling the forty-year itch when you're closer to sixty?"

I looked away, over the poplars and pine to the blue sky and–in the distance–the top of the château that gave the town its name. I turned to her and nodded as I left to go indoors.

"I'm sorry," she called to me. "That was pretty snotty. I should remember why we came here and just keep painting."

I said nothing, but nodded and walked inside. I had never told Lee how much I once loved Anne-Marie. She knew I had lived in Paris, knew I had women friends there, but never knew (though she may have guessed) Anne-Marie was the life-altering one against which all others — including Lee, I'm ashamed to say — would be measured. She certainly had no clue — none that I knew of, at any rate — of the extent to which I still

177

obsessed about her.

"I should do that, too," I said, stepping into the garden again. "Forget everything and write. The last time I had a serious ambition—as a painter, not a critic—was when I lived in France."

Lee nodded and her brush extended toward the canvas, coloring a yolky rush of sun behind the pear tree's branches. "You should paint, too. It'll take some of the slump from your shoulders," she said, as I walked back into the house.

For several days afterward, I painted in that garden beside Lee. I stopped and started for a while, then decided to work on something steadily for an hour or two each afternoon. I took brush straight to canvas, not bothering with charcoal or base colors, allowing my responses to dictate my subject and, to a certain degree, even my forms.

Don't expect a breakthrough for me here. I had no sudden blossoming of long-buried passion, or talent, although several of the canvases I did–ripe purple figs resting in the grass, a sliver of snake gleaming on a pebble walkway–captured something very immediate about the Lelandes' garden and our days there. Honestly, neither the pictures nor their techniques illuminated much beyond the colors of the place, and so they came off as amateurish yet not folksy enough to be interesting in their crudeness. Still I could not deny a personal joy–in both the work of the paint and the completion of the canvas. I felt no pressure, no need to reach the edge of anything (certainly not my talent), and allowed myself to revel in the pure, sensual delight of hand on brush, and paint spreading before my eyes. I did not have big orange suns or writhing clouds, but I had the minute shapes of small things under them and the enormous pleasure of urging them to life beneath my wrist and fingers. When I showed the completed pictures to Lee, her genuine smile warmed me with recognition of what I'd looked for in my youthful days–primarily from Anne-Marie.

"Nice," Lee said, simply, when she saw the figs resting in the grass. "I can sense your happiness coming through."

We made love that afternoon, a throwback to the ease of our early times together, and somehow, in perhaps a cowardly way, I felt it made up for my afternoon with Anne-Marie. The tight grip of Lee's hand, the comfort and joy I felt in her naked body next to mine, gave me the sense that she had something to make up for too — whether another lover or a simple wish for one, I would probably never know. So you could say we made up without ever having parted or argued very much, and for most of the rest of the summer we shared a lovely, friendly intimacy that sent me back many years. Despite the crazy things going on.

I worked steadily on my book during that time, the hour or so of painting every day along with the family closeness freeing some reluctance inside. I felt less inhibited, had a less tentative approach to the material and my ideas — even when I discussed them with Zach. I still drove Misha to Mouriès each morning, still had coffee at the little café there or in St. Rémy, but for the rest of that summer I wandered less in reverie, even while seeing Anne-Marie and Zach from time to time.

One day a young girl threaded her way through the tables toward me, and while she looked vaguely familiar as she sat down at a nearby table, I had no idea who she was until I glanced up again to see Anne-Marie, serious and determined, follow the same path toward her. She passed me with a friendly, yet distant, nod and sat next to the girl. After a few moments she motioned me to their table.

"Celestine," she said, as I pulled my chair next to hers. "This is an old friend of mine, an American, Ben Alto."

"Celestine," I repeated, rising and taking her hand in real surprise and kissing it. "How charming. Now I know why you looked familiar to me."

Nodding, she murmured an indifferent *"Bonjour"* and offered a formal, cool pump to my fingers after the kiss. The girl had her mother's looks but with the softer stuff toned down, darker, less compelling hair, and adolescent firmness in her face and trunk. Clearly Celestine's grandparents fed her very well. But there was perception in her eyes that, touched with bitterness, showed her very much her mother's child. I had never known her father, of course, but I assumed her less attractive features, along with her bitter smile, came from him.

"Are you here for long?" I asked.

"Here? A few days."

She shrugged, saying nothing so that Anne-

Marie had to add that there was illness in the family; a great uncle had fallen ill in a city west of Paris, and Anne-Marie's parents needed to go there to care for him.

"A perfect opportunity to visit me," said Anne-Marie with a hapless shrug.

"And also to see the South," I said. "It's my favorite part of France."

Celestine shrugged as haplessly as her mother and then stared out at the plane-tree-shaded street. A bicycle rider glided past, followed by a car with an impatient-looking driver.

"Have you been here before?" I asked.

Celestine nodded, staring angrily at the car and telling me what I already knew–that she had spent years here with her mother–until Zach had interfered. She said it that baldly, adding, with another hapless shrug, "I don't like it here at all. It's too dry and much too hot. Sometimes the people..."

"But the light and the sounds," I interrupted, inhaling. "And the incredibly lovely air. It makes the heat worthwhile, don't you think?"

Celestine shook her head, her mouth turning down in a classic Gallic scowl, so unlike her mother. "The people are slow, no matter what they do. I prefer the North."

"Oh, Celestine, people are people everywhere," Anne-Marie said.

"They're worse here, Mother. And very stupid."

Her glare said more than her words and, of

course, spoke personally to Anne-Marie. We sat for a bit, all three of us stunned by the explosive anger, but in the end neither Anne-Marie nor I could find the words to cut through it. Luckily, the waiter stopped for our orders.

"*Deux expresses*," I said, after checking with Celestine and Anne-Marie, "and a tea with milk for the young lady."

When the waiter left, we stared at each other for a short while. Anne-Marie expressed some interest in a performance by a couple of visiting American musicians later that week, but Celestine, her face wearing a deeper angry frown, shook her head. "I detest American music," she said, "especially jazz."

"Darling, you're insulting my friend, as well as the man I love."

Celestine turned from her mother, eyes wide, as mine were, I must admit, because it took me a moment to realize Anne-Marie had meant two different men.

"I won't take it personally," I said. "But Celestine must be the only young person in France who would say such a thing. French children love our music—more than I do."

Anne-Marie dropped her hand to the table. "This has nothing to do with music or any other art. It has to do with her Mama's time and attention."

"And whether the Mama is crazy," Celestine said.

Anne-Marie shook her head. I turned to Celestine and, thinking to clear the air, told her flat out that I had met Zach and liked him very much.

"I don't care what others think," she said, looking away from me now.

"Well, you should. He's a great musician and a wonderful person. He's told me some very nice things about you."

"Him?" Celestine stared into my eyes. Hers were large, blue-green and piercing, like her mother's. "He doesn't know me at all, and I don't want him to."

Another long, uncomfortable tremor of silence, this one interrupted by the arrival of coffee and tea and the little paper receipt. I glanced at Anne-Marie, who naturally looked very upset, but I could see her working to keep control of her anger. I tried to think of something soothing. Of course I'd already mentioned the weather and nothing else came to mind. I took a shot at school and, to my surprise, Celestine's eyes brightened. Her face broke into a beautiful, genuine smile.

"I love my school," she said. "My grandparents send me to a very special one where I learn karate and horseback riding as well as the usual subjects."

"I pay too," Anne-Marie said, glumly. "It is not all done by your grandparents. That's why I clean other people's houses."

Anne-Marie looked at me, and I didn't know what to say. Finally, I decided to try to help: "Your mother wants you to be happy," I said. "She sacrifices quite a bit of energy and time for that."

Celestine's smile dimmed, but I was glad to see she did not frown. After a sip of my coffee I asked for

183

her favorite school subjects, and she listed karate first, then went onto French, French history, literature, and art.

"Like your mother," I said, then added with a smile, "Do you enjoy writing?"

"It's not bad." She glanced at Anne-Marie, acknowledging the connection with a bona fide frown. "But not as much as karate and other sports, especially the horses."

She talked about riding in a show, describing the competition for points and the variety of moves she and the horse had to make to score well. *"Bullion,"* she called her horse. "He loves the work as much as I do. He has the finesse, but we have to work on timing so that he follows my signals without delay."

"You must be learning that with him as well."

"He is my lover." Celestine said that without embarrassment. "But with the goal of giving me everything I want."

"Like everyone else in your life, apparently." Anne-Marie stared at her coffee. "I hope you are at least more grateful to him than others."

We sat for another fifteen minutes or so, sparring like that until Anne-Marie and Celestine rose suddenly to attend the market in St. Rémy before it closed. I stayed at the table and worked, reacquainting myself with the words on the page and the principle idea (suburbs, I had to remember) that had driven me to put them there. The mutual scorn, Anne-Marie's helplessness to change it, and Zach's good-natured friendliness despite everything kept intruding–along with my own less serious family concerns.

I burrowed in, recalling the stone ruins I'd seen that week, imagining the lives they'd once nourished, the spirits that still seemed to hover above them on a cloudy night. Out of that I tried to make some realistic sense. That we erect structures against nature and then let our own natures, individually as well as collectively, destroy them seems uniquely human, and I wondered as I sat there how much was from necessity.

I sat for an hour with such conflicted torment in my heart that I could do little more than jot down self-critical notes. Finally, I left the café and drove the winding back roads impatiently to Anne-Marie's house, hoping for some reassuring thoughts but not from her. I found myself looking for Zach.

"I'm here to say hello," I muttered, tapping him on the shoulder first as he fussed with earphones and a player out on the terrace. "I need some soothing words."

"From me?" He laughed, hoarse and whispering. "You must be desperate."

He motioned toward a chair beside him. I took it immediately, comforted by the rolling fields and mountains before us. He offered me a drink from a pitcher full of ice water, and I remarked to myself that he had sat before all this with his eyes closed and senses turned to sound.

"Your own stuff?" I asked, pointing to the CD player on the ground between us.

"Hardly." He laughed, a little shame-faced.

185

"This is not music — just words, hope, that sort of thing. — I need them more than you, I bet."

He showed me the plastic CD case, and I read the title, *A Future Without Walls*, covering my surprise with a nod and smile. The illustration showed a mild blue sky with three absolutely clear white clouds providing form.

"The end," he said. "Mine, I hope. It makes me think of Satchmo playing happy."

I felt the melancholy of his words, and I cancelled my own need to talk. The voice on the CD belonged to one of those inspirational speakers who, while not formally Christian, seek to portray the afterlife as personal prayer satisfactorily answered.

"Coltrane felt it," Zach said as I studied the cover, probably looking doubtful. "'A Love Supreme.' I need to find it in words somehow, maybe pictures. It ain't gonna be in my music anymore."

He inhaled, wheezing, then hacked up some phlegm and, after an apology, spit it out.

"Does this sort of thing really help?" I asked, nodding toward the CD box.

"If I let it." He grinned. "Most of the time not." I felt the urge to reach across the chair arms and shake him. Then, to my surprise, I stood up, bent over, and, blushing, hugged him the way I had hugged my own father on his death bed when I was a boy. He had lung cancer, was tied to an oxygen tank with plastic tubes in his nose and throat, and still had trouble finishing a sentence, even a short one. He could hardly take my hand and weakly squeeze it. I wanted my hug to

186

express all the loving tenderness of a son.

Zach smiled and said thanks but went through, I think, the same squeamish sadness I did. I thought of Anne-Marie again and wondered how much I hugged her instead of my father in Zach. It was a strange moment. I stepped back, staring into his eyes, trying to see something of myself in them.

"Good man," he murmured. "I've needed something like that for quite a while — a brother."

He took a swig of ice water and motioned me to sit again. When I did, he brought up Celestine, but in obvious impatient tones. "She's carrying a chip on her shoulder," he said. "And I don't see any gentle way of knocking it off."

"She's as stubborn as her mother is," I said, nodding, "and, I guess, as strong."

He shook his head. "You got that right. But Anne-Marie can handle it. We'll have to see about me."

I thought about him dying (leaving Anne-Marie alone, really), wondering what I should do when it happened. I felt the impasse he must have been considering when I arrived: A Future Without Walls. He rose from his chair and motioned me to follow. We went around the hedge, came to a slight drop off and walked slowly down a path that wound through high bushes and brush. Before us lay a patch of harsh, dry land, an acre or two with a shepherd's hut on one edge of it. Zach led us through the pebbles, clay, and fallen pine cones to the hut.

"My refuge," he said, "when things get too hot

187

in the house."

He found a key above the drain pipe and unlocked the door, pushing it open. Inside, I let my eyes adjust to the dark as he opened shutters to the window on the far wall. I saw a chair, a battery-controlled player, and a cot with a huge bass standing next to it. When the light came in, I blinked for a moment before seeing the stone walls covered with hand-drawn images: a life-sized head with large dark eyes staring out at me; a landscape of farmland covered with blooming flowers, a man and a woman strolling in an overgrown garden with darkness above and behind them as if they had just come out of a frightening place.

"Anne-Marie," Zach said. "She did these just after I got sick. First to be with me while I played, then to help me not feel alone. She said the room looked too much like a prison cell." He pointed to a couple places and grinned. "I put in a line or two, and a smudge of color here and there. But it ain't my music."

I nodded, appreciating the working of chalk and paint around an oak door that gave on to a room or storage area, although I did not find much actual comfort in the images. The beauty–and they *were* beautiful in their own way, although that's certainly not an objective judgment–carried a weight and a mood that reminded me too much of dungeons and caves. Clearly, Anne-Marie had drawn and painted them in a somber mood. Zach's refuge was not an escape to happiness and, to be truthful, the pictures made me wonder just what went on in the two lives that brought them into being.

188

"Do you come here much?" I asked.

"Less than I used to. Since I got really sick, she's given me something more that I need—not just images."

He stopped, looked out the window, and waved his hand.

"I know what you mean," I said. "I'd be the same."

He grinned, weakly. Uncomfortable, I stared at the picture of the man with the sad dark eyes and wondered how I would feel with it hanging over my desk. Anne-Marie had something to express—that's for sure—but I wasn't sure I liked the message.

"I don't play this much anymore," Zach said, standing near the bass and fingering the strings. He plucked a note, a "C" I guessed, its deep plunk resounding like a stoppered kettle drum. The expertise in his fingers—weak as they looked—startled me, and I could only imagine what he must have felt in his lost strength. He took a bow from the cot and let it run across the strings with a light and lilting touch. A drone filled the room a second or two and stopped, leaving a larger silence than before. He threw the bow down suddenly and stood for a moment, letting the bass rest against the wall. "I lean on it instead of the other way around," he said.

He sat on the cot, his head in his hands, and for a long moment I watched his braids quiver.

"Let's go back to the garden," Zach said, standing beside me. "It's a little too much to stay here today."

189

We headed back around the hedge and settled in our chairs to drink more ice water. I left after an hour of near silence. Still he smiled as I walked to the car, telling me he would go on the road again soon, to feel "the life", as he phrased it. Then he stood silently, waving as I drove away.

XV.

After that visit, I spent morning after morning on the Mouriès café terrace working on my theme. Once or twice Anne-Marie stopped by the table to have a coffee, and of course we talked about Zach and Celestine. Things went better at home, she told me, especially now that Zach had gone on the road for a while. He had left within a week of our meeting because of Celestine, she said, so that mother and daughter could share some private time. But then they fought because, as Anne-Marie put it, Celestine refused to forgive her mother and see beneath Zach's curls and chocolate skin.

I confess there was little about Celestine to make me like her, or even want to know her better, but out of respect for her mother I expressed some interest. I offered to take her on an excursion to Vaison-la-Romaine, about fifty miles away, whose exhibit of Roman ruins was beautifully laid out to show the structure of an ancient town. To my surprise, Celestine immediately agreed to go when her mother brought it up, and three mornings later she sat next to me as I drove toward Avignon, then to Châteauneuf-du-Pape and the wine fields beyond until we reached Vaison. Celestine loved the ruins, especially the remains of shops and bars for Roman-age tourists, and when we drove out of town to see the medieval mountain village of Séguret, she reveled in the cobble stone streets, the galleries, and the shops with handmade Santons of Provence peasants for sale. It was like a quaint shopping mall, I thought, a place Misha would love, and of course that made me like her better. We stopped for lunch at a restaurant with a clear view of the surrounding valley, and Celestine showed such pleasure with the waiters, the food, and the view that I felt a father's pride in accompanying her.

"You look lovely," I said at last, adding gently, "very much like your mother."

"A darker version," she answered, smiling, "not with the luck of that burning hair."

I shook my head. "You look more French than her, which is not a bad thing."

She laughed, scooping up a stray piece of onion from her salad, and the happiness in her eyes shone so brightly for a moment that I couldn't resist the impulse to press her on it.

"Do you feel better about your mother now?"

"*Oui,*" she said, "at least for the day." But then the glow in her eyes dimmed considerably. "We get along properly without that terrible man here."

"Zach," I said in spite of the frown on her face. Her eyes swept beyond me to the surrounding countryside, and she didn't answer. For a moment I felt like reaching for her chin and turning her face back toward the table. I spoke in what I hoped was a gentle, fatherly voice: "She loves him, you know, and his illness is not going away. Ever. Your mother must be concerned."

"But not for her daughter?"

"She is very concerned about her daughter, I assure you. Any mother would be, but she has other things to think about–as any mother would. You have to understand."

I could see from her eyes that she had stopped paying attention, so I motioned to the waiter to bring more bread. We ate for a while, hardly going beyond polite commentary about the food and requests for salt or some other condiment. I sipped a glass of white wine to go with the local lake fish, and Celestine sawed and chewed away at half a *poulet à l'estragon* along with bottled water.

The other tables moved through their menus in a more vocal manner, with one group of shirt-sleeved businessmen hurrying themselves and the waiters as they joked with each other and wrote in notebooks, passing printed sheets of paper one to the other. The sun shone through the leaves of the *marronnier* above us and gave everything a filtered bluish glow. I tried to engage Celestine in a conversation about French movies, music, and painters, but she showed very little interest although I admit she seemed knowledgeable for her age.

"Celestine," I said, finally, "you can't hate your mother because she has fallen in love. Your father and she separated. She's entitled to some other happiness."

She placed her fork and knife carefully on the plate and turned her blue-green eyes on me. Once again, they reminded me of Anne-Marie and at the same time displayed a youthful innocence I couldn't resist. I smiled, but she did not return it with any pleasure or

193

warmth.

"Would you say that to your son, if your wife should leave you?"

I blinked at first, taking a deep breath. "I like to think I would—especially after several months... maybe years."

"Even with a man who casts her under a spell?"

I braved the icy blue-green glare of her eyes while I chose my next few words. "You don't mean that, truly, do you?–You mean the spell of love, not witchcraft, I hope. This is not the land of Harry Potter."

"My grandmother says that... that man has cast a spell on her–she's no longer herself."

I said nothing. I knew little about Rastafarians aside from the hairdos and Bob Marley's music, I confess, but from what I'd seen and heard of Zach I certainly couldn't see him having magic or evil in his soul. As to Anne-Marie, I can only say that despite the years I still saw her as the woman I once loved, too much.

"I've known your mother a long time," I said. "To me she has not changed. I think..."

"And you loved her," Celestine interrupted, smiling wickedly.

"And I still do love her," I answered, "but as a friend. I know she's not easily put under spells."

Celestine giggled—at my embarrassment, I think—and looked away. She drank her water and turned to the table full of businessmen along the terrace's edge. They stood now, shaking hands across the table and bidding each other fond good-byes.

"We are all friends. Zach is my mother's friend, too, and was my grandparents', and even my father's. But what about me?–None of you thinks of me as a friend or having friends. I'm just a child — inconvenient and spoiled."

I didn't answer that, mainly because I did not want to sound false. Celestine stopped herself with a sob and looked into the middle distance while sipping on her water. Once again I took a deep breath.

"You are no one's inconvenience, least of all your mother's. And no one thinks you're spoiled — at least I don't. But you ought to appreciate what your mother does for you, how she plans her life around you-and that is more than anyone does with friends, of any kind. Besides as I understand it, you left your mother because of Zach, nothing else."

"Oh, that drama: My grandparents convinced me it was the right thing. And I agreed."

"Why?"

"I ran away–really I just didn't come home from school one day–because I knew he would be there. I didn't want to see him with her — holding hands, kissing."

"Had he touched you, or done something to you that you didn't like?"

I hated myself for asking that, but at the moment it seemed important to get clear. Celestine just shook her head. "I didn't like the way he touched my mother, or looked at her, or even talked to her. I knew it wasn't wrong, but I didn't feel like seeing it. I don't know

195

why."

I nodded, considering my own actions with Lee in front of Misha. He seemed to take our affection as the most natural thing in the world–with an occasional giggle maybe, but only because human life–at least among adults–had some pretty funny stuff.

"They seemed very reserved to me," I said, "the one day I saw them together. I can't imagine them as offensive to you."

Again Celestine shrugged. I found myself in the unenviable position of wanting to help someone whose judgment I considered questionable at best. Her sullen looks along with the flat, critical tone of her comments made me fight to believe her because I rejected everything she said. Asking details seemed invasive — of Anne-Marie as well as Celestine.

"What exactly have your grandparents told you?"

Another shrug. "They tell me I should not live with her."

"Their own daughter? That makes no sense. What have you told them?"

Again Celestine shrugged, making me wonder what she held back. Anne-Marie's mother held some odd religious views herself, I remembered, much like the Bernards; she had sent pamphlets to Anne-Marie monthly, asking her to distribute them among her friends. *La Vérité* always sprawled across the top of the front cover, and though I'd never read articles in their entirety, I remembered teaser heads that cried out about a "plan" and warned readers to be prepared for the world's imminent day of reckoning. Not quite a Mayan star-gazer's prediction, but just as convincing.

"*She is crazy*," Anne-Marie always said about her mother. She had dismissed the pamphlets with an embarrassed laugh, throwing them out almost as soon as they arrived in the mail.

Her father seemed more rational, at least as Anne-Marie described him, but he tended to make old-fashioned, authoritative moral remarks that stemmed from his age, I guessed, as well as his experience fighting Nazis in World War II. "In my father's world men are weak and evil," Anne-Marie told me once. "He believes that human will and self-sacrifice can save us all."

I didn't ask what we needed to be saved from, of course, because the implication of real human evil always brought a chill to my backbone, making it hard for me to discuss, unless surrounded by art, as in a Crucifixion, for example, or Goya's etchings of war. Anne-Marie always let the subject drop at that, implying that both her parents were a little dotty and not worth taking seriously. She had spent her youth trying to live free of their strictures, which made the arts, writing, and me, to a certain extent, I think, important, but now she faced her own daughter in a cross-generational agreement with them.

"I don't know what you expect of your mother now that she lives with Zach, but you ought to realize that it doesn't change what she wants and feels for you."

"For me? What about what she wants and feels for herself?"

I nodded. "She puts you before all other things–for herself or anyone else."

"She should not force me to live with that man."

I stared at her, trying to separate her angry teenage thoughts from those of my own generation. Were her differences with her mother due to individual preferences or hormones? I thought about Misha, the absolute sense of comfort and belonging I could feel with him despite our different blood ties and genes, and wondered how Anne-Marie had failed to achieve it so far with Celestine. — Was her daughter under the grandparents' spell?

"Apparently you are not being forced," I said, "so I don't see your point. It is you forcing the issue, along with your grandparents."

"That man — Zach — makes me very uncomfortable."

I didn't know what to say. Once again, my sense of Zach, although I had known him briefly, and Anne-Marie made me doubt Celestine's sincerity. Of course, I knew how common mis-impressions could be, especially among child abusers, but I saw absolutely nothing frightening in Zach, except his dread locks. I had to ask again, directly, although it almost made me ill.

"Does he, uh... Has he touched you inappropriately?"

She paled and, without pretending, I think, shivered. "I wouldn't let him come near me, even if he tried."

"Has he tried?"

Celestine shook her head, angered. "If I can help it, I don't let him stay in the same room with me. That hair, the skinny arms, the helpless slope of his shoulders... He is old; let him be attractive for my mother. He disgusts me."

"Celestine..." I stopped, not wanting to continue. I asked about her father, what she thought about him, but she replied with the same indomitable force.

"I don't want to be with him either," she cried. "I don't trust him or his new young wife."

Something almost infantile in her eyes touched me when she said that, and I simply let my shoulders slump while I looked out sadly over the landscape before us. Children suffer everywhere, and I know that some children exaggerate their parents' punishments into unjustified cruelty, but I had no idea where Celestine fit in. Crossing her anger off as blanket emotion, I simply called for the check and paid the waiter without asking another question.

"We have more sights to see," I said, "perhaps something natural and less tied to human weaknesses."

She said nothing, but as we walked from the restaurant, staring into the green valleys and stone gray mountains surrounding us, I could see her face soften and relax a little. Beauty, natural or manmade, has an effect, I remembered someone saying once.

"Celestine, have you ever seen *La Gorge de la Nesque*?" I asked.

She shook her head, grimly, but I saw the beginning of a smile and felt encouraged.

"Well, you should. It's a perfect day for it. We'll drive through it on the way home. You'll have perfect views of the *Gorge* and, maybe more important, romantic sights of Petrarch's *Mont Ventoux.*"

XVI.

Weeks rushed by quickly that summer. Warm days connected mornings and nights in a weave of comfort and good feeling that turned Monday into Friday in a wink. I wrote fast for a while, catching and riding the wave of my idea in the Provençal surroundings I walked through each day and waked to each morning. I read this timelessness, or its impression, as the key to many suburban pleasures, seeing the ancient presence of Rome combine with the more ancient presence of mountains, plain, and gorge to reveal how humans depended on both for peace and grace, but craved civilized products for security and a sense of progress.

I visited the *Pont du Gard* several times and stood before its magnificent expanse, not even remembering, until I returned home and organized my notes, that this lovely piece of stone and brick had carried water for miles and so possessed function as well as art. People boated for pleasure beneath the arches now, took walkways above and beside them, or gawked in admiration and snapped pictures, or perhaps sketched them, as Lee and I did while Misha stood in awe and studied an olive tree near a sign that said the tree had begun growing as far back in time as the *pont* itself.

"Here they are, dear," Lee said to him, "olive oil and water — two precious liquids that the Romans used

201

daily and valued. And they're still here for us now."

Misha took a picture of the tree with the *pont* looming behind it, then studied the digital display on the camera's back.

"Really old," he said, proudly. "Do you think this meant something to Julius Caesar?"

"Augustus and his successors, you mean, not Julius," I told him.

Lee laughed. "Dad the teacher. The liquids probably had more meaning for the people who lived here than the Caesars.-They ate or drank both."

Misha could not take his eyes off the tree and asked many questions about the building of the *pont*, the people using it, the lives enslaved and lost in getting it to stand. Moments like these made me proud of my son-and Lee and me for bringing him home. In truth he had been reluctant to come to Europe, and the daily grind of answering his need for other children and giving him something to do when he didn't attend camp wore all of us down, making our work on book or painting—or just growing up—difficult sometimes. On days like this everything came together. The glow of the river and our feeling of belonging to the structure spanning it, as well as each other, somehow permeated Misha's life.

Lee felt it too, I know, producing sketch after sketch of the *pont*'s details, eventually turning it into one of her largest, most successful paintings, its combination of blues and greens, yellows and golds filling our living room with a special glow when we got home. Guests and family members feel it too, apparently. "That's

202

nice," they'll say gaping before the canvas. "Where did you buy it?"

Misha beams. "My mom painted it," he'll say, "from a picnic we had beside that river in France."

But something reductive often happens after that, something like my own shameful envy of Zach. I watch people's mouths tighten; I see their eyes narrow, and somehow their faces change, as if they feel tricked. "A souvenir from vacation," one of our colleagues commented.

I don't know how to respond to these reactions in any friendly way, mainly because I've felt them myself. Lee caught something about the *pont*, a feeling, and made it glow in a colorful image. In a certain sense the painting works on people like the *pont* itself-a convergence of elements that arrest the eye and heart, yet somehow the question of value intervenes.

"Am I missing something?" I said to one colleague recently when he reacted that way. "I like Lee's painting a lot. It's exquisite. What's more it says something—about aspirations caught for one moment in the flow of time. What's wrong with that?"

Lee dismissed the argument that followed, but whether it's the academic in me or the protective husband, I wanted to defend her work.

It was an academic party. My colleagues generally nodded and begrudgingly glanced up at the huge canvas again. They nodded their heads, but with frowns still doubtful and worrying.

"If the eyes—and heart—remain open, people

will see it," Lee said. "If not..." She shrugged and gave a little grin.

"If not... What?" the colleague asked. "Is it technical, or just something lacking in the subject?" He smiled, mockingly.

"If not, then you don't love art—or even life itself," Lee said.

That kind of living—and loving—reaction arrived almost daily for me that summer in Chataurenard. At the same time, I felt the brutal sadness in Anne-Marie's life, one I might have shared and still wished to share despite the sadness. Sometimes I worried that she might give me a simple, welcome sign— a smile or nod of her head–and I would throw over all my years with Lee and Misha, just to feel the romance and drama she lived alone. Such is desire, I guess, of the unreturned, foolish kind, and because of it I kept visiting Anne-Marie at her house every few days. We rarely spoke of our past, and never that afternoon in the early summer, but both memories clogged the atmosphere between us. When Zach returned from his long road trip along the Atlantic coast up to Bordeaux and Normandy, the mood among the three of us became more complicated although I couldn't say exactly why. I drove over soon after he returned, but surprisingly Zach did not come out to greet me. He stayed in his bedroom–sleeping, Anne-Marie said; and after a short while I left, telling her I would return to see him in a couple of days. When I did go back later in the week, he remained in his room again, and Anne-Marie excused him again, saying the trip had worn him down. "He says hello," she told me. "But he cannot leave his bed."

Her shame-faced look said more than the words, and, although I didn't return to the house for close to a week, I did see Anne-Marie one day running errands in St. Rémy. She looked pale and drawn. When I saw her leaving the pharmacy near St. Martin's in the town center, I could see the sadness weigh heavily on her shoulders.

"I hope that does some good," I said, pointing to the pharmacy package she carried. "For both of you."

She shrugged. Her weary eyes looked on the verge of spilling over. When I touched her arm, she shook her head. "Let me help you," I offered. "What happened while Zach was away?"

She turned her back to stare at the windows of the pharmacy and the bakery next to it. I embraced her.

"I'm sorry. Tell me how I can help. Maybe, with Celestine, I…"

She shook her head and pulled herself from my arms, brusquely. "She is horrible. Her miserable behavior is—inexcusable." Her voice grated harshly, and I felt the words as if directed at me. Dropping my hands to my side, I stepped back and studied her face.

"She has run away … again," she said.

"What?—"

"Because she couldn't stand the attention I give to someone dying."

"Zach? Is it…"

She shook her head again. "He doesn't want anyone to know. The trip was too much, and he had to come home early. He must attend to his health."

I stood beside her and put my arm about her shoulders.

"More chemotherapy," Anne-Marie said. "And oxygen. Now the doctors say there is nothing else they can do."

I squeezed her tightly and looked down at her face, repelled by my urge to bend toward her lips and kiss her. "I'm sorry," I said. "Really. I had no idea."

She looked up toward me. I felt stupid, I must admit. But I also felt pulled toward her and made sure to hold my head away. She stepped toward the church and pointed past the plane tree leaves toward the steeple, surrounded now by a glaring, bright blue sky.

"I keep looking for some hope from that. I never believed in it, but now there is nothing else. And nothing comes."

"Time..."

She turned as if to give me the lie, but buried her face in my chest. Meanwhile, passersby, tourists mainly, had begun to stare, thinking, I was sure, that this was a typical French lovers' quarrel. I held Anne-Marie close and shut my eyes against them, feeling a bitter sexual desire along with a wish to be with her alone. At that very moment, somebody tapped me on the lower back, and when I turned, ready for an insult, I looked into the wide open, curious eyes of my son.

"Dad, we're visiting the museum and monuments today. I thought I might see you."

Down the road toward the *périphérique* exit for Avignon, I saw a bus parked with a crowd of children

206

standing beside it. I felt Anne-Marie step away, and immediately I let my hands drop to my sides. Misha's eyes darted toward her, then back to me. "*Bonjour, Anne-Marie,*" he said sweetly, his face showing he knew the moment was weighty.

"*Bonjour,* Misha." She mastered a pallid smile.

With another glance at me and then at Anne-Marie, Misha stepped forward and touched her wrist. "Is my Dad bothering you?" he said. She looked at him. "Did he hurt your feelings?"

"No, Misha, no." She laughed, almost angrily. "Your Dad wants to help me. I've just heard some awful news."

Misha's smile turned into a frown.

"Dad–?" He gasped.

"It's just not good news, Misha. Anne-Marie's very upset."

He looked at her carefully, reminding me once more of how attentive he could be. For a brief moment I caught a glimpse of him as a young man not quite comfortable with an emotional woman. "Her daughter, Celestine, has left," I said, not wishing to tell him about Zach.

Misha let out another little gasp, his mouth forming a sympathetic "O". For whatever reason, adoption, his reading of fairy tales, or just something in his character makeup, Misha has always feared separation from home and parents more than any other danger.

"Where did she go?" he asked, handing his blue

handkerchief to Anne-Marie to dry her tears.

"That's the point. We don't know."

"Oh..." He looked puzzled, turning from me to Anne-Marie. "But why–?"

"We don't know. We have to find her," I said.

"Honey, children run because they're upset with their parents." Anne-Marie reached out to touch his shoulders. "Thank you very much for your concern, but I think I know where she went."

Misha's eyes opened wider. He could never hide his need to know and understand such horrific things, and I thought for a moment he would once again blame me.

"She's with a friend near here, I think, someone she rides horses with. She has stayed with the family before."

I wondered if Anne-Marie believed her own guess, and apparently she did. She crossed the narrow lane toward the center of town, and beside a huge plane tree took out her phone. I watched her search for a number and, using her thumbs, dial. She talked for a few minutes as Misha and I waited, then returned and stood before us.

"There?" I asked.

Anne-Marie nodded, but her eyes filled again.

"Is she all right?" Misha said.

Anne-Marie nodded, and frustration clearly showed on her face. She wiped her eyes, blew her nose, and with another pallid smile patted Misha's cheek. "Thank you," she said fondly. "Celestine is fine."

"And...?"

I spoke directly into her silence. She turned toward me, wavering for a moment, I saw.

"She wants to return to her grandparents. She's called them to come get her immediately–which my father will most happily do."

"Without seeing you?" I said. "Or Zach?"

"Without seeing me or anyone else. She will call the police if I or a friend – I think she meant you – comes to get her."

I walked Misha back to his camp bus and then returned to Anne-Marie to talk more openly. She had decided to go see Celestine in person, and when I asked if she needed help she suggested I come along–in case. I knew that I could not turn her down at that moment, but I had no idea what use I would have. We walked to my car in the lot across from St. Martin's and drove around the *périphérique* until the route to Les Baux, taking that road past the monuments and through the hills toward Mouriès. We turned before we got to town and drove along a narrow back trail through vineyards and wild land until we came to an even smaller, dustier one on our right. I turned, saw a large herd of sheep eating its way toward the white hills ahead, and then abruptly, after a sharp curve, we arrived at a corral with half a dozen horses in it and a large gray stone barn beyond. We parked next to a Japanese SUV, then walked around the barn, arm in arm, toward a red-tile-roofed house nearby.

I could feel the tension in Anne-Marie's hand as we approached. Her fingers dug into my wrist, and she cast a wistful glance at me as we stepped beneath a large poplar near the front of the house.

"I'm not sure this is right," she said, "but I have no choice. Do I?"

I nodded and patted her hand as we mounted the terraced landing. She knocked on the door.

"She's gone," Anne-Marie said, after a long moment's silence. "Now I won't know where to reach her. My parents…"

At that moment the door handle turned and the great slab of oak and brass opened, letting the sunlight shine on the dark interior. Celestine's face peered out.

"*Bonjour, chérie.* I hope you don't mind."

"*Maman,* I don't want you here, and I'm sure I won't talk to you in front of him."

She inclined her head toward me, her voice gathering that same undertone of hurt and anger that she had projected with Zach. *Him*, as if I had an unmentionable name. I said nothing, having decided already that this family quarrel was hardly my business.

"We need to talk, Celestine. The time is too important to shut down."

Celestine pushed the door almost closed and opened it again as we stood there, not moving. Sun beat down on our backs, and I felt a wave of hot wind, crossing the mountains from the south.

"*Cherie,*" Anne-Marie whispered, "you can't just leave your mother like this. Life is too short."

She stepped toward the door. Celestine held it steady a moment, then, very grudgingly, pulled it open.

Most of the interior shutters had been closed, but

after our eyes acclimated we saw a couple of beige couches, a dark Henry II armoire in the corner, a low table with a TV, and a white stone fireplace with a wrought-iron mobile horse made of stirrups and spurs dangling above it. An oil of a chestnut horse hung on the wall behind it, and to the right, beside a chair, an English-style saddle rested on a wooden stand.

"So?" Celestine said.

"You need to stop hating me," Anne-Marie told her. "Your father and I failed each other although we're doing our best not to fail you now that we're apart. You must cooperate."

Celestine closed the outside door quietly, but she remained near it after we entered. I half-expected her to dash into the yard and disappear again, but she turned, her face a mask of keen disappointment in her world. For the moment I felt torn between two primitive urges: to shake her out of her anger, or embrace her to give her more human comfort.

"*Maman*, I'm going up north again to live with *Grand-Maman* and *Grand-Papa*. It's the only solution to make me happy."

"We have a good school here, Celestine. We also have riding, and I'm sure we can find you a karate master easily. Besides..."

But Anne-Marie's word caught in her throat. I laid my hand on her shoulder and stepped near while Celestine remained at the door, ready to fling herself out.

"I'm sorry, *Maman*, but I don't have anything

more to say. Everything's been brought out between us already."

Anne-Marie nodded, with tears running freely down her cheeks. She held her hands out, reaching for her daughter as if to an infant just learning how to walk. Celestine glanced past me toward the window across the room. Pain clouded the space around us. I let my hand drop from Anne-Marie's shoulder and turned toward Celestine.

"Your mother would like you home, I think. This is a particularly hard time for her."

"I know. For me, too."

"Celestine..."

"We need each other! Don't you see?–And I need my mother more than she needs me!"

I glanced at both of them together. Anne-Marie's face rested in her hands, her shoulders slumped forward as she shook her head. I don't know; perhaps it was the coward in me — or the family insider wishing for outside — but at that moment I felt ready to run from the house. I took Anne-Marie's elbow, stepped toward the door, but to my surprise she yanked her arm away.

"Celestine, tell me exactly, what do you want?"

Celestine paused, holding her breath a moment, and then spoke in a loud, unstoppable flow. "I want to be home with you, *Maman,* but I want to know that I'm the most important person in your heart. I want that man out of our house."

She looked at me, fiercely, as she said, *"that man,"* and I felt my neck and back tingle with the urge to respond. Misha might hear a comment like that someday, I thought, and so I searched for something to put it to rest—permanently. Anne-Marie spoke before me:

"He's going to go soon, *Cherie*. Perhaps in a matter of weeks or a very few months. He has never harmed you. Why–?"

"I've said it already!–I want to be important, and I've never, ever felt close enough to you."

Anne-Marie winced. She took another step toward Celestine, her arms extended again, and to my surprise Celestine moved forward, a little grudgingly at first, then allowed herself to fall into her mother's arms. They stood together a long time, softly sobbing, and I, quiet, walked into the yard.

XVII.

They solved the problem easily after that, in a way that may have pleased even Zach. He moved permanently into the shepherd's cabin behind the bushes while Celestine and Anne-Marie stayed together in the main house. I have no idea how they lived on a daily basis — their habits; how well they got along — but on the days I visited they all seemed content. Zach, quieter than he had been, always an oxygen tank dangling from his shoulder, smiled easily when the four of us sat on the terrace to drink and talk. He usually left early, retreating to the cabin for some rest if he started coughing. Anne-Marie said the chemotherapy wore him down, but I saw a slump in his shoulders and a shrug that said he carried more than medicine and an oxygen tank to weigh him down.

Celestine smiled a lot, her body and face aglow with a youthful health that seemed to belie ordinary human illness and death, as she helped her mother around the house and at work. Together they drove to Anne-Marie's clients, including the Lelandes, of course, and cleaned bedrooms, kitchens, and baths: "Twice as quickly," Anne-Marie said, "and many times more happily." They returned to spend afternoons and evenings tending the garden surrounding the patio and traveling into Mouriès and other towns to shop for food.

Often I spoke to Anne-Marie and Zach

separately during that time, finding the sadness and fatigue of their personal lives quite palpable. Zach started strongly, despite the plastic tubes in his nostrils, giving a large smile and a hardy greeting whenever we met for a prescribed twenty minute walk. But I noticed that he quickly took on a tired, deadpan tone that turned more distant as we talked, as if he knew the immediate future and wanted to get past it.

"He is very ill," Anne-Marie reminded me almost daily. "He listens to music, his own above all others, and sleeps as much as he can."

Neither had very much to say and, as I look back, I wonder if I didn't take advantage of their welcome. I felt Anne-Marie wanted me there as a bridge to a happier time, but I never quite figured what she, or Zach, or Celestine, for that matter, expected of me. Was I wearing out my welcome? Zach usually came out for his walk but not much else before he wandered off on a solitary amble back to the cabin for a nap. He carried the oxygen tank as if it were a punishment, and as he opened the cabin door one day, I thought the stone walls—especially with the gloomy painted images— added weight to his already burdened shoulders.

Warm air surrounded the *bas Alpilles* that summer, the wind from the south often warmer than the air it replaced, but Zach had begun to wear a jacket or sweater whenever he stood outdoors. The sight of him, dark and shaky against the bright sun and fields of the surrounding landscape, carried a particular sadness that I could never quite escape. When I remembered the

215

sounds coming from his contrabass, the words, friendly and articulate, that I had heard just recently from his mouth, I could only consider that some unbelievably unfair chain of events was occurring–not in Zach's life alone, but for all of us.

"My man," he said to me one afternoon as I walked with him. He smiled and raised his arm, sweeping it toward the sky, taking in the sun, the perfume of the lavender, and the rich red of the poppy fields to our right. "We can't ask for more than this, despite everything."

I nodded but with a pang of awful remorse. Zach opened the door to the cabin, allowing me to enter before him. It had been altered now that he lived there, with large speakers on the floor and a shelf full of CDs with a battery driven player and two or three large stand-alone tanks of oxygen in one corner. The walls looked brighter, newly whitewashed, and, in place of the images that the paint now covered, three large canvases hung from the walls. I knew them immediately as the work of Anne-Marie though they looked little like the pictures she had painted on the walls. The colors washing over the canvases conveyed a more cheerful character than the murals had. Zach nodded when I mentioned that. Anne-Marie and Celestine had hung them a day or two before he got back from his trip.

"She works fast," I said, "and they're not bad — in fact, they're pretty damn good."

He nodded again. "She's held them in her head for years, I think."

The images looked autumnal, despite their

216

brightness. Dark greens and oranges brought to mind October harvests, and her brushstrokes added roundness to the forms that indicated grapes and grains — in a sunny October — on the verge of falling.

Zach turned on the stereo and collapsed on a gray leather couch across from the door. Without apology or explanation, he lay back, lifted his feet from the floor, and closed his eyes. I stared at the paintings as I listened to the familiar music–his contrabass primarily, uniquely light, floating with a bright summer swing to it, and felt what I imagined he wanted to take with him as he faded.

"A good place to check out," he muttered, his eyes half-open when I turned toward him. "Like a pharaoh's tomb ... with windows."

I smiled, heard his complicated laugh, and because of it couldn't reply. The room felt chilly, and I wondered how it affected him, even with a sweater and jacket.

"Are you comfortable here? It must get a little damp at night."

Zach shook his head. "We open the window to dry it. I've got blankets. It's warm enough."

"It's going to get colder in the fall."

He shrugged. "We'll deal with it. Maybe by that time something will change."

I stared at him.

He shrugged. "Something." His eyes widened. "Look behind that chair over there. See what they brought home for me."

In the corner behind a caned wooden chair leaned a square of wood against the wall. Antique, pock-marked, and slightly warped, it had dove-tailed planks and looked to be a panel cut from a shutter. I pulled it out, turned it over, and looked directly into a faded, painted image: a man, dark, on his knees with arms extended toward the sunrise, a diapered child, and the blue folds of a woman's pleated, full length dress beside him. It did not look like the work of Anne-Marie. It looked more like some shutter paintings I had seen on an earlier visit to an antique shop.

"It's old," I said. "Where did they get it?"

Zach sighed. "Ask Anne-Marie, or Celestine. They found it–not far from here–up in the hills beyond the house. Believe it or not, it was in a little cave."

"A cave?" I shook my head and looked at the image, seeing no signature, front or back. "Do they know anything about the painter?"

He laughed. "It was in the cave alone. Probably some shepherd who liked to draw left it there last century. Or even earlier. Anne-Marie and Celestine are researching it, but so far nothing."

I nodded, thinking of the museum in St. Rémy, and wondered what kind of archives it possessed. I had seen such paintings in their collection, bucolic scenes mostly, but I had never done much in the way of research into their files–nothing about painters except the obvious one, Van Gogh. They had nothing on him, though I was sure every painter and visitor who came through town thought principally of him. Sunflowers in various states of life and death made up the town's principal twentieth century painted image–that with a little lavender or poppies mixed in.

"I've always liked folk art–especially painting on wood," I said, "and they have a few good ones down at the museum."

Zach nodded, mentioning that Anne-Marie often visited antique dealers lining the road between St. Rémy and Mouriès. "They haven't found anything else like it," he said, "but she wants to check the records at city hall to find out about the house and this cabin–who the landowners were because a hundred years ago they probably owned the cave."

"A shepherd must have lived there, or maybe just spent time in the cave."

I shrugged, shaking my head. Zach said nothing. "A nearby cave certainly gives it possibilities."

We talked about it and built a story around the shutter after a while, imagining the painter-shepherd carrying his work with him as he moved through surrounding pastures with his sheep. "Might have rained one day as he worked," Zach guessed, "and he hid it in the cave to keep the paint dry. He probably just forgot to go back for it."

"Or intended to go back to work on it some other time."

Zach nodded. "Something stopped him." He said. "I know what that means."

After a long, silent eye-to-eye look we turned away from one another and let the subject drop. I know the pastel figures moved me, completed or not; the

219

child's face, against the background of the mother's skirt had a saintly quality I could only associate with Madonna and Child. But the man's features — Arabic or Roma probably — begged for a colorful top, like a fez, the kind I'd seen Arab farm workers wear in the local café. This was not a picture of a Christian family.

The colors looked faded, some of the pastels nearly erased, and a side of me fancied it imitation Vincent Van Gogh. His St. Rémy painting, "First Steps," copied from a drawing by Millet, came to mind, especially with the father's outstretched hands and the baby wobbling at her mother's feet. But in this painting only the mother's dress showed, and the child, a smiling boy, strode from it as if before a blue-velvet stage curtain. Meanwhile, the father's violet hair and ochre arms extended from a seemingly alternative world.

I studied the brush strokes and paint, letting the familiar rough-edged energy Van Gogh's technique managed to convey enter into my thoughts. I knew it wasn't a real Van Gogh, of course; it didn't have that much vibrancy or unique energy. Still the painter knew something about form and had managed, with changes of patterns and point of view, to create a fairly gripping family image.

"It's a beauty," I said, finally. "What a shame they can't identify it."

Zach opened his eyes. "Ask Anne-Marie about it. She's found a couple bits of information somewhere out there. Nothing definitive, a letter or two, I think. Maybe a card from some woman who used to live near here."

"Saying what?–She had been painted?"

Zach shook his head. "More like she saw someone painting. I'm not clear on the details. You have to remember, this is a project to distract Celestine. I've got other things going on."

I looked up quickly and found no bitterness on his face. He folded his hands across his chest, and for an eerie moment I imagined Zach as a corpse on the couch. He laid one foot over the other, and the casual pose, even after his stiff-legged effort, cast the illusion aside. Soon he began to snore, quietly at first, then louder, and I decided to leave him to his nap. But I did carry the sawed-off and glued plank of wood into the light.

The colors glowed more fully out there. I saw the brush marks much more clearly and felt the peculiar energy in the paint. I turned my back to the sun, held the board before me, and studied the surface carefully, detail by detail. No pencil or charcoal lines marked it, and no apparent attempt to mix in colors. The painter had applied color directly, without a grid, without a guide of forms or shapes. It was a spontaneous sketch–though probably not from life–made with oil and paintbrush instead of lead or charcoal. The result, of course, gave the instantaneous "found" quality that provides Van Gogh's canvases so much freshness.

I returned the board to its spot behind the chair and left the cabin again, after checking to see that the oxygen tank was working. I drove to the café in Mouriès to work the rest of the afternoon, but the image of that painting on a board stayed with me–as it would for days, reminding me not only of the impact of a picture, but the quickly fading zest for life Zach must have been experiencing. The crouched man reaching for youth and bloom, the unknown woman above and behind leading it to him. Van Gogh's canvas of the coal mining family at table, "The Potato Eaters," his landscape in St. Rémy of a couple walking through wooded undergrowth, and "First Steps," in the garden, all struck me with longing, as if Van Gogh were peeking at a world he wanted desperately to enter. His letters to Theo express loss–and isolation–"*seul*" is probably the most frequent word in them–and I think paintings such as the three I've just mentioned show him attempting to leap the wall he felt around himself all his life.

I had written about Van Gogh more than once and, of course, planned to include at least a few pages about his work as I discussed St. Rémy and the Roman suburbs. But I never quite looked at him as a man needing family love, and gradually, as the painting in Zach's cabin weighed on me, I began to see him in that light. The gloom in his interiors of St. Paul de Mausole asylum reveal an empty, isolated heart, and the outdoor scenes of the rocky Alpilles with ghostly clouds and views of a much diminished St. Martin's steeple in the town's center reveal a world of craggy beauty that seems very separate from the viewer and expresses no sense of ready human warmth.

During nights afterward at dinner with Lee and Misha, I felt in my own life the richness Van Gogh so sorely missed — and what Zach must have felt draining away inside him. I had always seen Van Gogh as a devoted artist, one who easily gave up family love for his painting–and had killed himself because he thought he had failed in his work. Now I was beginning to see a failure of another kind, and it made me judge my own life's gifts in a better light.

Or, as I still ask myself from time to time, was it all (the happiness, the family comforts) really just a bunch of hidden shadows? In the next week or two, I went back to that question daily, and my thinking wrapped itself around one subject as I worked: Suburbs. Were they natural, an organized way of curtailing human pleasure?–It had been years since I first read Freud's "Civilization and its Discontents," but now his raw image of frustrated men and women forgoing basic carnal needs to make something better of the world forced its way into my plan.

Discontent became a major emotion for Freud, and sacrifice–to an idea, a small, human one like family, neighborhood, children, and art–raised itself as a hopeful sign of human fate and progress. Whenever I spoke to Lee about it that summer, she nodded, but her no-nonsense expression always regrouped into a familiar bemused one: "Dad's thinking too much again," she'd announce to Misha. "He's stuck in his writing and has that look." At which point Misha would squat on a chair, prop his elbow on his knee, rest his head on his fist, and assume what we all called the "Thinker Pose".

"Enough," I often said, shifting my gaze from food on the plate, Lee, or some distant place in the garden. "Let's go fishing."

I remember spending a week with Lee at a *gite* in a little village in Normandy several years before we went to Russia. It was a stone house attached to a stone barn and, although the house was spotless and newly painted, we could hear–and smell–the cattle through the massive, thick wall separating us from their stables. One of my freshest memories, still, is waking to the lowing of sheep in the morning, dressing, and then walking out the back door into a pasture filled with grass-munching animals who parted unhurriedly as I walked through them on the way to the village for breakfast bread. I began to feel close to the animals during that week, a cozy family feeling that eventually led to dog, birds, fish, and, yes, my son, as if the Biblical encouragement to be fruitful had finally outpaced my youthful exuberance for painting and no binding commitments. That week in Normandy, Lee and I have often said, initiated Misha's gestation—although it occurred at least five years prior to his birth.

The basic act of painting had begun to fade in importance for me, and I sensed myself switching from creator to provider. I wrote earnestly for money, sought paid assignments on easy topics in newspapers and magazines, and came to see income (what it could yield) as a measure of my success. I felt reasonable about it, but I also recognized that raising money through hard work was a lot like the farmer—or shepherd— husbanding products to provide food for his family throughout winter. Although I had wanted to emulate Van Gogh's artistic mission for years, the choices I began to make from that point on took me in Theo's, not

Vincent's, direction.

One night late that summer at the Lelandes', I decided to tell Lee about the afternoon I had spent in bed with Anne-Marie. I hoped to set things right between us, and to my surprise, she took it calmly at first, but in a sudden fit of anger (and real sadness, I have to think) told me about important afternoons in her life. To my surprise, there were many.

"Is this revenge for Jean-Luc?" she said, finally. "Because if it is, I don't want any part of it. That stuff's all over for me, and it has to be for you."

"It has nothing to do with Jean-Luc," I said. "Or any of the others."

She looked at me, wondering.

"Lee, it was just a collapse, or relapse — into other times, where I hadn't grown so old and still had energy to paint."

"Mmm... And do other things, too, I guess."

I said nothing. How could I respond without some kind of smirk or leer of my own? To her credit, Lee kept her eyes squarely on mine. Measuring words with her no nonsense stare, she said, "I know you've been distracted all summer long. I also know it hasn't been from writing alone. Did Anne-Marie feel that same fallback in time? — And the rewards?"

"Rewards? There were no rewards — not after that day, I assure you. It's been hell."

I shrugged because, when I thought about it, I really didn't know about rewards. Or the hell. "I never thought of leaving you–or Misha — if that's what you

225

mean. It never occurred to us to plan another afternoon together. Or an apartment of our own. If Anne-Marie had asked me to, I'm sure I would have refused."

Lee frowned, angrily, and at that point picked up her brushes to return to work. Dazzled by a fog of doubt and guilt I got in the car and drove into town.

XVIII.

Most of Lee's affairs—at least the ones I now knew of—had been more about the heart than adventure, I think, and may not have always ended in a real affair. One was with a single colleague of mine whom we had to dinner several times and always seemed enamored of the qualities that made Lee special, especially to men: her warmth, her unselfish willingness to help others, the abundant table she set, and her practical, hands-on interest in the way paint works. She had done a close-up portrait of this colleague, and the splashes of color she worked into the skin of his face provided a rough-hewn, thoughtful quality to his expression that, according to all who knew him, caught his character perfectly. He sketched her in the near-nude shortly afterward. She appears draped in a classical toga of blue cotton that dramatically sets off her amber skin and black hair. Of course with all I knew and read about artists and models, I suspected the outcome although I waited for Lee-or the colleague-to bring it up first. She did that night in sunny Provence.

Her second adventure was different, a surprise, she said, occurring as an aftermath of her time with my colleague. We had a handyman, an excellent, artful carpenter who installed a dozen hand-built cherry wood cabinets in our kitchen. Barely five feet tall, but well-toned and muscular, he immediately took to Lee's slim, graceful figure, I could tell, although his head barely reached her shoulders. Standing beside her, discussing kitchen layouts for form and convenience, he clearly strutted to impress her, his buzz-cut head and wild Brooklyn brogue taking her in through a combination of physical animal power and aesthetic gentility–at least as I imagined it.

"It was only once," Lee said to me in Provence, "an afternoon's celebration of domesticity."

"Completing the kitchen?"

"Our collaboration on making something beautiful together." She shook her head. "You should understand."

I said nothing although I, too, had had a few exciting opportunities, ones that I am happy to say passed over. A side of me congratulated her for choosing well–both my colleague and our handyman were okay, I thought—but of course another side hated what that said about Lee and me. Me, really, especially after the affair with Jean Luc. Didn't she love me? After all these years, did she find life, and bed, with me unfulfilling?–Was she unfulfilled because she hadn't born a natural child? I knew I could turn aloof and dreamy when I thought about an artwork or my own writing. I also knew that time with paintings often drained me of emotional and physical energy for Lee–a mood that neither she nor I begrudged each other, I had thought. Did she, in her solitary moments in the studio, long for some passion and strength that centered on her rather than abstractions like texture, colors, and line?

"Dad's thinking too much," she had said,

228

laughing, to Misha a few weeks earlier. Now that I remembered the comment, I wondered how much her laughter (and his silly Thinker pose response) hid. Time passed slowly for one or two weeks, a kind of summer sadness. Both Lee and I felt blinded by the sudden invasion of light into a dark corner of our marriage, and for most of July, with no agreed upon plan, we ambled through daily tasks and chores—even with Misha—as if an old ceremony had turned meaningless through repetition.

Misha noticed something, I was sure, and as summer advanced, I felt increasingly stupid about our behavior. How could we have allowed it? How could I? Anne-Marie, her distinctive beauty and my vivid memories of our youthful time together, loomed way out of proportion to the life Lee and I had made. And when I thought about my dumb behavior with her, the book about suburbs took on a different meaning for me. It provided a shaky bridge to connect two important landmarks of my life—and without allowing me to see the real traffic surging in the waters beneath.

"Dad," Misha said to me one hot morning toward the middle of August, "Mom's not forgiving you, is she?"

"Forgiving? For what, Misha?"

"For spending time… so much… away from us."

I looked at him. We sat next to each other in the car, just about ready to leave the Lelandes' yard for the drive to camp. He had witnessed Mom and Dad's casual, and distracted, morning farewell, the lack of embrace, the friendly voices turned cool and at the edge of ice. Misha's lean face, clear blue eyes, and loosely-cut hair struck me as fresh and handsome, and for a moment I swelled with pride and envy. But with his question the pride immediately turned to shame.

"I didn't think she was angry," I lied. "Maybe just a little sad."

He nodded, started to say something, but thought better of it.

"Mom wants us to be more close," I told him. "The three of us. Unfortunately, a writer often has to work alone."

I stared at him, but I could not tell what he was thinking. "She's not mad at you for something else–like maybe she's ... uh... jealous?"

"Jealous?"

"You know, seeing Anne-Marie, and maybe Zach, too much? You always talk about visiting them."

I shook my head, but I remembered very clearly the day he saw us embracing in St. Rémy. "Mom might not like it, Misha, but she knows that Zach is sick and Anne-Marie is troubled."

"Yeah..." Misha turned to stare out the window. After a long pause, he added, "It's everything. Mom wants us to be happy, and there are things taking too much of our time. Your time."

I nodded, wondering what "things" he meant.

"Bummer," he said. "And here I am going off to camp instead of staying home with her." I reached across the seat and patted his shoulder. I thought he must have questioned Lee before that morning, but I didn't want to hear her answers. Instead, I backed out of the driveway and turned at the roundabout, taking the route through St. Rémy and over the bauxite hills toward Mouriès. I had planned to work in the café that morning, thinking the sense of small town French life would help me back to the chapter I was writing. But after I left Misha at his camp and headed down the main street, I turned toward Anne-Marie's house instead, driving through the farmlands toward Eyguières. When I reached her house, I saw Anne-Marie working in the garden and, still unsure of my motivations, turned into the drive slowly, parking in front of the garden shed.

"*Les américains sont arrivés*," I said, trying for lightness.

Anne-Marie grinned, straightening up from a bean bush she had been picking. She turned and caught my eye as I walked over.

"Are you okay?" she asked, studying my face. "You haven't been here in days. I thought you might have gone back home ... without saying good-bye."

I shrugged, throwing out an empty line. "Busy— all of us. Doing separate things."

Anne-Marie looked at me—directly—for a long time. I smiled as if "separate" meant nothing and inquired about Celestine and Zach. Anne-Marie turned toward the bushes, in the direction of Zach's cabin, and said little had changed. "Celestine is ready to return to Paris with my parents, and Zach spends almost all of his time in the shed listening to his music. Soon I will be in my house alone."

231

Her smile hardened, and "alone" sank like a stone landing in very still water. I felt like retreating to the car and driving away, but Anne-Marie returned to the bush and, despite my many doubts, I opened the gate to join her. She moved a flat garden basket to the ground between our feet, and we picked the thin green beans and tossed them into it together. The sun baked my neck, and gradually sweat moistened my shirt. Anne-Marie wore a sunhat, sandals, and a long, flowing yellow dress with a blue and red pattern of lilies and poppies. When we finished the beans, she pulled off one or two yellow squashes and several tomatoes, picking up the basket to go inside.

"Do you want some tea?" she asked. "I put a batch in the refrigerator to cool this morning."

I nodded and followed her inside, certain that I should turn in another direction. Still, her loose flowing dress, the comical smudge of dirt on her toes and sandals, and the weight of the vegetables we had picked slanting her shoulders as she carried the basket took the glamour from her appearance. Sweat and mud on my shirt did the same for me.

We entered the kitchen door, and Anne-Marie left the basket on the counter top, pouring us both glasses of fragrant tea. Noticeably cooler indoors, we both seemed to relax, and we sat at a little table near the door that looked out on a range of mountains, one of which was Mont Ventoux. Seeing it, I reached for her hand and held it.

"It's been nice seeing you again this summer," I said. "I mean it. I'm sorry the circumstances are so sad."

232

She blinked, sipping the tea. For several minutes, we remained silent, the sound of a fly buzzing at her window trivializing the somberness of our moment. We simply stared at each other a good long time and, at least for me, desired.

"I'm glad you've been here," she said. "I don't know anyone else who could give me what I needed. Both Zach–and, yes, Celestine–like you very much. It's a shame we couldn't have been better hosts."

I waved my hand. "We've had some great conversations. I've learned a lot–from all three of you. I'm just sad it will all end very soon."

Anne-Marie nodded doubtfully and looked away. Her free hand reached out and covered mine. "How much longer will you stay? Zach's sleeping now, but he'll certainly want to see you before you go."

I looked into her eyes, puzzled at first, until I realized her full meaning. Just the thought of going opened a void in my stomach, and I shook my head to answer her. "A little less than a month," I said. "And I'm already missing everything—especially Zach... and you. We've had a wonderful time."

"Come see us one of these afternoons. Zach sleeps most of the time, but he is usually awake at four. Musicians' hours, he says. And some days he's strong enough to do more—even go into town if you bring along oxygen. You can talk for a while somewhere. He'd like that."

Somber, I nodded. "But I also want to talk to you. We have so much to go over."

She inclined her head, a grim ascent that filled me with real remorse. She squeezed my hand. "At this time," Anne-Marie said, looking directly into my eyes. "I don't feel I have anything to give you. We've both moved on to different lives. But..."

I waited, unsure of what to expect. "But—?"

"But we don't want to spoil yours. I have to move on with mine, no matter what the conclusion. I have a young girl to raise, a young girl who says she hates me."

I sighed. Anne-Marie did, too. The conversation could only get darker, and for several moments we sat with our hands folded over one another. My spine tingled and swelled. I felt a wave of regret wash over my whole body. I had carried her inside so long that it seemed impossible now to admit another, perhaps permanent, separation. Celestine was my daughter, too—at least as I sat there—and the woman beside me was one I wanted to hold and spend a life with. I have no idea how Anne-Marie thought of me, but I can say the emotions of that moment appeared clearly, powerfully, on her face.

She raised her hand, placing it on my neck and then rose from her chair, leaning forward to kiss me on the lips. I stood immediately, pulling her close, the two of us together for quite some time. I wanted to, but did not, free my hands; the fear of what might come next cut across my thoughts. I looked out the door toward the west and tried to feel something other than desire.

I placed my hand on her cheek and, closing my eyes, stroked her forehead. "There's not much we can count on," I said, "but we know children will be there–will need us–no matter what the circumstances."

"And our wonderful spouses, too."

Anne-Marie leaned back, trying to make sure I understood. "In a short while Zach will be beyond need. He and I both know that. He's already freed me–as should Celestine."

"She doesn't want to face it," I answered. "And maybe she shouldn't."

Anne-Marie placed her finger on my lips and, with a truly lovely smile, held it there. I felt the urge to make things change and, in her arms, I was caught for a few breaths between worlds, aware that I could only hurt her and myself. Sighing, I took the chance anyway. Closing the door to the house, I lifted her in my arms and carried her–both of us self-conscious, laughing, even shaking a bit–across the floor and into the room she had shared for several years with Zach.

XIX.

Most of the time, when I reach a sex scene in a story, I have to admit I skip over it, not out of prudishness, but boredom. "Oh, jeez, what else is new?" I'll say. After all, how many permutations can there be? — When we were young, Anne-Marie and I had probably achieved most, if not all, of them, at least among heterosexual (and monogamous) possibilities. So what could a novelist, or any writer, show me? We had attempted vertical, horizontal, and slanted — sliding head-first down a haystack in Normandy, for example. We had done cars, bathtubs, pools, and even bicycles (never a plane in flight, but the World Trade Center roof, as I remember it, was like the wing of a low-flying aircraft over New York City). Name the position: We'd taken it. And somehow through it all we felt no sense of sleaze, probably because everything seemed like innocent fun between us, a natural consequence of all that beat in our hearts when we saw each other, when we wanted to see each other, when we heard each other's voice on the phone or across the room, and, most certainly, when that little electric charge leaped between our skins as we finally shed our clothing and touched.

So, what can I tell you in this confessional rendering about that afternoon, our shameless behavior so many years after our original Parisian bumps and grinds, that will illuminate and not take away the beauty of the mystery existing between us?—The attraction that made me change my life so many years before and, once again, seemed to egg me on. Yes, I was ready to change my life one more time. Forgive me, but Lee was out of the picture, Misha was out of the picture, God knows the Roman suburbs were not even considered part of the picture, and my job, our house, even the noble Vincent, my wonderful, devoted companion on daily western New Jersey walks, were as good as consigned to the trash heap—an S.P.C.A. of once important animals now ready for the dreadful needle.

I wanted Anne-Marie. To achieve that, I wanted Zach, Celestine, and all of Provence airbrushed from her life. I wanted to go back in time, through the World Trade Center, Katrina, the Clinton-Lewinski debacle, the collapse of the Berlin Wall and the rest of Communist Europe, the Reagan-Bush happy no-taxes talk, to Iran, the assault on the American embassy, and the stringent, moral Carter years when we seemed freer because of rock and roll, though prices rose and the brow of the President sank increasingly lower, past Nixon's scowling dour expression. That's when Anne-Marie and I met on the banks of the Seine while I painted and my sensual, emotional, and aesthetic life flew in the face of everything we read in the news.

Strip, no clothes on, the occasional wrinkle on our abdomens disappeared, cellulite slid backward into the maw of time, hair naturally restored, color refreshed, skin cleared—taut, robust, and ruddy were

237

the descriptive words. The two of us rode this wave again as sweaty shirt, flowered granny dress, socks, clogs, and even jewelry flew, caught up in the wind of our eagerness, and we felt ourselves celebrating on the *rue de Vaugirard* across from the Luxembourg Gardens instead of here in a remote stone *mas* in Provence.

We had energy and strength; both of us were supple. Anne-Marie's long, shapely legs had not turned angular; my testicles had not sagged; my gut had not expanded; the energy in our thighs, fingers, tongues, and lips matched our imaginations as we spun, crawled, covered, sucked, pushed, pulled, entered, exited, and then entered again, the movement and drive as hectic — and primitive — as a bordello in Avignon for Picasso and as restless as a dark blue Provençal night with whirlpools of light illuminating the writhing clouds within it for Van Gogh.

White sheets swirled around us like billowing clouds, the pillow cases collected our saliva and sweat, and the mattress and spring echoed our cries, my shrieks, her soft pleas for more. I don't remember laughing so viscerally, not belly laughter but something more full throated and free, since the days we called them gonad laughs during our afternoons in Paris. Here we are having just "taken our feet," as the French say (that is, our joy and pleasure): Anne-Marie sits on top of me bellowing with her head back and her hands on my shoulders, pressing them down. Her belly shakes. "I can't stand it. I love it!" she shouts, and I, with my hands clutching her muscular hips, can only howl. To me it's the laughter of the gods. I have never known my

238

life to be so perfect, never known how perfectly Anne-Marie fit into it, never even dreamed that the two of us—just like those spoiled, bratty gods—would never change, lose our beauty, never get sick or age.

With a loud shout to her stippled ceiling, I struggled to sit up, embraced her with my elbows floating along her sweaty inner thighs, and—still coupled—buried my face between her neck and shoulder. Just the smell alone fulfilled me. There was warmth and sweetness, along with a hint of pine, as well as the moist ambrosia of a field of lavender. She rocked, pulling my shoulders close to her breasts, and without a moment's thought or hesitation, we rolled with the wave of a second emotion, swaying with each other's body as if we were a pair of mooring skiffs.

"Love," we both murmured; "never forget you," we both blurted; and the words that followed came out with as little thought. Our lips combined, tongue and liquid blending, and our legs, crossed, pointing in different directions, rising and falling, spreading, closing, as our bodies talked and whatever shook them inside continued to shake.

"Oh," Anne-Marie said, after we separated, her calf lifting over my head as she fell to my side and rested her arm across my lap. I closed my eyes and remained upright, with my hands and arms behind me for support. Sounds from outside gradually began to enter the room—a magpie hopping across the gravel, wind rustling through poplars and umbrella pine, and of course the insistent, overwhelming hum of the *cigales*

239

in the trees. As the sounds swelled, the room took on its former cubic shape, walls and ceiling creamy white, the floor the yellowish-orange of Provençal oak. I turned and fell to my elbow, nuzzling my face into her ear and hair. "I'm not sure how this happened," I said. "If I weren't naked and exhausted, I'd probably run out the door."

"I'd run out after you." Placing her hand on my neck, she turned and kissed me, lightly, her affection broadening into a friendly, open smile. "And I'm sure I'd catch you," she said.

"Probably because I'd want you to, if I had any sense."

We embraced again, enjoying the cool softness of our naked bodies, but at the same time feeling the world we knew outside rapidly coming back to the present.

I heard a car rumble on the road nearby. Then a military jet screamed across the sky, probably toward Toulon. I lay back, resting on a pillow, and Anne-Marie settled her head on my shoulder. We said nothing, breathing quietly together for a long time. At one point she rose to bring in two glasses of our unfinished, now tepid, tea, and we sat up to lean against the wall and sip them. I tried not to think of anything but Anne-Marie and her room at that moment, but each sip of tea I took, every subtle switch of body position she made, seemed to open a door or window into something larger. At one moment I thought I heard footsteps outside; then a phone or doorbell seemed to ring; and finally, something I knew was real, the softly distant music of home—a piano, some drums, and a singing bass.

"That's Zach," Anne-Marie said, standing near the window. "He must be awake and playing his music."

"He'll know I'm here. He knows my car."

She nodded, bending to pick up her underpants and step into them. I glanced around the floor to find my own. As Anne-Marie slipped on her dress, I began to gather my outer clothes and put them on. "He wouldn't walk nearby without knocking, wouldn't just walk in," she said. "He's just listening to some music while he reads."

I nodded, but the mood had changed for both of us, and I very quickly slipped into my shirt and jeans. I finished my tea and, without so much as a touch or whisper, we walked together into the main room and put on our shoes. "I have to go now," I said, frowning. She nodded, frowning too, and as we stepped out of the dark house I felt the sun on my face again, blazing. It seemed to fill the sky. Anne-Marie took my hand and handed me a basket of vegetables, lavender, and beans.

"You and I have certain things to hide, I think," she said.

I smiled, nodding, and thanked her for the basket, taking a handful of lavender, squeezing it, and scattering it at her feet.

"Your boy, Misha," she said. "He has a bright, wonderful personality. Enjoy him and your wife. You have nothing to regret, with me or anyone. Your life, your work, the world you have made for yourself. It makes me happy–genuinely happy–just to see it."

241

"Sometimes..." I couldn't say anymore but leaned over to kiss her cheek.

She pressed my lips again, first with her finger, then her mouth, both very softly. My eyes closed, and my whole body flooded with a heat and motion I really cannot name: love, desire, even anger, but mostly relief at the lack of expectation from them. "*Sometimes,*" Anne-Marie said, "is nothing. For most people, regret and failure fill every moment of their lives. Don't let it happen to you."

"Not with you," I said. "I hope it's not going to be that way in your life either–especially with Zach."

"We won't let it. I promise you."

"Good, but why..."

She shook her head, smiling. "One of these days we'll have to talk — to straighten things. This just isn't the right time."

I nodded, but even with the few weeks I knew I had remaining in France, something told me this might be our last moment alone together–at least like this–for a long, long time.

PART FIVE:

WHEATFIELD WITH CROWS

XX.

I did see her again—quite often in that summer of many good-byes—and in truth I'm not happy to tell about it. When I returned to see her a few days later, no one was home–not even Zach. The main house looked empty, and when I went through the bushes to knock on the door to the shepherd's hut, no one responded. The door held firm, as did the large oak door on the main house. So I left, assuming a family outing as the best case scenario while really fearing a sudden revelation about us or a necessary hospital stay for Zach.

At home I found no messages from Anne-Marie, and when I returned a few days later, I stopped at a neighbor's for possible news. She was a sweet woman, with a deep, booming voice and a tendency to speak vaguely. Tending the vegetables beside her house, she answered with a classic Gallic shrug. "Oh, I don't know," she said, at first, pulling a weed beside a tomato plant. "I haven't seen anyone there since last week."

"Madame hasn't worked in her garden–like you?"

She shook her head.

"Didn't you hear anything?–See any cars?"

She looked at me, then past me, down the road toward Anne-Marie's house. "To speak frankly, I did see something, but it's not my affair." She looked me in the eye and then turned her attention to another tomato

244

plant.

"An ambulance?" I asked, again thinking of Zach.

She shook her head. After a moment she answered, "Police." And to my puzzled frown she responded, "But there was no siren, no emergency."

I looked in her eyes, and the worry on my face made her add something: "The daughter. I think they were here because of her."

"Celestine?–But why..."

Madame closed her eyes and looked up to the sky. "Trouble," she said after another Gallic shrug. "A friend in the market said she ran away—again."

"Again...? But she had gone to Paris to stay with her grandparents."

"Ah, but she ran away from home up there. That's the way she is."

I stood quiet for a moment, stunned. With Zach so sick, Anne-Marie could certainly use help rather than added trouble. But how could I, or anyone, help her? I thought of going to the local gendarmerie for information, but I realized they would have every reason to refuse since I was not a family member. Thanking the neighbor, I left, and as I went to my car I decided to call the Lelandes instead of the police since they might have news that related to Anne-Marie's work.

Monsieur Lelande answered the phone, quickly telling me, before I had a chance to ask, that "the girl," Celestine, of course, had gone to Paris but had not come

245

home to her grandparents a few nights before. Now Anne-Marie and Zach searched for her along with the police.

"Where?"

"Who knows? Anywhere in France I suppose."

"That's ridiculous. Isn't anyone helping them?" I remembered how difficult it was for Zach to travel. "Have they gone up to Paris?"

Monsieur Lelande paused a moment before blurting out, "What can they, or anyone, do, my friend? Especially you. It's a family affair. Best leave it up to them.–The daughter doesn't like the man, Zach, so she's run off. With a boy, I bet."

"A boy..." It stopped me short, and I felt sick in the pit of my stomach. Celestine had just turned fifteen.

"I can help find her, I suppose. I can give them some support. Do you know how to reach them?"

Monsieur Lelande sighed into the phone. "Well, I don't know where they are or how to call. And I certainly have no idea where to look for the girl — or her boy. If I were you, I'd do my work and leave it all to them, as well as the police. When they call, *if* they call, I'll let you know."

"He's sick," I said. "Anne-Marie needs somebody — other than Zach — with her. And Celestine... Well, her life is about to fall apart."

Another pause... Lelande's silence seemed loaded with all sorts of premonition. Perhaps I was revealing myself as a foolish, overly nosey neighbor; perhaps I revealed much more than that, I don't know. Whatever I showed, Lelande ended his silence with an agonized *"pfff...,"* and then simply added, "It's their affair, my friend. If I were you, I'd leave it at that."

I drove down to the gendarmerie in St. Rémy and got nowhere with the officers there, but as I climbed into my car parked on the *périphérique*, I saw Anne-Marie and Zach pull up to the curb and behind them, going at a slower pace, a small police car with Celestine's girlish, tear-stained face conspicuous in the rear seat. At a quick glance, I saw no boy.

I went to Anne-Marie's car and saw her, as grim and tear-stained as Celestine, staring at me through the window. Beside her Zach looked pale and unhappy, his face showing no sign that he saw me or even the street outside.

"Ben," Anne-Marie said, barely holding back a sob.

I tried to open the car door, but it was locked and she made no attempt to unlock it for me. Zach looked up and nodded, finally opening his own door, which automatically unlocked Anne-Marie's. "Not a good time," he said, struggling, with the oxygen tank dangling on his shoulder, to stand at the curb. "Maybe we ought to..." He groaned, leaning heavily on the open car door to pull himself to his feet. Anne-Marie stretched across the seat to assist him but couldn't work up much leverage. I walked around to his side to take his arm. He thanked me but quickly shrugged himself free of my help. Meanwhile, two police had left their car and walked toward us with Celestine between them. She frowned at me, sniffled, and turned away to avoid

247

eye-contact with Zach and her mother.

"*Célestine, nous t'aimons, tous les deux,*" Anne-Marie said. "*N'oublies pas.*"

Celestine glared at her mother, glared more ominously at Zach, and then followed the police into their building. Zach and Anne-Marie looked after her and then turned to me in resignation. "A court order," Anne-Marie said. "From my own parents."

"What for?"

Anne-Marie shook her head. "It's my fault, although she ran away from them. They say she can't stay with me as long as Zach is on the property. Now they want her to go back to Paris to live with them, no matter what I say. — All because of the child."

"Child? She's already fifteen," I said.

She closed her eyes. Zach put his long, thin arms around her and held her close, his chin resting on her head as he looked at me for sympathy. On first impression, he seemed too weak to offer much support, but as I looked into his dark brown eyes and saw the genuinely tender expression in them, I felt that he gave her exactly what she needed.

"*Her* child," Anne-Marie said. "She's pregnant, if you haven't already guessed."

"Pregnant...?"

She nodded, her fists slamming down on her thighs as Zach held on.

"Are you sure?"

She nodded yet again, angrily. "I've talked to her about this many times. She knows what she needs to do. It was her choice, I'm sure."

"I'm going to move out," Zach said, turning her to face him. "Completely. I'll find a nurse to look after me. It'll work out. Celestine — and the baby — can stay with you."

I saw Anne-Marie's shoulders shake as she hunched forward and buried her face deeper in his neck. Zach stroked her hair, his fingers a pale contrast to her flushed skin. "We can do this, love," he said. "Celestine can, too."

"But I can't be there when you really need me," she said. "I won't be able to help you."

"Celestine and the baby will need you more. I can take care of myself."

I felt the situation tear at my own conscience, and I could only imagine what it did to Anne-Marie's. We returned to our cars, and I followed them to the Lelandes' home in Châteaurenard, where Zach and Anne-Marie arranged to move Zach to a small apartment the Lelandes owned near St. Rémy. Then we drove to Anne-Marie's, gathered Zach's clothes, CDs, and oxygen tanks from the hut, and brought them back to the apartment. The place was small, but neatly furnished–a bed, an armchair, an oak table in one room and in the other an adequately equipped kitchen with a couch, another armchair, and a huge walnut armoire that must have gone back to the early 1800s.

We settled Zach in the armchair with a heavy blanket, set up a selection of CDs on the Bose player we had also brought, and left him there smiling as he listened to Coltrane's "A Love Supreme," telling Anne-

Marie not to worry about a thing as we went out the door. A nurse would arrive in the next day or so; meanwhile, the Lelandes had alerted a neighbor in a nearby house who would check on him regularly. "And," Zach said, reaching inside his shirt pocket, "I've got my phone."

"How that brave man suffers," Anne-Marie said as we walked down the stairs to our cars. She was driving home to call her parents and report that Zach had moved out completely. I had agreed to follow her and, after we arrived, went into the living room with her while she made the call. They seemed to accept the news at first, reluctantly, but as I stood next to her, listening, she shook her head vehemently over something one of her parents said.

"Oh, the ignorance of that woman!" Anne-Marie said after hanging up. "Now this is all Zach's fault. My mother says he is a witch, and that he's cast a spell on me to inherit their money and eventually seduce Celestine."

"But the baby?"

"The devil's. She swears it will turn out black."

.   I looked at her and shook my head. Before I could think of anything, Anne-Marie took out a broadsheet much like one the Bernards had given me at the *Maison au Crau*, and pointed to a picture of a Rastafarian on the front page. Dark skin, dread locks, and the giant headline, "*VOODOO EN FRANCE*" dominated the page. "They read this and immediately called to warn me against him. My father says he's changed me, made me devious, and my mother fears

250

he's done the same to Celestine. She's a fifteen-year-old witch—who's pregnant!"

I could barely restrain an impulse to laugh and pass this talk off as the stuff of imbecilic fairy tales. But I couldn't because, clearly, Anne-Marie—as well as Celestine and Zach—suffered. That talk had changed their lives. All the good reasoning–or sly comments about her parents–could do nothing, especially with French law majestically behind them. Zach, an artist, a dark-skinned single foreigner, and, from what I heard, a man with a known, but minor, record of drug use, might be in too strong a position to influence a young mother and her baby. I also knew he was not Rastafarian. "I just like the braids," he had told me once. "The rest is just a throw-away beat."

"Do you notice how different he's made me?" Anne-Marie asked. "How I've changed?" She raised her hands, cackled, and pointed her thumb and forefinger as if to cast a spell.

I smiled, laughing as always at her outrage over narrow-minded French thinking. "But for the better," is all I could say. "There's no comparison to the woman you once were."

She shook her head and went on with her mimicry, but real anger immediately returned. She started sobbing again, and, during the next half hour or so, I did my best to comfort her, deciding finally to talk to Celestine again though with little hope for results. The sense that I had about young people of that time— open-minded about race, as well as extra-marital sex

251

and women's behavior—would not necessarily carry over to Celestine: "I want a home–with a mother," she told me the afternoon I took her to Vaison, "not a friend, not a baby sitter, not someone who wants to find a man and start a second family."

"As I understand it," I replied, "it's just the opposite. Your mother has never abandoned you–for Zach or anyone else."

"Each time she sees him she abandons me!" she shouted, her face turning an absolute crimson red. "He's not like a father at all! He's her lover."

After a while, Anne-Marie and I moved outside into her garden, where we sat in the shade of a huge umbrella pine to map a strategy. The most important thing was to find a lawyer to represent her against her parents. She didn't care about money or their houses. The *mas* she lived in here sufficed, she said, and she felt sure her work as cleaner and manager of rental properties would continue to grow since Provence still attracted tourists from around the world. Of course, her life with Celestine would change, and Anne-Marie would have to work at getting it under control.

"Her father?" I said. "How does he fit in? You almost never mention him."

She blushed and looked away toward the house. "He doesn't fit in at all, Ben. He came well after you."

"Is he French? From Provence?"

She shook her head. "Polish," she added after a moment. "I met him in Paris when he needed French lessons." She laughed, bitterly. "I conducted them on the pillow."

252

I said nothing, thrown off by her bitterness more than anything else. She said he was a writer and had returned to Warsaw well after the Solidarity victory in the 1980s. "He wanted to restart his life and career there," she said. "Celestine and I were holding him back."

I looked away, almost ashamed. "Doesn't he keep in touch now–with Celestine?"

Anne-Marie shook her head again. "Not even a post card–for years," she said, "or a note for her birthday. He's found another woman and started a family with her while publishing his books. My father is her only father now."

I frowned, angry. All I could think of at that moment was that I, too, had started another life–for her, I thought at the time, when I left Paris for New York– but with terrible results at the top of the World Trade Center.

"I'm sorry this happened," I muttered, trying to block out all my personal disappointment. "I'm sure you and Zach have tried. But now this–a baby."

She nodded, but the look in her eyes registered her–and his–limits. "I kept hoping this would work out as Celestine got older. Right now that's impossible to believe."

"Will she have it, you think? Do you want her to?"

Anne-Marie looked at me, and tears welled up in her eyes as she turned away. I put my hand on her shoulder but felt her stiffen at my touch.

253

"Do you know the boy—the father?" I asked, letting my hand drop to my side.

She hunched up her shoulders, cupping her hands over her mouth. "He's a friend, a family friend, someone she's known for several years. Now, suddenly, it's love." She shook her head and turned away, giving me a nasty, aggressive look.

"I'm sorry. This is none of my business. I should keep my questions to myself."

"Ben, my husband wanted me to do that to Celestine. An abortion—get rid of her! You have no idea what the thought of that did to me." The anger in her eyes turned to cold terror and then, gradually, sadness again. "After that he wanted me to give her up to another mother—in America. I threw him out of our apartment immediately, and I wouldn't let him back in."

She took a deep breath and held my hands. "He went back to Poland, happily. Since then, nothing— except for clippings of news articles about him or one of his wonderful books."

She shook her head and moaned. As I seemed to do throughout that awful afternoon, I took on his guilt, regretting Anne-Marie's obvious pain and somehow feeling responsible for it.

XXI.

I remember vividly the day Anne-Marie and I first met. It was cool, clear, with an early fall light turning the pavement gold and scattering jewels of bright color on the Seine's gray surface. Young, enthusiastic, and new to Paris, I had carted my easel slung over my shoulder, my box of oils and brushes in one hand and a blank, primed canvas in the other, from my small apartment near Porte Orleans, past the stone lion at Denfert-Rocherau, through the Luxembourg Gardens and beyond until I reached the river near the *Ponte des Artes*. I knew it was a corny choice, and that I sought inspiration from an overused placement. But I also knew I had to start right there. My first Parisian oil would not be of the Louvre across the way, or the river with the Notre Dame and the *Ile de la Cité* appearing like a huge ghost ship pushing upstream. No, I would paint two or three of the barges moored along the southern bank, catching, I hoped, the mood and minutiae of life lived there in the shadow of all that art: clotheslines full of underwear, jeans, and dresses; a child's tricycle, handles vertical, leaning against a red smokestack; cats nibbling on fish, shaking themselves and stretching contentedly near a cardboard litter box.

I set up the easel on a relatively level spot along the quay, scraping away pebbles and debris to provide a solid footing for the tripod's legs. Meanwhile, traffic

255

blared above on both sides of the river in that curious, hornless Parisian fashion. "Focus on the 19th century," I told myself, staring at the boats. I set the canvas on the easel, secured it with some string, and opened the box of paints, brushing grayish blue on the bottom of the canvas, modulating to beige, white, and cobalt blue on the top half. As I began quickly and efficiently to sketch in more precise details–proud I could do it fresh with a brush and no charcoal to spoil the immediacy–I sensed, as I had seen with other painters in the city, a spectator or two stopping to stare over my shoulder, and a couple more prospective ones talking loudly along the quay.

"*Parles a moi*," a woman behind me whispered; then louder in English: "Pretend you know me, please."

I felt a hand on my palette arm, and when I turned I saw a burst of burnished sunlight hovering at my shoulders. Then I looked into a pair of blue-green eyes and pale pink lips that I have always remembered as the primary colors of my life with Anne-Marie.

"Just smile—and look friendly," she said, gripping my forearm as if she needed my support.

It was the easiest thing in the world to do, and when I heard other voices, men's, pause for a moment behind us, I turned, laying aside the palette, and put my arm around her shoulders. Two young men with shaggy hair and dirty clothes stared at me, checked out the canvas on the easel, shrugged, and spit their still-burning Gauloise butts into the river. Hands buried in their pockets, they mounted the nearby steps to the street.

"At last," Anne-Marie said. "Thank you. They've

been following me for blocks. One of them tried to take my arm. The other said something ugly, so I came down here as soon as I saw you from the bridge."

I smiled, flattered that so much beauty would come to me during my first few hours painting in Paris. "I'm very glad to help you," I said in French, the bad accent shattering my dream of going native. Anne-Marie stepped away, and automatically I reached for the palette again, wishing her a stiff good day. I continued painting, assuming she would mount the steps and continue along the quay, but instead she stood beside me and watched for several minutes, eventually squatting down and sitting on the pavement behind me.

"It's a very interesting view," she said after a while. "It shows a simple, necessary life beneath the glamour of the city."

"Thank you," I said. Then, after a few more strokes, I added, "It's really about things I like. It relaxes me because it seems so quiet."

Quiet herself, Anne-Marie said nothing, and I continued painting in details, not wanting to break my concentration or the intense good feeling. With a beautiful young French woman squatting behind me to watch and appreciate my work, I felt spurred on to paint quickly, spontaneously responding to the image of barges in the afternoon light. I couldn't paint the sound of tires, engines, and flowing river, but I felt their pace and energy and tried to let my brush strokes respond to them.

"Nice," she said when I paused, stepping back

for a moment to sit on my haunches beside her. "You see how things fit together. I like that."

I looked at her, nodding as I studied her eyes and face. A side of me believed we talked on a movie set at that moment, or perhaps in some personal, surreal daydream. I sensed something important happening and — young enough to believe large forces worked — our two gazes seemed to intersect in a knowing, familiar way. I found it hard to risk another word. Nodding instead, I stood and stepped back to the easel, wiped off a couple of brushes, then hooked the palette on my left thumb and went back to the canvas. After painting in more of the background, adding a few new details of the boats and clarifying others, I put the paints, brushes, and palette back in the box and locked it up.

"You must be exhausted," Anne-Marie said as I stepped back to look at the picture again.

"It's not bad. I'm a beginner, I confess, especially with live Parisian scenes."

"Even so, you've done very well."

I glanced at her, relaxed, probably because I really did feel tired. "You are very kind," I said, changing to the familiar *"tu"* from the *"vous"* I had been using. Then mentioning a good café near St. Placide, I asked her to join me for a drink.

"I walk right by there," she said with a happy smile. "I live on the other side of the Luxembourg Gardens."

"Then let's go."

I folded the tripod and picked up the paint box. She offered to carry the canvas as we started.

Things moved swiftly after that, so quickly you would have had to describe both of us as swept away. Large forces were indeed at work because we experienced an extraordinary sense of comfort and ease with each other in no time: two strangers from two different continents who happened to fit–and please–one another as if they had shared a lifetime. We both loved art and liked to spend hours in the Louvre and other museums. We both enjoyed walking, trudging through the city, neighborhood to neighborhood, without resorting to bus or Metro lines. In three successive weekends we completed a circle, on foot, around Paris. It is still one of my peak traveling experiences in France.

Anne-Marie loved all kinds of music–as I did– and we attended performances at the Opera, concerts in various halls by Leonard Cohen, Joni Mitchell, and Paul Simon, and jazz in night clubs, bars, and one or two city parks. She did not read as much as I did, didn't paint or perform, but had a natural insight about things she saw and heard that I very quickly saw put my own stilted responses in the shade. In addition she read people and sympathized with them very well, making her a delight when she liked you, but also made her assumptions about your character infuriating because she believed herself more than she believed you.

"I don't feel the impulse," she said, when I asked why she didn't paint or play an instrument. "I like to move, I like to go out among people and interview them. An artist needs to spend too much time alone."

She danced very well, but had too many years behind her already to begin lessons for a professional career. Besides, though she liked people, she liked their company, being among them, not standing in front or above them. "I like being appreciated," she told me once, "but for simple things, not for grand ones."

I had no easy response because, at that time anyway, I felt committed to fame and success. I knew there was a huge leap between my work and the thousand, even one hundred, dollar canvases we saw in various galleries. Still, I told myself, I will put my time in, patiently learn craft picture by picture, make some important contacts in this wonderful, aesthetic city, and through them meet some wealthy patrons. Eventually, by sudden or gradual means, people will want my work on their walls and compete feverishly to buy it.

"Your grandchildren, maybe your great grandchildren," I told Anne-Marie once as I painted her, seated with her back to the window of my studio, "will be proud to own this. They'll never believe their granny could be so beautiful when she was young."

"Yes, and with her two pink *Cavaillons* exposed to the world." She laughed, turning to look back over her shoulder at a window full of Paris rooftops.

"I could paint more than those juicy melons, my love. Every part of you is worth seeing."

She crossed her legs, folded her arms across her chest, and smirked, which made us both laugh–at the joke as well as the ease and comfort between us. Looking back at that time now, I still wonder why we couldn't make it last. We were young at a time and in a city that seemed to value youth and all its freedoms. She admired my commitment to art and my willing apprenticeship to it without looking for immediate rewards. I admired her strength of character, her writing, her willingness to have fun with sex without looking to build a couples life. But, and here is the rub although I didn't see it until much, much later, we couldn't always live without some kind of personal limit.

Within an hour of our talk in the café near St. Placide, I knew that she shared an apartment with another man. I also knew he was a childhood sweetheart to whom she felt loyal without being committed as a mate. Her openness in saying all this over coffee in a public space made me immediately assume she would leave him in time–to be with me or someone else. Yes, I was certain she would choose to be with me.

Their apartment on *rue de Vaugirard* near the south-western end of the Luxembourg Gardens had one large room with a mattress on the floor, a foyer next to the kitchen where they kept an eating table, and a boom box with hundreds of tapes that constantly filled the room and foyer with music: Stevie Wonder, Steely Dan, Django Reinhardt, Duke Ellington, Ella Fitzgerald, Yves Montand, Edith Piaf, and Jacques Brel, along with an assortment of classical opera, orchestra, and chamber music. A small bookcase next to the mattress held French literary journals and paperbacks–classical novels and poems along with contemporary writers like Duras,

Robbe-Grillet, and de Beauvoir. I felt like I could slide right into the place, bringing my paint equipment, some pictures, and a few additional books. Within a day or so, after she had visited, I felt absolutely certain she would easily fit into my place too, her body and spirit adding a rich light and color to my paintings and my walls.

We always felt at play when we saw each other. Anne-Marie worked in an office somewhere in Les Halles, just off the rue Francs-Bourgeois. She typed, filed papers, kept track of manuscripts and correspondence, and generally, as she phrased it, had to "Hustle my ass so none of the jerks will pinch it."

We saw each other for lunch daily, either in a restaurant near her office or down at my apartment, where I learned the beauty of a two-hour lunch period. When we met near her office, we'd tour the Pompidou Museum, window shop the Jewish stores in *rue des Rosiers*, or visit FNAC, the discount store where we bought more music, journals, and books.

After work she'd travel down on the Metro and spend the evening with me, though more often than not we'd end up at her apartment on Vaugirard where I'd say good-night, occasionally after drinks and conversation with her roommate, Joseph, and then walk home. During those walks I'd think how lucky I was in my affair with Anne-Marie, how wonderful it was to be alive, young and painting, in Paris, and how important it was for me to make the most of it. "If I can't accomplish something now, in these very lucky circumstances," I wrote to one of my friends in New York, "I might as well just give it all up. It's not going to get better."

And looking at that message now, more than thirty years later, I still think it's true. I had no other issues: my sensual life was uncommitted and nearly perfect; I had saved money in America and at the exchange rate then I had more than enough cash to live on for two full years; I had every day to paint, all day to paint if I wanted to, and no job or responsibility except to fulfill that need.

"The problem," Anne-Marie told me frequently when she stayed overnight, "is that you have no one to talk to—about your art or anything else. You stay alone too much."

"I have you," I reminded her, "though sometimes not enough. I don't need anyone else."

She frowned at that, genuinely annoyed. "Ben, you're a few years older than I, but sometimes you sound very young."

"You tell me what you think of my work, don't you? And it's honest, not always a compliment."

"I can tell you what I think of a painting, but not what you need to do. You need others. I'm not smart enough. I don't know the craft, or how to challenge it."

"You're my inspiration," I said, smiling.

"Oh..." She frowned. "So I'm a muse. My cunt is a muse for your painting."

She said that in English, shocking me.

"Everything about you is a muse," I said. "Especially your spirit. I can't tell you how much it means to me to know I'm going to see you when my

263

workday is done."

She gave me a forced smile. I saw it immediately, although I confess I pushed the idea from my mind because I wanted to think of other things. As if she felt the same way, Anne-Marie turned to look out the window toward the street.

Now, just remembering that brief moment as I write it, I see the beginning of our final separation. The frozen joy, the evasive glance toward Mansards and gray cement, the silence that followed because neither of us knew what to say. Sure, we (or at least I) loved, and lusted, but suddenly–and again I just see it now–the question was, *Why?* And *For what end?* Then, *How?* and *In what manner?*—Basic questions neither of us could answer, so how could we plan a life? I don't remember how much I thought those things through consciously, but in my memory I didn't give them time at all. We'll continue seeing each other, I thought; keep having good times; circumstances will tell us what to do.

Anne-Marie had other conclusions, I suppose, and soon came to let me see them all too well. She spent nights with me less frequently; lunch hours now yielded to occasional "important" appointments; and, yes, she stopped posing for me, fully clothed or not. I continued painting, dropping in on classes at the *Ecole des Beaux Arts* to work on live human figures, and I began to do live outdoor scenes again around Paris. Lunches, dinners, and long, dark evenings increasingly went empty without her, and the urge to paint quickly turned to dull habit.

Sometimes visits to museums helped; occasional

trips alone to Florence, Rome, Madrid, or Provence would boost me for a week or two; and, of course, as Anne-Marie had said, meetings with other artists, by accident or design, refreshed me, especially if they took one or two of my canvases in exchange for theirs. I gathered a nice collection that way and eventually, as our affair cooled still further, I wrote three or four profiles for art magazines in New York and London. Yes, as I had thought, circumstances began to dictate what I felt I could do, and eventually that led to my work in art criticism.

"I'll probably go home soon," I told Anne-Marie one afternoon in my apartment. "But I want you to know I'm not leaving you. At least I don't want to. You can come and live with me if you like. If not, I'll come back as often as I can. There'll be summers and Christmas holidays, and…"

She nodded, as if this was not new information, but with no expression I could read for inner feelings. Even then I could tell how dishonest I must have sounded to her, how silly to say I would leave Paris without leaving her. Effectively, I had completed slicing us apart–once with my comment on inspiration and now with this final one about returning to New York.

"I can't leave Joseph," she replied, with a helpless shrug. "He needs me still. Besides, he can't pay for the apartment by himself. It's expensive on Vaugirard."

"He could move, or find another roommate. Maybe he has one in mind already."

She shook her head.

"Anne-Marie, you've been seeing me for a year and a half. Maybe things have changed with Joseph, and you don't know it."

She shook her head again. "He loves me," she said simply. "Not for sex. Joseph has loved me since we were ten years old."

I nodded but said nothing, the full weight of her life with another man weighing on my shoulders. I was afraid because, I thought, anything I said about love and sex had to invite disaster. We went out later that night to a dance performance in the northern part of the city. Baryshnikov and Nureyev joined in a manly *pas de deux* along with dancing bits from *Romeo and Juliet* and *Firebird*. But little of their beautiful performance registered–at least on me. I kept thinking about the afternoon I had met Anne-Marie down on the quay of the Seine, and how naturally our lives seemed to fall together afterward. I knew about Joseph from the beginning, just as she knew about my work and commitment to it. Her childhood love and my career ambitions kept us aligned for a while, but very clearly that period had now passed. I understood that I needed to counter with something special, some kind of new adventure or sacrifice she could admire and, maybe, share. But apart from living together in Paris or New York, I could think of nothing. Then I realized that by living with Joseph, Anne-Marie had chosen a completely ordinary, risk-free path, and I decided that I had read her incorrectly from the beginning. I needed to prepare my own zone of safety now, financial,

266

emotional, and geographic. When I was ready I would present it to her in the most generous–yet still romantic–way. It would work, I thought: Once I was settled in New York and opened my arms, she would leave Joseph for me. I was sure.

As we walked away from the theater that night, I had another one of those remarkable moments when my life ahead seemed to reveal itself before me: large forces, again at work. Perhaps Anne-Marie felt a similar sensation; or perhaps the beauty of the music and dance that night had lifted her soul. She beamed at me as we walked down the street toward the Metro, held my hand, and playfully kissed my ear as we descended the steps. No question she'll stay with me tonight, I remember thinking. As we entered the station and bought our tickets, I reminded her of a show I wanted to see in Montmartre next day. Without hesitation she agreed to accompany me there, but, as I might have guessed and hadn't, she said she needed to spend this particular night with Joseph to lift his spirits.

We took the train down to St. Placide, walked along the Luxembourg Garden fence to her apartment building, and kissed — urgently — good-night. Next day, in Montmartre on another beautiful autumn day, we talked about memory, performance, and–by extension–children. But you remember that story, I'm sure, because I've told it already. Not long afterward I returned to New York to begin my new life — this present life, I should add — a life that, as an artist, I never wanted to lead.

XXII.

We talked alone for more than an hour at her home in Provence that afternoon, with a phone call or two coming from a lawyer Anne-Marie had contacted. She felt depressed, but the lawyer's confidence gave her hope because he felt Celestine's need for a mother at this difficult time would easily win in court. I found myself wishing for more than that to boost her spirit, but, by the time I left, I realized it was all she could expect. I spent several days away from her, occasionally calling for news of Celestine or Zach, and offered a sympathetic ear. Celestine had left on a train for Paris to be with her grandparents, and Zach remained in the apartment near St. Rémy. Anne-Marie's lawyer recommended strongly that they remain separate until the situation with Celestine and her grandparents became clear. "I can only visit him," Anne-Marie said, "and never stay the night. The lawyer says that if anyone sees me there, my suit is finished. What if he gets sick—if he needs something at night?"

"Doesn't he have a nurse?"

"The doctor recommended two, but neither wants to stay overnight for a full week. They claim he can call them or an ambulance if he has trouble."

I talked it over with Lee and Misha that evening. With their reluctant, I should say generous, consent, I volunteered to spend a night or two a week with Zach.

268

The long couch in the main room would give comfort for the nights, and, since I liked rising early to write, I'd be able to start right away without disturbing Zach. If the nurses could share the other five or six nights, then he would be covered—at least for a while.

I felt awkward at first, but Anne-Marie gladly accepted. Lee did too, with that exceptional kindness and unselfishness at her core that I have often taken for granted. Very quickly Anne-Marie found three nurses who agreed to a rotating schedule, and so I soon found myself leaving Lee and Misha after dinner on Tuesday and most Thursday evenings to drive fifteen minutes toward St. Rémy to spend the night.

Zach welcomed me, happily smiling and shaking my hand with a hardy slap on the back the first week or two whenever I arrived. He'd bring out a cool bottle of rosé, pour it into a pair of wineglasses, and then turn on a couple of his favorite CDs. We talked a bit, but mostly he got lost in the music and responded to sounds and combinations of sounds that passed me by until he pointed them out. For me it was like being a student again, loading up my senses with a complex artist's work and hearing about subtle shadings and colors for the first time although I'd stared at canvases (or heard performances of music) most of my life. In one piece Zach bowed contrabass on Ellington's "Mood Indigo," and his dark, silky sound blended so deeply and certainly with the line of the saxophone that I could have sworn the two became one player.

"We put it together there," Zach said, after we

listened through the third or fourth repetition. "Nailed it. It was one of the times when the music played the musicians, not the other way round."

On another track he bowed through "September Song" on his own, a solo performance that began with the lowest, deepest moan, as if perceiving a black abyss before him, but he gradually worked his way up the ladder of notes so that the end of the song became a dance, a maypole dance in spring, as if he looked across the abyss and saw a happy, fertile other side.

"I don't know how you did that," I told him after a long pause when he had finished. "I want to click my heels because I see white blossoms at the end of it."

He grinned broadly, with genuine pleasure. "Hmm. Got to watch that rosé," he said with a laugh. Then, "It was just something I wanted to do." He paused, glanced in the glass and then up at me. "It was a very bad, desperate time of my life–with women, a good friend who was dying, and even the hard stuff – drugs. I wanted to see if music could lead me through it. That performance did – for a bit."

The look on his face, gray, wistful, said something important to me, but I also felt cut off. Did he wish for a requiem or somber fugue to put a triumphant finish to the life he had led? Was there some type of New Orleans dance, or march, he could swing into? I glanced in the corner near the window and saw the large case that his instrument stood in. We had brought it in with the rest of his stuff although he was sure he would never use it. This particular contrabass had no classical pedigree that he knew of, no famous craftsman as its builder, but he had carried or rolled it on the sidewalk in front of him throughout his career and regarded it as a special friend. He could barely hold it upright now, but its presence brought him comfort. "Not a bride," he said after I carried it through the door. "But it'll keep me company out here." Yet whenever I offered to remove it from the case and bring it to him along with his bow, he shook his head as if he'd been insulted.

"No possible way I can play it," he said, frowning. "It comforts me just to know it's there."

The frown dropped into a deeper mood. His bent head and the absolute sorrow showed how much he missed his life. I could only imagine the added burden of missing Anne-Marie as well.

"Celestine is in Paris now," I said, trying to turn us toward a more positive subject. "Maybe Anne-Marie..."

He waved his hand, pushing the idea aside as if a night with Anne-Marie was impossible, too. "Don't want to jeopardize anything," he said. "It's too important. Besides, this..." he waved again probably to push off any further comment. "This thing is something I have to face alone."

That shut me up altogether because I could think of no way to a happier train of thought. But I would come back to try again, phoning him almost daily for the next couple of weeks, even on days when I didn't stay over. He needed me. Anne-Marie's lawyer constantly repeated the advice to keep apart, and Zach paid scrupulous attention, rarely calling Anne-Marie, never appearing with her in public day or night. "We have to convince more than a judge," he told me. "We have to convince her parents and, most important, Celestine."

Of course, he was right. The lawyer agreed and traveled to Paris regularly to meet with the grandparents and Celestine. Anne-Marie's mother, a tall, fair-skinned woman from Alsace, as I judged from photos, seemed to lean toward a settlement to unite her family again, but her husband felt more suspicious, and the lawyer said Celestine, who remained quiet during every meeting, seemed to agree.

"He thinks I should talk to my mother," Anne-Marie told me once, and she too thought her mother's sympathy could eventually sway her father and Celestine. "My father's stubborn, but not really impossible. He wants to make my mother happy, and with a great granddaughter coming—even this way— she naturally leans toward family."

"Stay away from me, then," Zach said. "I'm behind a door they don't want to open and walk through."

Anne-Marie sighed deeply when he told her that. "What choice do we have? There's just no logic to the way they..."

The words caught in her throat. I kept quiet myself because the frustration of her situation was so obvious. "We're staying a little longer than we had planned, Anne-Marie. I received an extension on my stay—until the first week of September. Lee has some canvases to finish, Misha can learn more French, and I, of course, still have my book, although I admit I haven't written a hell of a lot lately. So I'll just keep coming here a couple of nights a week and go off to write early in the mornings. I'll let you know when that changes."

She smiled happily while Zach glumly turned toward his feet. "I don't know where this comes from," Anne-Marie said. "But I want you to know we ... I ... feel this care ... It means more to me than I can say. A lot more."

Despite myself, my breath caught at her words. I had to struggle to hold my tongue. "I have always cared," I said, whispering. "Never doubt that." Then I turned away to Zach and shook my head.

"Ben..."

"Frankly, I'm doing this for Zach, as well as you," I mumbled, opening my eyes.

"We're both indebted to you," Zach said. "We know that."

I shook my head. "You owe me nothing, my friend. It's just my turn to do something right."

Zach said nothing but looked at Anne-Marie again. She took my hand and beamed, smiling beautifully now, but with a single tear rolling down her cheek. For the first time since her startling September 11th email, I had begun to feel my life grow orderly again. But I was angry at that moment. At myself, not them. I had been aware for months (years, really) that some kind of shadow followed me, sulking as I walked, loudly complaining that there should be another path, *was* another path I needed to take. And now, well, here that shadow self stood again, helpless, because I was still nothing more than a friend—hers and her present lover's.

"I'm sorry," I said, completely disregarding Zach. "Things have happened in my life that I've never been able to let go. You're one of them."

Anne-Marie's face lost all of its brightness. She looked over at Zach and then at me. "Oh, Ben... You've gone on to do so many good, even wonderful, things. How could you ... ?"

"Not what I wanted," I said, despite her hopeful smile. "Nothing at all like it. You made it impossible, and now..."

I stopped because the warning look on Zach's face showed me how much my words would hurt. Now, as I reached for her hand, I touched his shoulder, and—more gracious than I—they both let me hold them.

"You can always paint," Anne-Marie said. "You have such skillful, wonderful vision."

"Not since you—not seriously—and I probably won't ever again." Then I added, trying for my own graciousness, "It's not your fault. I just haven't done any."

She lowered her head, as if there were nothing more to say. Zach looked up and put his hand over ours.

"Ben, I was afraid of myself, of what I had become. Of what you would find out about me."

I looked at her. Anne-Marie stared past me—over my arm toward Zach. "What would I find out? I knew everything about you — I thought."

Her eyes caught mine, then quickly dropped and turned to Zach again. What could I say?

"I was pregnant in New York," she said loudly, nearly shouting. "I arrived pregnant, and I left pregnant because I couldn't do what I had planned."

I said nothing, breathing heavily for a moment as my mind raced. Finally, as calmly as I could, I asked, "You wanted to abort it? You wanted my help?"

She shook her head, then lowered it, mumbling.

"Anne-Marie..."

"I wanted to trick you," she said, still looking at Zach, rather than me. "You were going to be her father — after I came home."

"You thought I would marry you?"

"I knew you would." She looked directly into my eyes now. "But after the Towers, after your proposal up there, I couldn't do it that way."

"Jesus, Anne-Marie..." Zach said.

She let out a long, mournful groan.

"What about Joseph? Wouldn't he — ?"

She shook her head, wringing my hand. "He had already left."

"What?" I waited. "And? — "

Zach nodded, and she did, too. "I went to London after I returned, spent the weekend in a hospital, and came back to France ready for a new life — alone. I stopped writing those stupid articles and started cleaning other people's houses, having made such a miserable mess in my own."

275

XXIII.

That was the bullet through my heart. Often, when I think of that conversation on the wing of the World Trade Center, I wonder how I would have responded had Anne-Marie told me the whole story then. I like to think I would have leapt at the chance to marry her and, together, raise a child. But I was young and had so many other things going on—a degree to finish, articles to write, and, vaguely, fondly, getting back to painting—that I have to doubt it.

A child would have had very little place in my world back then—in New York or Paris. Besides, everyone talked about zero population growth, women's need to fulfill themselves in the workplace, and the idea that there was more to life than parenting, especially for an artist. But clear and committed as all that sounds, I look back now and doubt that I could have turned her down, even though I'm sure much of my subsequent youth would have been spent wallowing in self-pity, a regret more painful than the one I have in fact carried with me through the years. In many ways I was very lucky.

By contrast, Anne-Marie struggled under a cloud of guilt over the sacrificed baby, the attempt (which she planned on her own, she told me) to make me accept responsibility for her actions, and of course the bad marriage she made to a man who abandoned her and his daughter, a daughter who now threatened to turn the tables on her. Luckily, a musician she had heard play in a nightclub near Juan-Les-Pins came to her rescue, and the man she had always felt closest to before him arrived once more to give her support—and continue the rescue as the musician started final bows.

But that wrenching talk with her and Zach ended everything for me: painting, secret second self, life as an ex-patriot in France. Our summer in Provence rapidly ran to its conclusion, and Anne-Marie soon would be left on her own—with the additional burden of a new baby in her life in far from joyful circumstances. As I drove home that afternoon, I wondered what to do. I wasn't angry, but I had no real responsibility toward her—just the opposite, you might say—yet I always sensed that Zach hoped I would look after her somehow.

"She's a tough lady," he had said to me once, "but she's got a lot of difficult stuff ahead of her. Most of it isn't her fault."

I knew he thought of Celestine and Anne-Marie's parents when he said that. Zach and I were the main sympathetic people in her life, and my sympathy had just weakened. Her brother, hostile to Zach, hardly spoke to her, and for whatever reason she had few close friends around Châteaurenard and St. Rémy.

"You and Gilles will be the only ones to hug her at his funeral," Lee said to me when I mentioned all this to her one day. She smiled, but the undertone in her voice and serious look on her face put me on notice.

"I'm sure there will be others," I said. "Her parents won't let her stand alone for long. They have a granddaughter — and a great grandchild — to consider."

Lee's eyebrows rose. "Maybe — if the great grandchild's living with her instead of them. But it sounds like they see Anne-Marie as difficult, if not impossible, and would just as soon let her go."

I looked at Lee, my wife of almost twenty years, wondering if that was her assessment rather than theirs. And also if it were true. I smiled across the table in the Châteaurenard garden and squeezed her hand. In time I came to agree with Lee about the parents, and I spent afternoons and evenings the rest of that August considering what Anne-Marie would do — with and without Zach. The Lelandes said they would continue to employ her, in fact had recommended her to several property-owning friends. Celestine would eventually come home with the baby to live, I figured. The key problem would be her lonesomeness while she waited, and I decided there was little for me to do about that.

"Anne-Marie's not stupid — or weak. That's for sure. She'll work it all out," Lee said to me. I agreed, but reluctantly. I had my own family to think of, and Lee, who had shown little anger about my spring and summer with Anne-Marie, began to complain openly, while Misha, whose bumptious nature masked a growing boy's needs, might explode at any time because of my neglect.

"There are two sides to me," he often said, as if it were something we should think about. "So far you've seen only one of them."

It was a clear warning, I knew, yet I continued to visit Zach pretty much daily though I stopped spending nights when one of the nurses volunteered to stay with him for extra money. Zach slept a lot day and night, and his alert hours began to turn more inward. He'd call from his room; the nurse (or Anne-Marie, if she was there) would help him out of bed. He would emerge into the larger room in jeans and slippers and with closed eyes fall into his chair near the speakers, waving his hand for music.

He'd listen with a soft smile on his face but usually fell asleep before the disc had reached its second track. "Medication," the nurse whispered, when she turned off the player and, checking her wristwatch, took his pulse. She'd tune the radio to some French pop station and smile contentedly at me as she knitted. For a good part of an hour after that, I'd stare sadly at Zach, an icon of French and American jazz: His mouth hung open; his eyes quivered while closed; his voice remained still amid the brassy, optimistic rhythms now filling his apartment.

XXIV.

A little less than one month after that, September 14 to be exact, as Lee, Misha, and I prepared to drive home from Kennedy, Frederick Zachary Douglas (as the next day's *New York Times* obit named him) died. Nothing dramatic happened. Anne-Marie wrote to me afterward that he simply lay on the floor and fell asleep before the speakers one afternoon. And quietly stopped breathing. He had weakened enormously, walked and talked far less, slumped more deeply in his reclining chair and always, always listened to music, sometimes his own, more often than not the music of others: especially "A Love Supreme".

"Not much time left," he said to me on one of my last visits. "I want to take as much with me as I can."

Around the first of September, on a gorgeous sunlit Provence afternoon, the nurse had announced that she thought his heart might give out any time. That seemed incredibly casual, even for a somewhat disinterested nurse, and I urged Anne-Marie to call his doctor. He responded with the breathy equivalent of a French shrug, Anne-Marie told me, then he added, "We are doing our best with a situation that is almost without hope, Madame. The nurse has talked to me. We can only try to make him comfortable."

"Shouldn't we take him to a hospital?" I asked after the call ended. "I know there's not much hope, but..."

Anne-Marie didn't hesitate: the patient would not have it. "For our comfort, maybe," she said, "but Zach is stubborn, a fatalist, and no one can change his mind." She lowered her head and then looked up at me. "I think he's ready, Ben."

"People who love him might want to help him anyway."

She paused a long time. "I have to prepare myself. Maybe you should, too. The cancer is extremely aggressive."

I left Anne-Marie's house soon afterward, not wanting to discuss Zach's illness as a dead end. When I saw her again, I offered to drive her to his apartment anytime she wanted, thinking my presence would work against any attempts in the courtroom to link them romantically. The timing would be complicated, because Celestine had promised some visits to her mother from Paris, a practice Anne-Marie's lawyer had worked out to ease the daughter's resistance.

"She's coming down tonight for a week," Anne-Marie told me. She smiled at my surprise, adding, "It's the effect of becoming a mother herself."

"Well, you can see him whenever you want. This afternoon will be fine. We'll let my car stand conspicuously outside the house."

She agreed to go, finally. Absurd as it may sound, I was prepared to testify, if the lawyer asked, that I stayed with her and Zach the whole time and never let them out of my sight.

281

We drove past the farm fields on the highway toward St. Rémy, and when we arrived at Zach's apartment, I parked the car near the road, walking slowly, hand in hand, with Anne-Marie to the front door. The nurse, a gray-haired woman with a bundle of knitting wool in her hands, let us in. She said that Zach was sleeping and then left for a couple of hours when we told her we would stay with him.

Anne-Marie glanced around the apartment nervously, especially at the plastic CD boxes piled up and lying near the sound system. She stared at an enlarged photograph of her and Zach seated on a large rock somewhere above the Rhone near Avignon. Then she went to the contrabass, opened the lid with a neat flick of the latches, and studied the instrument for a long time. "In the beginning we felt sure he'd get well enough to practice again," she said, shaking her head. She plucked a string and sobbed; the sounds reverberated ominously in the open case.

I pointed to the chair he generally sat in. Facing the speakers and a window, it provided a distant view of the blue Alpilles and, through a second window, a clear image of the snow-capped Mont Ventoux. Zach's bedroom door was closed, but Anne-Marie kept glancing at it as if she expected him to emerge.

"Usually, he calls," she said. "Because he needs help standing up."

I nodded, biting my lip.

"I call every morning," she said. "Or sometimes drive over and wait in the car for the nurse to come out."

"I'm sure someone would let you know if it was really bad news."

She shrugged, looking out the window as if to avoid the subject. Then her head fell forward and her shoulders slumped, drawing me to her side. I took her in my arms. "I don't know what I would have done without you this summer," she whispered. "You've been a very good friend."

She turned up her face and looked in my eyes. "I often think of that week in New York," she said.

"It was so beautiful and true," I said, "that I knew–I was absolutely certain at the time–it couldn't be real."

She smiled into my obvious anxiety, raising her arms carefully and putting them around my neck. "Ben, you were very ambitious then. How could I have helped you?"

I let my own arms drop to my side and shook them. "I wanted to marry you, Anne-Marie. It would have helped a lot to say yes."

She frowned suddenly, her eyes flashing with bitterness.

"It sent me reeling–for weeks, months. Sometimes I think I'm reeling still.–It would have been *our* baby you carried. I assure you."

She stood apart, looking down at her feet. "In those days I doubted everything–happiness most of all. I'm still not sure we did the right thing."

"*We?* Anne-Marie, you turned me down."

She nodded, the frown, a confused smile

283

replacing the bitterness for a moment, gave way to a blank, level-headed stare.

"Anne-Marie, you can't..."

She raised her hand, touching my lips with her finger to quiet me. "You looked so grand, adventurous that day, as if it might be fun to try marriage out. A French girl and an American—an artist/professor— reaching out to embrace at the top of the world. Had you planned that moment?"

I shook my head, trying not to look at her. I let my hands fall into my pockets to hide my clenched fists. "I adored you. In many ways I'm not happy about, I still do."

She looked away, silent for a long time. "We had too much joy," she answered. "I knew it then, and I still think so now."

"Too much joy!"

I stepped closer, my hands immediately reaching for her shoulders, and, against all my instincts, felt like shaking her and tearing her apart. In some ways I understood Celestine more than ever before. I dropped my hands again, fearing I might do something stupid. "Your answer–the complete silence behind it–crushed me. With my child or someone else's, you still could have had me. I deserved an explanation."

She smiled openly, galling me enough to make me turn my back.

"Ben, I didn't want to live there. I still don't. My soul is French. How could we have compromised?"

Without a word, I nodded and stepped toward the door, pulling it open. I still wonder, as I remember that intense silence telescoped over the long moment on the World Trade Center's roof: What makes you love and commit to share another person's intimate life?

"I am happy now. I honestly love Lee; and Misha. I have no wish except to spend my life with them." Now impulsively, I crossed the room and held her close. "But I see you once after too many years, and I wonder how much different my life would have been."

Anne-Marie raised her arms behind my head, smiled happily, and pulled my face closer to hers. She looked into my eyes; in place of words, she brought her lips against mine and brushed against them. Our thighs pressed together, and I felt myself struggle to keep my feet.

Fred Misurella

286

PART SIX:

FIRST STEPS

XXV.

That, in fact, was the last time I saw Anne-Marie.
Yet this remained:

"Ben,

*"My shame, my horror is enormous. Zach, my love,
the man I felt I would end my days with, passed away nearly
a week ago, alone, helpless, not even a nurse to hold his hand
during his final breath.*

*"Did I love him enough? Did I do enough to save
him? The nurse had been called away, for medication, she tells
me, although the pharmacy certainly would have delivered,
and so she left him in his chair while she drove into St. Rémy.
An hour later, she says, she returned and found Zach on the
living room floor, his head lying against a speaker with his
own music playing directly into his ear. He had been sleeping,
the doctor said. It was not a fall.*

*"My poor, wonderful love. I don't know what his
final thoughts were, if he spoke any final words, or even heard
the music as a sign of happiness or despair. I hadn't seen him
for several days, maybe only twice since you left. Celestine
had arrived. I spent time with her in preparation for the baby.
Now, with the season turning fields and woods around us
gold and brown again, I play his music every morning, I look
out the back window to the shed he stayed in for a while, and
I thank whatever power–or powers–there may be for letting
Zach into my life–even for so short and difficult a time.*

"Celestine attended the funeral with me, as even my

288

parents did. They now apologize almost daily for making the last two years so difficult. I keep wondering what has made them change, if they want something from me, in fact. But apart from love–and I have always, always, loved my parents, as well as Celestine–I can't really see anything else. Sometimes I sit at the kitchen table with my head in my hands and cry when I think of Zach's lonely end, or listen to a particularly touching passage of his playing, and almost always–as she did this very morning–Celestine will sit by me, take me in her arms, and as if our roles had reversed, caress me, put my head on her shoulder, and let me cry until the anguish passes.

"'I'm sorry, Maman. It's my fault. If it weren't for me, you could have been with him.'

"She's right, I suppose, but who can blame her, especially me? And so I never speak of it. Instead, I give thanks again to the power–or powers–in control that she has come back to live with me. Permanently, Celestine says.

"I hope you, your lovely wife, and wonderful, charming son are well and have a good, productive year. Let me know how the book turns out. Perhaps we'll see you again next summer at the Lelandes, maybe even in New York. I look forward to it, my old, my best, my very meaningful friend. I'd like to meet you again, in a happier time."

...I folded the black bordered letter, replaced it in the envelope, and thought back to the past summer's days. The uncompleted manuscript, *Life in Medias Res: A History of Suburbia*, lay on the desk before me with a handwritten list of corrections and additions alongside. Like all deaths after long illness, I think, Zach's passing came as no real surprise, came as a relief, in fact, and yet it still shocked because we (or, at least, I) have never accepted that this life should ever end. I lowered my head when I thought of him dying in his room, tapped my chest twice in a kind of *mea culpa* motion, and dropped the letter beside the manuscript.

I put a recording of "September Song" in my Bose player, regretted that it lacked Zach's amazing up-tempo solo, and listened, carefully trying to imagine how, when, and where he would intersect with the playing and let his instrument sing. I glanced through the window at sun glittering on the reddened leaves of a maple tree outside, and then I looked up at the two paintings hanging above my desk. One was Lee's, a still life of fruit, plants (one small ficus among them), a gorgeously three-dimensional red plate with two walnuts in it, and a pair of my favorite novels–*Madame Bovary* and *Portrait of the Artist as a Young Man*–next to them.

But the other painting held my attention more: my own, of Anne-Marie, nude from the waist up, her brilliant hair spread on a dark background, her face a neutral expression of acceptance, comfort, and desire. In a trick of perspective I'm still very proud of, her arms and hands seem to break free of the canvas's flat surface and grasp the viewer somehow, by hands or head, just as she once grasped me.

"I'll always be with someone," Anne-Marie said when she saw it completed during our early days together in Paris. "As long as that painting lasts, and hangs, someone will be with me in a room."

Surprisingly, Lee admires the painting too, as a

290

strong woman's portrait, she says, but she feels that hers somehow better represents a man, the one I have become. "It's the life you inhabit now," she told me once, with a thoughtful frown, "a man of responsibility — and books." I acknowledged the suggestion her words make about ordinary life and love, but in quiet, saner moments I still see passion in her painting, while in my own I read loneliness, longing, and a different kind of accomplishment.

Sometimes I wonder what Zach would say about the paintings, how he, consummate professional and sideman that he was, would sort them. I see him bringing the two together somehow, blending the genteel, the fecund, the hominess of Lee's approach with the all-out lust and excitement of my portrait of Anne-Marie. In my life I've never been able to hold the two together very well, because for me, somehow, desire, physical desire, inevitably launches into the larger world while the stuff of home, its mood, its quiet, turns me inward to smaller, subtle things.

I remember sitting down with Zach one cool afternoon outside his cabin near Anne-Marie's and staring at the surrounding mountains. I felt like we sat in an empty bowl waiting for something–soup? vegetables?–to pour down on us and bring more comfortable warmth. Zach still looked fairly strong then, his eyes alert, his smile relaxed yet bright with happiness, his expression genuinely alive with satisfaction. In certain ways, apart from his music, this is the most positive memory I have of him.

"This is the life," he told me. "I have all this to look at every day, a pal like you to visit, my favorite music whenever I want to hear it, and that woman over there, bless her, to comfort and keep me in line when I feel depressed."

He looked at me and laughed.

"I know that feeling," I said. "Sometimes I wonder why it took me so long to find it–to let it find me."

He grinned. "It sneaks up, I know. When I was on the road, I thought it would choke me. I thought I'd never be able to play, never be able to feel anything strongly enough to put in my music. Then I met that red head in the house over there. Hearth took on a lot of heat."

He smiled more broadly. At that moment Anne-Marie emerged from her back door carrying a basket. She wore a white gossamer blouse with flowers embroidered on it and, I saw with a little shock, no shorts, her bare legs extending under the blouse from what must have been either a white bathing suit or underwear. In sandals, she walked to her garden to gather vegetables and flowers.

Zach and I both followed with our eyes, our hunger unacknowledged, watching something tinged with magic as Anne-Marie smiled at the sky, stretched arms and basket toward the sun above the mountains, and then squatted to her haunches. She picked some tomatoes and zucchini, used a pair of scissors to snip bits of basil and rosemary, and then cut what looked like a dozen red roses from a bush she kept beside the bed of herbs.

"That just turns me on," Zach said, laughing. "An earthy woman like that just possesses a lot of soul. I find it moving."

He called out to Anne-Marie, motioned her through the hedge to join us, and then rose to go into the hut. At first I thought he meant to leave us alone, which made me a little uneasy, but soon he came out with three glasses and a large bottle of Evian.

"Have some water," he said, pulling a chair beside him, as Anne-Marie arrived. "We're just talking about the comforts of home."

"Women," Anne-Marie said with a wry grin. "I know what you're discussing."

"You," Zach said, with a sweet smile, "and how much you've brought to me." He held her hand, filling the three glasses with water.

"If only my daughter would agree," she said, without a hint of forethought on her face. Her shoulders shuddered, bringing the magic moment to a halt, as she smiled painfully and shook her head.

Zach looked pained himself for a moment but said nothing; although Celestine didn't concern me, I too felt a deep sense of regret.

"Well, on this beautiful late spring day, why don't we do something?" Anne-Marie asked. "We don't have to let my family problems block the sun."

Hesitant, I suggested a ride to Arles. In the Provence paper that morning, I had seen an advertised exhibit about Van Gogh in an outdoor square near the

Arles Coliseum, along with a festival of buskers staged on corners throughout the city. "It could be fun," I said. "Music and pictures."

"You must bring Lee and Misha, too," Anne-Marie added. "They'll love it, I'm sure."

Zach nodded, and Anne-Marie brought out a phone from the house. I felt uneasy although I knew that Lee held little against my past with Anne-Marie. This summer might have been a different matter, but as I remember she had said nothing about it so far.

"I'll be happy to go with you," Lee told me, "and Misha, too. I'll call him and get ready right away."

We took my car to pick her up at the Lelandes, returned to Mouriès to retrieve Misha early from camp, and then headed out to the auto route for Arles. We arrived in a little more than an hour, parked in a lot near the reconstructed yellow house where Van Gogh and Gauguin lived for several months, and then entered Arles center through the ancient Roman walls. Music filled the streets around us, and as soon as we started toward the Coliseum, we saw vendors' tables lining the walkways–food, clothing, Provençal cloth, and antiques the primary wares. We bought Misha some ice cream at a café and then walked along the Rhone until we came to a little bridge to Trinqueteul, one of my favorite Van Gogh landscapes because of its Japanese-inspired fastidiousness, its unwillingness to utter anything to the viewer except a simple message: "Look. Take it or leave it, but look."

Misha tossed a few stones into the water beneath the bridge, and then we turned back into the city. We found the exhibit on a little hill near the *Ecole des Beaux Arts*, a few rooms on two separate floors, each dominated by one or two Van Gogh originals along with dozens of knock-offs, copies, and parodic interpretations by local art students. We saw sunflowers in all colors; hayfields dead and alive; dozens of sowers with different kinds of sun and seed; hippie portraits of Joseph Roulin, Van Gogh's philosophical mailman friend; Dr. Felix Rey, his physician in Arles, with white and brown spots splattered all over him; and several of the painter himself in various bizarre outfits: top hat, Indian headdress, straw sun hat and sunglasses, winter *casquette* with earflaps down (and pistol in his mouth), and simple, naked, red-headed Vincent with beard, looking fierce and competitive from his flinty eyes.

"Wow, all these Vincents," Misha said. "One after another."

"Repeated and repeated until we're sick of him," Lee said. "A man whose work no one wanted while he lived."

"See the painting of this man?" I said, pointing to the original of Dr. Felix Rey. "His doctor. And Van Gogh gave this portrait to him as payment for care. Years later it was found in the family's chicken coop, patching a hole."

Misha's eyes widened in surprise and momentary anger. Stepping closer, he glared at the knock-off white and brown spots, while Zach laughed beside him. "The value of art," he said. "At least it got him some medicine and provided a few chickens with

295

shelter. That's more than a lot of this stuff does."

After the exhibit, we wandered through the city, following a marked Van Gogh trail haphazardly to see a café he had painted at night, a garden of poppies and other flowers, the graveyard at *Les Alyscamps*, and of course the Rhone and its banks at various spots that he had memorialized. Misha and Zach seemed to lean into the sites we visited, as if they looked over the shoulder of an artist actually at work. I envied Zach's easy comments, his ability to identify with the painter rather than the object.

Misha had a similar approach, his eyes bright and darting, as if he evaluated and planned the work immediately while standing before the scene. Once or twice I saw him close his eyes as if to make a mental note.

"Would you paint that?" I asked at one spot along the Rhone, "—if you didn't know Van Gogh had already done it?"

He thought for a moment, and then nodded.

"What about it catches your attention?"

"The people. And, I suppose, the colors. I just think the whole thing is interesting. Why did Van Gogh paint it anyway?"

Ah, and here the learned critic could finally lecture the son, Dad showing off his knowledge of artistic principles, the *Zeitgeist* Van Gogh lived and breathed in, how he and his peers sought to change it. When I was done, Misha looked at me, his blue eyes muddy and narrow (not unlike a flinty Van Gogh without a hat), and replied loudly, "I'll bet he just liked

296

it, Dad. Why else would he paint it?"

Lee smiled, obviously proud of Misha. Anne-Marie caught my eye with a sympathetic smile. "Your dad painted with that kind of feeling too—one time," she said. "And he did some very, *very* beautiful things."

Lee nodded, quietly adding that it depended on the subject. She looked out at the river, not at me or Misha, certainly not at Anne-Marie or even Zach. I realized that much of what we did, and still might do, that summer would make Lee feel excluded. I stood beside her, put my arm around her shoulders, and held her tightly. Even Misha knew it as a Van Gogh moment—one to appreciate but probably never get to paint.

"You're the one who taught me to appreciate these scenes," I whispered to Lee. "I owe you everything because of them."

She shrugged, her smile grudging, but without the anger I had seen when her eyes first turned toward the river.

XXVI.

"Now the physical suffering is over," I wrote several weeks later. "But you won't be done with the rest for a long, long time. Nor will Celestine, if she's honest."

Anne-Marie's letter about Zach had arrived in late September that year, not very long after we returned from France and I read the obituary in the *Times*. I called her immediately, with regret from all three of us, and learned a few more details.

She had his body cremated and then scattered his ashes, as Zach had requested, along the road through the hills to Les Baux: "The route of the Troubadours," he had called it. Celestine accompanied her in the car and remained with her afterward, returning to school briefly before taking a year-long leave of absence. She talked of attending university after the baby arrived to learn about art history, spurred on, her mother said, by their research around the painted shutters in the shepherd's hut. Anne-Marie felt the urge to leave Provence herself and live in the north again. "Perhaps in Paris, where I met you, my old friend," she told me. "I'll be lonely at first, but at least in the city there will be people to see and many, many more things to do than tend a garden or people's houses. Celestine and the baby can live there, too."

She had no specific idea of how she would work,

or if she had to. Zach had left his whole estate to her, a small but decent sum of money from record sales, and she felt that would last until she found something useful to do, maybe return to writing. "I'm ready for a new start," she said. "I see this as an opportunity to grow. Visit us in Paris next time. I'll let you know when I have a new address."

That was close to ten years ago, and I have no idea how much she has changed or grown. She lives in the 14th Arrondissement now, near Porte Orleans, not far from my old apartment, and works for an internet journal—web and paper page layout and design, not writing. We email occasionally, usually Christmas and birthday greetings, little more, but there's always the sense–at least on my part–that one of these days, in Paris, or maybe here in New York, I will turn a corner and involuntarily catch my breath. I can't picture it, what I'll say, or what we'll do, but there is a frisson of inevitability about it that keeps me on the alert after all this time–especially downtown New York, around Ground Zero.

I feel it in other places too, I suppose, and before certain kinds of images, which probably says something about my time with Anne-Marie. I feel it on clear, beautiful autumn days with just a hint of smoke in them, when the leaves on maple and oak begin to fade slightly before their final, colorful burst. In my mind at least, it is Tuesday, September 11th again, but in a blessedly different year, and now I sit in western New Jersey, reviewing my life, thinking more realistically of

299

my sixties and trying to understand what all that experience years ago has to say about beauty, along with horror, and the human delight I revel in when life unfurls its full potential.

Some one or two years after that first September 11th, on a bleak October day when we kept Misha home from school because of a cough and runny nose, I sat in our family room reading while he rummaged through a pile of toys in search of something to do. As I dipped into a textbook to review one of the assigned readings for my students that day, Misha pulled open a side table drawer and found a white cardboard jewel box that had once held some inexpensive glass brooch. With a cry of delight, he opened it, letting the contents fall to the floor as he turned toward me. Half a dozen or more bluish-black, springy ringlets spread and settled at his feet. They bounced and rolled like little live eels, and he called out as we looked at them, wonder flashing in his bright blue eyes.

"Dad! — *What* are these?"

I rose from the chair, book in hand, and stood next to him, knowing immediately what he had uncovered.

"Hair," I said, laughing. "Curls, from when I was your age–actually younger. They're no longer alive, I'm afraid."

"Yours — at *my* age? — " He stared, eyes darting, I could see, to the top of my head and the graying, thinning cloud floating there. Distinguished-looking, Lee likes to tell me; sometimes she'll even say, though half-mockingly, "prettier than it used to be." But

300

"distinguished" is not an expression Misha knew, and certainly didn't appreciate, that year. Even more so presently, I'm afraid, he'd prefer a dad who's "really cool."

"It's mine," I told him, "for sure, from my first haircut, when I was three or four years old. Aunt Rita saved them, and when Mom and I brought you home from Russia, she was so pleased she gave them to me to keep for you."

"For me?–*Your* hair?" Misha stared again, his face so filled with puzzlement that I could not read him. "From preschool?" was all he said.

"About that time, although I never went to preschool."

"Dad, they look like Zach's curls. Does that mean you're...?"

He stopped, his eyes lighting with a new awareness.

"They're mine," I said. "I'm sure there's some African in there somewhere. Sicily's right across from its continent. Now look at me: a big American guy with a wonderful family."

He laughed, but slightly fearful and with a nervous edge. After a few seconds, he added, "Like I'll be, maybe?"

"You will, absolutely. I know it. You're already my American guy." I squeezed his shoulder, then hugged him. "And I hope you have as wonderful a family–and son–as I have." I hugged him again, tighter.

"Dad!" With a wild look of something I could not

name, Misha pushed himself back, and then lunged toward me, dropping his head as he reached for my waist. He squeezed my hips, fiercely, nearly sobbing. "I love you, Dad. I don't want you to leave. I don't want you to die!"

I don't know; perhaps, I tear up too easily in these later years. I've lost something of my critic's objectivity, I admit, but my eyes still moisten whenever I think of him saying that. As with that evening in Lee's studio a couple years before, when I learned of her affair with Jean-Luc, I felt one of the most piercing stabs of loneliness and weariness I have ever known.

But also intense happiness this time.

At just ten or eleven my son bore such awful knowledge, sharpened by stories from Grimm, movies from Disney, and, during that terrible fall and winter of 2001, daily images of tragedy from TV news. He cried often as a toddler, covering his eyes before the screen when he first saw Snow White keel over after biting the poisoned apple; or when the stepmother and stepsisters cruelly turn Cinderella into a household drudge. And, yes, the Wicked Witch of the West still made him turn his eyes from the screen until her famous meltdown relieved him of her threat. Too imaginative? Unable to separate reality from fiction? Some people might say that. At home that fall of 2001, even with me beside him during the dark days of October and November, he refused to walk in our backyard after sundown because he feared whatever might lie out there or, maybe, fly down at us from overhead.

Smart, I would tell people. "Nature over

nurture," I might add today. Misha showed little fear of other children, even bigger, athletic boys three or four years older at school. In his private dramatization of "The Nutcracker Suite" one December, he donned a green cap, raised his glowing Peter Pan sword (along with an added prop, a magic wand), and, with Tchaikovsky's swelling notes egging him on, attacked the forces of disharmony as personified by a large rubber puppet he called "the Mouse King." Clara (Lee, holding paint brushes at that moment) hurled her "slipper" (a dry brush, of course), crying "Leave my Nutcracker alone!" And Misha-turned-Nutcracker-turned-Peter-Pan began a showy chase, diving over backs of sofas, stabbing pillows, keeping the season's brilliantly lit tree, his electronic toys, Lee's painting studio, and Mom and Dad's family life an energetic but safe haven for another ageless winter night.

He embodied the image of happiness and love for Lee and me, despite world events: trading knock-knock jokes with his mom while playing cards, singing *"Toréador, en garde!"* in mock baritone with Dad while listening to *Carmen*, whirling dizzily to the bounce of ballet or other classical music as we ate dinner — sometimes clutching a violin beneath his chin to draw the bow continuously along the A-string: a zinging, deliberate count of four.

"Whole note," he'd whisper, squinting, with a smile of satisfaction, at the cringing look of horror on our faces.

And then came the following autumn's

Halloween: "Guess what I'm going to be this year, Dad—a witch!"

"A witch, Misha?"

"A wicked witch. An *eeevil* witch! Snape!"

"Not evil," I say. "You can't be evil. I won't allow it."

"Snape's not really evil. Everybody knows that. Besides, you can't stop me if I want to."

His eyes narrowed. For a moment their brightness took on a fiery, cartoonish hint of hell. I inclined my head, annoyed because I wanted to get back to a book I was reviewing. Then I smiled, benignly, I hope.

"Trick or treat!" he cried.

"Treat. Go ahead. One more Tootsie Roll can't hurt."

He cackled a bit and, kitchen broom between his legs, howled like a wolf, galloping to the kitchen to pull out a two-step stool and place it near the cabinet where we hid his candy. For a moment at least, the ambiguous Snape had left the room.

"Let's play Headless Horseman," Misha shouted. "You be Ichabod!" He raised his hand, pulled his witch hat low on his eyes, and rode the broom, trotting toward our couch while I, bumbling teacher, sauntered by whistling beneath what must have been a cloud-covered Halloween moon.

More than Zach ever had a chance to, I think, I have reached an age when I am heartened by such moments—autumnal cold, a hint of melancholy, but with a lingering remembrance of the dance of spring. I

304

am willing to accept one of the darker rules of life—let go while enjoying things. Anne-Marie and Zach taught me much of that, I think, but mostly Lee and Misha. And now, how could I return the favor—especially to my son?

Last year, on September 11th, more than ten years after that first awful one, I tried, driving Misha and his new friend, Jamie, along with Lee across New Jersey, parking near the Hudson in the early morning mist, and staring at the river from its banks. We took it all in, a couple of boats, the gulls, two or three crows swooping after them, motor traffic zooming up and down the opposite bank, and then, inevitable it seemed, a dark cat strolling quietly toward us along the railing. On our right, far down past the new structure marking Ground Zero like a giant narwhale, we could just make out the Statue of Liberty, a glowing, copper colored Ishmael, basking in the early light.

"Disappear!" Misha shouted, laughing beside me. "Disappear!"

His shoulders level with mine now, Misha waved his arm toward the water and shore while embracing Jamie, a gymnast, runner, and dancer. She spun away from him and let fly with an athletic Pulcinella leap.

Gulls and crows, startled by the sudden movement and Misha's louder, second shout— "Disappear!" he repeated—suddenly changed direction, careening away from us, crossing to mid-river before circling and returning.

305

The cat hissed, lowering its head before dashing beneath a nearby juniper.

"Misha," I said, nodding toward the cat. "Give the animals some peace."

He stopped mid-call, his hand above his head, and, smiling, let his chin sink into his chest.

"That's just Charcoal, Dad. But I couldn't resist. I don't want anything—anything—to disappear. Certainly not that little ghost."

I embraced him, wrapping him and Lee in my arms, while Jamie, looking bored at first, took out her phone and snapped a picture. We walked up the ramp past the tollbooths toward the center of the bridge. And at the center, as with hundreds of moments since Lee and I first met, I felt a shiver of surprise, not from cool wind or the view, but from something more personal: joy—pure joy—in her, our commitment to each other and Misha. Not in a rush of blood and breath, or predetermined genes, but in an infinitely more fulfilling, yet mysterious flow. It happens to me still, as I write this. Misha flashes blue, intensely serious eyes at Jamie. She laughs at his obvious loving interest, then spins and gestures to some silent music surrounding us.

"I love this place, Dad," Misha whispers. He opens his arms, and Jamie, like a little Misha for a moment, charges into him. A barge ploughs toward us from downriver, nudged by a red tugboat behind it. A sailboat tilts and begins to drift like a seabird for the Jersey shore.

"Someday I want to paint all this," Lee tells us. "On a huge three-part canvas."

"I love it," I answer, smiling. "Just breathing it all in."

We continue east, admiring the shallow sunrise as we walk: a narrow view of a second body of water beneath the sun and finally what I think of as shifting ocean dunes and marshes farther out.

"We're going to dance tonight," Misha exclaims. "I know a place down in the Village. We've got to go there. You, too, Mom. Dad."

"Let's do it. It's your time to lead us," Lee tells him.

I put my arm around her shoulders.

Someday, maybe, we'll explain: Sure we've stumbled, but here we are, walking and trying to dance with the younger kids. There is no magic, not a lot of drama. Just a series of perfect, balanced moments with plenty of air and space between.

You need to be ready, always, we'll tell him. Hold on as long as you can, then — simply, lovingly — let go.

And that, we hope, will be that.

Fred Misurella

ABOUT THE AUTHOR

Fred Misurella has published two novels: *Arrangement in Black and White,* the story of an interracial marriage; *Only Sons,* a novel about two contemporary Italian-American families; *Lies to Live By: Stories; Short Time,* a Vietnam war novella; and *Understanding Milan Kundera: Public Events, Private Affairs* (a critical study of Kundera's work). His stories and non-fiction have appeared in Partisan Review, Salmagundi, Kansas Quarterly, Voices in Italian Americana, L'Atelier du roman (in France), The Christian Science Monitor, The Village Voice, and The New York Times Book Review. His essays on Primo Levi appear in *The Legacy of Primo Levi* and *Answering Auschwitz.* He is the current book review editor for VIA (Voices in Italian Americana), a Fulbright Scholar, and graduate of the University of Iowa Writers Workshop. He lives with his wife and children in East Stroudsburg, Pennsylvania.

Learn more: WWW.FredMisurella.com.

If you liked *A Summer of Good-Byes,* please help spread the word. Write a review at Amazon, GoodReads, Facebook or Twitter. Better yet, tell your local bookstore to order it for their shelves. Thanks.